r. Attentio

tion. Defici

eit. Disordo

a novel

BRAD LISTI

 SIMON SPOTLIGHT ENTERTAINMENT
New York   London   Toronto   Sydney

To my parents, Frank and Peggy Listi

SIMON SPOTLIGHT ENTERTAINMENT
An imprint of Simon & Schuster
1230 Avenue of the Americas, New York, New York 10020
Text copyright © 2006 by Brad Listi
All rights reserved, including the right of reproduction in whole or in part in any form.
SIMON SPOTLIGHT ENTERTAINMENT and related logo are trademarks of Simon & Schuster, Inc.
The text for this book is set in Life BT.
Manufactured in the United States of America
First Edition 10 9 8 7 6 5 4 3 2 1
Library of Congress Cataloging-in-Publication Data
Listi, Brad.
Attention deficit disorder : a novel / by Brad Listi.—1st ed.
p. cm.
ISBN-13: 978-1-4169-1230-9
ISBN-10: 1-4169-1230-4
1. Young men—Fiction. 2. Funeral rites and ceremonies—Fiction. 3. San Francisco (Calif.)—Fiction. 4. Loss (Psychology)—Fiction. 5. Suicide victims—Fiction. I. Title.

PS3612.I864A95 2006
813'.6—dc22
2005022697

My thanks:

Lauren

Erin

Phil

Madison

Kari

Merlin

Erin Hosier, my incomparable agent

Ryan Fischer-Harbage, my trusted friend & editor

Jennifer Robinson, Jen Slattery, Julie Amitie, & all
of the great folks at Simon Spotlight Entertainment

Sharon Davis

Susan Compo

James Ragan

Aram Saroyan

Hubert Selby Jr.

The University of Southern California professional
writing program

And all of my family & friends.

Absence makes the heart grow fonder.

—Sextus Propertius

Familiarity breeds contempt.

—Syrus

A penny saved is a penny earned.

—Benjamin Franklin

You can't take it with you.

—Moss Hart and George S. Kaufman

God must love the common man, he made so many of
them.

—Abraham Lincoln

God must hate the common man, he made him so
common.

—Philip Wylie

I've steered clear of God. He was an incredible sadist.

—John Collier

There is a superstition in avoiding superstition.

—Francis Bacon

There's a sucker born every minute.

—P. T. Barnum

Man is a social animal.

—Baruch Spinoza

Man is a political animal.

—Aristotle

Man is the measure of all things.

—Protagoras

Man is a blind, witless, low-brow anthropocentric clod who inflicts lesions upon the earth.

—Ian McHarg

The main thing needed to make men happy is intelligence . . . and it can be fostered by education.

—Bertrand Russell

Learned men are the cisterns of knowledge, not the fountainheads.

—James Northcote

All paid employments absorb and degrade the mind.

—Aristotle

A perpetual holiday is a good working definition of hell.

—George Bernard Shaw

If you want others to be happy, practice compassion. If you want to be happy, practice compassion.

—Dalai Lama

Happiness? That's nothing more than health and a poor memory.

—Albert Schweitzer

A humanitarian is always a hypocrite.

—George Orwell

Sisyphus was basically a happy man.

—Albert Camus

Every actual state is corrupt. Good men must not obey laws too well.

—Ralph Waldo Emerson

What do I care about the law? Hain't I got the power?

—Cornelius Vanderbilt

Reality is a crutch for people who can't cope with drugs.

—Lily Tomlin

Of all the things I've lost, I miss my mind the most.

—Jimi Hendrix

There are two ways to slide easily through life; to believe everything or to doubt everything. Both ways save us from thinking.

—Alfred Korzybski

The no-mind not-thinks no-thoughts about no-things.

—Buddha

The art of living is the art of knowing how to believe lies.

—Cesare Pavese

Always be sincere, even when you don't mean it.

—Irene Peter

When a man has pity on all living creatures, then only is he noble.

—Buddha

I tend to be suspicious of people whose love of animals is exaggerated; they are often frustrated in their relationships with humans.

—Ylla

He gave her a look you could have poured on a waffle.

—Ring Lardner

The only really happy folk are married women and single men.

—H. L. Mencken

The body of a dead enemy always smells sweet.

—Aulus Vitellius

Rubble is trouble.

—Muhammad Ali

The trouble with our times is that the future is not what it used to be.

—Paul Valéry

A conclusion is the place where you got tired thinking.

—Martin H. Fischer

A problem well-stated is a problem half-solved.

—Charles F. Kettering

The certainties of one age are the problems of the next.

—R. H. Tawney

This is my death . . . and it will profit me to understand it.

—Anne Sexton

I'm not afraid to die. I just don't want to be there when it happens.

—Woody Allen

The universe is but one vast Symbol of God.

—Thomas Carlyle

Taken as a whole, the universe is absurd.

—Walter Savage Landor

Put three grains of sand inside a vast cathedral, and the cathedral will be more closely packed with sand than space is with stars.

—Sir James Jeans

When it is dark enough you can see the stars.

—Ralph Waldo Emerson

I.

1.

I was at Horvak's apartment in the Haight, a couple of blocks from Golden Gate Park, on Waller. It was late, and I was there alone. Everything was quiet.

Horvak had caught a flight to Aspen a few hours earlier. We'd passed each other in the sky. Horvak was in an idyllic mountain paradise, celebrating the holidays with family and friends. I was alone in San Francisco, waiting for a funeral. A defeated brand of envy was the only natural response.

Horvak didn't really know Amanda. He knew her peripherally through me, but he didn't know her well enough to mourn her. Nothing about her death was debilitating to him; none of it really affected him. Beyond the kind of standard empathy that occurs in decent people, nothing much would transpire within him on account of her passing. There would be no resonant impact. He would escape unharmed.

I'd arrived in town late that afternoon. Rented a car at SFO and followed Horvak's instructions door to door. He'd left a key in the mailbox. I walked inside and planted myself on the couch and sat there for hours in silence. Flipping channels. Smoking cigarettes. Tending to my confusion. The television was on, but the volume was all the way down. There was a stack of bad magazines on the coffee table, and sleep wasn't really an option. My head was swimming. I'd come to the conclusion that I had very little understanding of what anything actually meant. That right there was the extent of my knowledge.

Sometime after midnight, I stubbed out another cigarette and rose from the couch. I walked over to the window and pulled back the curtain. Down below, life was happening. Cars were rolling by, rattling and coughing exhaust. Christmas trees and menorahs were glowing in windows. Streetlights were shining. The fog was moving in. People were walking along the sidewalks, wrapped in hats and scarves. I wondered who they were, where they were going, what they did. I wondered what their stories were. I wondered what would happen to them. I watched them disappearing, one by one and two by two, lost in the direction of wherever it was that they were headed. And none of them even knew I was there.

The ancient Egyptians mummified their dead. They treated their corpses with spices, herbs, and chemicals, and then they wrapped them in cotton cloth and stuffed them inside of a wooden case. Then they put that wooden case inside of another case. Then they decorated the outer case with information about the life of the wealthy dead person. Then they painted it and adorned it with jewels. The entire contraption was then stuffed inside a coffin, which was then stuffed inside a sarcophagus.

The Parsis, a Zoroastrian religious community in India, place their dead atop twenty-foot-high stone structures called "towers of silence," so the vultures can more easily devour them.

Australia's Aborigines have been known to leave dead bodies in treetops.

In New Caledonia and among Borneo's inland mountain people, dead bodies are placed erect inside the trunks of trees. The bark of the tree is then replaced over them.

The Jivaro peoples of South America inter their dead women and children under the floor. This practice dates back ten thousand years, to the rituals of urbanites in Mesopotamia.

• • •

Muslim people bathe their corpses carefully, with warm water and scented oils. Male corpses are bathed by men, and female corpses are bathed by women. Both men and women can bathe a dead child. The corpses are then wrapped in a plain cloth called a *kafan,* placed in a casket, and buried underground.

Jews wrap their dead in simple cloth and bury them underground too. Once the corpse is lowered underground, family members often toss a few handfuls of dirt into the hole. They might also tear a piece of their clothing, or a black ribbon, to signify their loss. This practice is called *kriah,* a tradition that many believe dates all the way back to Jacob's reaction to the supposed death of Joseph.

In certain parts of Indonesia, it is customary for widows to smear themselves with fluids from the bodies of their dead husbands.

In central Asia, mourners often get masochistic, lacerating their arms and faces in honor of the deceased.

In Tanzania, young men and women of the Nyakyusa tribe customarily copulate at the site of a dead person's grave, as a show of respect.

In some nomadic Arctic cultures, a doll of the deceased is carved from wood and treated as though it were alive. The doll is often kept for years. It is placed in positions of honor. It is taken on family outings. Food offerings are made to it. Widows have been known to sleep with the wooden doll in their beds, in remembrance of the deceased.

3.

Earlier in the year, the filmmaker Stanley Kubrick and the baseball player Joe DiMaggio had died within a day of each other. Kubrick passed away on March 7, 1999. A heart attack did him in. DiMaggio died on March 8, of lung cancer and pneumonia. I learned about both deaths on the morning of March 9. My alarm clock went off, same as usual, and I heard Bob Edwards talking about their deaths on National Public Radio. I remember lying in bed, looking at the ceiling, hearing the news. I found myself feeling sad in a vague and peculiar kind of way.

Later that same day, I was driving around Boulder, running errands, headed north on Twenty-eighth Street, trying to make a left turn. Up ahead I saw two little girls standing on the side of the road, darling little Japanese girls, sisters holding hands. They darted out into the road, right in front of a guy in an Oldsmobile Cutlass. Traffic was thick, so the guy wasn't going very fast— maybe twenty miles per hour. He slammed on his brakes, but by then, it was too late. The nose of the Olds struck the little girls, and they popped up in the air like rag dolls. One of them landed on the street. The other one landed on the hood. It was terribly surreal.

Everything started happening fast. Suddenly, I was out of my Jeep and running across the street. I arrived at the scene, and the little girls were lying there. The younger one was wailing. The older one was trembling, in shock. Both were conscious, and there wasn't any blood. Onlookers were rushing in from every direction. Everyone was crowding in around the girls, trying to comfort them, asking them if they were all right. I felt nauseous. I looked to my left and saw a woman standing there. By the looks of her, she was a mother. She had her hands on her head, as though she were wearing a wig and the wind might blow it away.

"Oh my God," she kept saying. "Oh my God, oh my God . . ."

I took my jacket off and tried to drape it over one of the little girls, the older one. I'd read somewhere that people injured in accidents should be covered with blankets or coats, to keep them warm, to treat them for shock. The little girl wanted no part of my jacket. She threw it off her shoulders, looked at me, and started bawling. She said she wanted to go home. Having all of these strange adults around her was scaring her. I backed away, holding my jacket. I felt silly—dejected, almost.

Sirens rang in the distance.

The little girl sobbed.

"Don't worry, sweetheart," someone said to her. "Help is on the way."

"I don't want to go to jail," she said.

Everyone assured her that she wouldn't be going to jail.

The woman to my left crouched down and gave her a hug.

The driver of the Oldsmobile was short and middle-aged. He was wearing a Colorado Rockies cap, standing to my right with his hands in his pockets. He looked a little bit like Al Pacino, and he was oddly calm, talking to another onlooker.

"I didn't see 'em," he said. "I didn't see 'em at all. They came out of nowhere. I had no way of seeing 'em. I didn't see a thing until they were up on my hood. I didn't see a thing. All of a sudden I looked up, and *bam,* there they were. There wasn't even a crosswalk there. I couldn't have seen 'em."

An ambulance arrived, followed by two fire trucks and two cop cars. The circle of onlookers opened up, and the paramedics came through. The older girl kept saying that she wanted to go home and see her mommy. The little one just sat there crying. After a while, people started to disperse. I walked back over to my truck, climbed inside, and drove away. My hands were shaking, and I drove very slowly. It was a cold wintry day, and there were giant towering clouds rolling in over the mountains. It was a very strange afternoon.

4.

I dated Amanda during my sophomore year of college. She was a freshman. We started seeing each other in September of that year and kept it going all the way through the following May, at which point we parted ways for the summer. Amanda had an internship lined up back at home in the Bay Area. I was staying in Boulder to work a construction job and take summer classes.

At the moment of our parting, everything was fine. Saying good-bye seemed to bring out the best in us. We said we'd call, we said we'd write. We told each other we loved each other—the first and only time we'd ever done so. We said that we'd keep it going, but it didn't wind up working out that way, which was my fault entirely. I didn't hold up my end of the bargain. Somewhere along the line, I experienced a change of heart. The summer apart was no good for me. My imagination took over. I had too much time to think. I convinced myself that I wasn't ready for anything long-term, told myself that things were getting too serious, that I was too young to be this involved. I needed time, I needed space. Felt trapped. Got nervous. Didn't want to be tied down. At that point, Amanda was a thousand miles away. I was nineteen. I figured I'd deal with it later.

I went to visit her once that summer, on Independence Day. Amanda showed me all around the city—her favorite museums, her favorite parks, her favorite neighborhoods. She took me to her favorite café in Hayes Valley. On the night of the Fourth, we watched the fireworks from a hillside in Marin. I was feeling awful, completely phony. I wanted to tell her that I was having my doubts about continuing the relationship that night, but I didn't go through with it. I told myself the timing wasn't right.

When she got back to Boulder that August, I broke up with her poorly. First, I dodged her for a week. Then I returned her phone calls slowly, much more slowly than normal. It went on like this into September. We'd see each other, here and there. I slept with her a couple of times, knowing that I was going to break up with her. I pretended.

When I finally got around to telling her that I wanted to end things, it caught her completely off guard. She wept. She called me once a day for the next week, asking questions, hoping to reconcile. She wrote me a long, emotional letter and put it in my mailbox. In the letter, she told me that she didn't understand, that she hadn't seen it coming, that she wanted to try to fix things. She told me that I was breaking her heart.

I told myself that she was being dramatic. I called her up and we talked. It was painful and uncomfortable. I told her that I didn't think it was in our best interests to continue dating. I told her that I just wasn't feeling it enough, that my heart wasn't in it all the way.

"So why have we been sleeping together these past few weeks?" she said. "Why have you been having sex with me if you knew you were planning on ending it?"

I didn't have an answer for that. I tried to give one anyway, stumbling my way through a stilted and embarrassed response.

Amanda told me she needed to get off the phone because she thought she was going to be sick. We hung up a few seconds later. I felt awful. I wrote her a long letter that night, apologizing, trying to iron things out and put some sort of amicable end to everything. I walked it over to her mailbox at about two in the morning.

After Amanda read the letter, we had one more phone conversation. I told her once again that I was sorry, that I really wanted for us to be friends. Amanda said, "Sure." She sounded tired and wounded. I think she was crying. No sobs, just tears. I knew they were there by the sound of her voice. A little while later, we hung up. And after that, she stopped calling. In fact, she never called me again. Ever.

I called her one more time, a few weeks later, but hung up when I got the answering machine.

We hardly saw each other for the rest of our college days. She avoided me, I avoided her. The University of Colorado is a big school. Our circles didn't mix much. I didn't know how to approach her. I felt she didn't want to be approached. I wanted her to approach me, but she never did. Maybe she felt I didn't want to be approached either. Maybe she didn't know how.

We never approached each other ever again.

Last I'd heard, she was dating a wealthy ski bum up in Crested Butte, and they had a good thing going. Then she was gone.

5.

suicide *n.*

1.) The act or an instance of intentionally killing oneself.

2.) The destruction or ruin of one's own interests: *It is professional suicide to involve oneself in illegal practices.*

3.) One who commits suicide.

In imperial Rome, taking your own life was considered honorable.

In ancient Greece, convicted criminals were permitted to off themselves.

In France, suicide was illegal up until the Revolution.

In England, failed suicides were hanged right up until the nineteenth century.

Greenland has the highest per capita suicide rate in the world, with 127 out of every 100,000 people choosing to check out voluntarily.

China is home to 21 percent of the world's women. More than half of all female suicides take place there.

In the United States of America, suicide is the third-leading cause of all teenage deaths. A teenager commits suicide in the USA about once every two hours or so.

In 1997, a former music teacher named Marshall Applewhite convinced thirty-nine people to kill themselves in Southern California. Applewhite was the leader of a doomsday cult called Heaven's Gate. He and his followers believed that a UFO was trailing the Hale-Bopp comet. They thought this UFO was four times the size of the earth and that it was on its way to pick them up; so instead of waiting around for it, they drank apple juice and vodka laced with pentobarbital and died.

The sheriff who arrived on the scene discovered all thirty-nine bodies. Resting beside each one was an overnight bag and five dollars cash.

Suicide was naturally the consistent course dictated by the logical intellect. (Is suicide the ultimate sincerity? There seems to be no way to refute the logic of suicide but by the logic of instinct.)

—William James

Back in 1993, a book called *Kanzen Jisatsu Manyuaru* was published in Japan. I happened to read about it in the news one day. *Kanzen Jisatsu Manyuaru* means "The Complete Suicide Manual." The book offers detailed instructions on ten methods of suicide, including hanging, overdosing on drugs, electrocution, and self-immolation. It compares and contrasts the different methods in terms of pain, speed of completion, and level of disfigurement. In addition, the book offers readers tips on the best places to kill themselves, naming Aokigahara, a thick wood at the base of Mt. Fuji, as "the perfect place" to die.

In 1998, seventy-four corpses were found in the woods of Aokigahara.

The suicide rate in Japan rose by 35 percent that year alone.

Suicide prevention groups in Japan were convinced that *The Complete Suicide Manual* was a big part of the problem. The book's author, Wataru Tsurumi, saw things differently. "No one ever killed themselves just because of my book," he said. "The authorities are blaming me because they are unwilling to take responsibility for the economic, political, and social problems that are the real cause of suicides."

In a span of roughly seven years following its publication, the book had sold about 1.2 million copies. With very little advertising or promotion, it was already in its eighty-third printing.

"This goes to show that there is a demand in society," said a spokeswoman from the book's publishing company.

6.

I went to the funeral alone and sat in a back pew, terrified that someone I knew was going to see me. It was miserable being there. I wanted to disappear.

There was no coffin, just a table full of framed pictures of Amanda and some potted plants and some baskets of flowers. The church was packed. A capacity crowd. A fat man was playing a piano. A skinny woman was singing "Ave Maria." Amanda's parents were up ahead in the front row, leaning against each other, defeated.

"Ave Maria" ended, and the priest stepped up to the microphone. His face was red, and his hair was shockingly white. He talked about God, life, death, grief, friendship, love, and heaven. He spoke eloquently, with convincing sympathy and erudition, but I failed to find any real comfort in what he was saying.

From there, the priest called M.J. and Nancy up to the altar. M.J. and Nancy were Amanda's best friends from college. They looked like twins. Blond, petite, and attractive. I hadn't seen either of them in a long time. They seemed to have changed a little bit. Neither of them looked as bohemian as they used to. Both were dressed in formal attire, and each was holding one side of a prepared speech on a piece of wrinkled notebook paper. Their hands were shaking, the piece of paper was shaking. They were trying to keep it together, but keeping it together was pretty much impossible. M.J. started reading and lost it immediately. And when she lost it, everyone lost it. The whole church went with her. Everyone started sniffling and sobbing.

The woman seated next to me was kind enough to hand me a tissue. I glanced at her as I blew my nose. She was holding Tibetan prayer beads in one hand, and her hair was openly gray. She was an aging hippie, a real one, a Marin County authentic.

"I'm so sorry, sweetheart," she whispered.

I made a snorting sound.

I glanced up at M.J. Her jaw was trembling. She was trying to read into the microphone, but it was a lost cause. She couldn't get the words out. Nancy stepped in to help her, and together they were able to stammer through the rest of the page before stepping down. The text of the speech was hard to decipher. I was having a hard time concentrating. Didn't have a clue what it was about. The only part of it that I caught was the part about how lucky they felt to have known Amanda. The rest of it was lost on me.

Then the priest stepped up to the microphone again, said a few final words in closing, and the ceremony ended. Sting's "Fields of Gold" came on the church P.A. system, the recessional hymn. One of Amanda's favorites.

As soon as that happened, I was up and out the door in a flash, one of the very first to leave. I wanted some fresh air. I wanted a cigarette. I walked out of the church and down the concrete steps and moved away, over to the left, over toward the road. I pulled a cigarette from my jacket pocket and lit up. It was overcast outside, a Bay Area winter day, cool and crisp and pleasant. The cloud cover was thinning out, and the sun was trying to break through. Cars were going by, and a light wind was blowing through the trees. There was nothing too unusual about it.

7.

Fortunately, there was no burial, just a reception back at Amanda's parents' house. Amanda's remains had already been cremated. No corpse with makeup, no lowering of the coffin into the muddy brown hole. I was thankful for that. The worst of it was over.

At some point along the way, I'd decided not to go to the reception. I'd convinced myself that there was no need to go to the reception. I knew it would be polite to stop in and offer my condolences to Amanda's family, but I didn't think I could deal with seeing her parents, didn't think I could deal with offering my sympathies at a reception. I was sure her parents knew all about me, sure they knew about the breakup, my behavior, the fact that I'd broken Amanda's heart. I figured I'd write them a letter later and skip the reception altogether. I didn't have what it took to attend. Too much intensity, too much sadness, too many people, too much conversation. Everyone standing around, drinking wine, eating finger food, talking in hushed tones about how great Amanda was, how she would want her funeral to be a celebration rather than a dismal affair, how much life she had inside her, how much joy, how much light. Instead of navigating that madness, I was planning to simply drive back over to Horvak's place. I'd assume my position on the couch and watch television, and maybe later, if I actually got hungry, I'd order some food for delivery. And maybe I'd have a beer or two. And eventually, with luck, I'd drift off to sleep.

In the morning, I would rise and drive back to SFO, where I'd return my rental car and catch my flight to New Orleans. I'd rendezvous with my family in the Deep South to celebrate the holidays, and my life, unlike Amanda's, would continue on.

8.

I was standing around smoking in the church parking lot when I noticed Alan Wells walking toward me. Wells was another friend from college, born and raised in Berkeley. He was a big, bearish guy with lamb-chop sideburns and a head full of curly blond hair. He wore silver hoop earrings in both ears and had known Amanda for years. I'd first met him in Boulder, three years earlier, shortly after I started dating her. I always got the feeling that he didn't like me very much.

He walked right up to me, half smiling, and extended a hand. I shook it and we man-hugged, slapping each other on the back. We talked for a while, trying to sum up Amanda's death. It was a strained conversation. Nothing much was said. Suicide seems to leave you strained, with nothing much to say.

"She was the greatest," he said.

"She was," I said.

"I'm still in shock," he said.

"I feel remarkably dumb," I said.

Wells then asked me how I was getting to the reception. In a moment of reflex, I told him I was driving. I couldn't bring myself to admit that I didn't want to go. He asked me if I was alone. I told him I was. He offered to ride along with me, and I told him that would be great. I had no idea how to get to Amanda's house. For some reason, I couldn't remember the way.

Wells then excused himself momentarily and walked over to his father and stepmother, who were standing near the doors of the church, to let them know he was going to catch a ride with me. His stepmother, as it turned out, was the woman who had handed me the Kleenex during M.J. and Nancy's speech. Wells hadn't been sitting with them during the service. He'd been up in the front, with Amanda's closest friends. His stepmother looked over at me, gave me a pained smile, and waved. I waved slightly in response, shifted in my shoes, and averted my gaze. I took two small steps backward, dropped my cigarette butt to the ground, and stepped on it. Then I pulled a fresh one from my pocket and lit up. Then I looked up at the sky. And then I bent my arm as if to look at my watch.

I wasn't even wearing a watch.

9.

The house was nice, even nicer than I remembered it. Expensive furniture, expensive architecture, expensive art. It felt like a museum and it smelled like cinnamon. None of that really mattered, though. When push came to shove, all I could think about was the garage. I couldn't stop thinking about Amanda tiptoeing down the stairs in the middle of the night, in her nightgown, with her note, grabbing the car keys, heading out there.

I thought about Mr. Anaciello waking early for breakfast, walking into the kitchen in his robe, reaching for the coffee, stopping, cocking his head to one side, listening. Hearing the engine running. Making a face. Wondering. Walking over to the door. Opening it. Coughing in the cloud of exhaust. Eyes burning from the fumes. Panicking. Reaching for the button, opening the garage door. Running over to his car, one hand covering his mouth and nose. Finding Amanda. Dead. Blue. Stiff as a mannequin. Heavy. Lukewarm. Gone. Screaming for his wife. Screaming for help. Screaming for someone to call an ambulance. Shaking Amanda. Trying to shake the life back into her. Screaming her name. Weeping. Pale. Carrying her back inside. Attempting CPR. Pounding on her chest. Saying something along the lines of, *"Breathe, goddamnit! Breathe!"*

It was pointless to think about those things. But I couldn't stop.

• • •

There was a receiving line in the living room. Wells and I were standing in it, advancing slowly on Amanda's parents, Jack and Nora. Nobody in line was talking. Everyone was preparing themselves, dealing with their fears, their discomforts, trying to figure out what to say. An impossible task. No words would do. There was nothing to say in a situation like that, nothing that would make them feel any better. The best you could do was say how great Amanda was and how terribly sorry you were that she was gone. In many ways, saying these two things in conjunction would only serve to heighten the sadness.

Jack Anaciello was doing the greeting. His eyes were glistening with tears. He was shaking well-wishers' hands, whispering to them warmly, thanking them for their presence. He seemed to be holding it together somehow. He was wrinkled and tired. His eyes were bloodshot from tears.

Nora Anaciello was down for the count, laid out on the couch. She wasn't greeting anyone at all. She was dazed, looking off in the distance at nothing in particular, holding a glass of white wine. She was barefoot and appeared to be medicated. Her high-heeled shoes were sitting side by side on the floor.

Strangely enough, when I stepped up to greet him, Jack Anaciello didn't even recognize me. He had no idea who I was. Or else he couldn't remember. Or else he didn't care to. Or else he was so out of it, he couldn't put two and two together. When I told him my name, it didn't seem to register. But he pretended that it did.

"Ah, yes," he said to me. "Of course. How are you, Wayne?"

And then I started talking about myself. Started rambling. Told him about Boulder. Told him about my degree. Told him about my plans for the future. I felt as though I shouldn't be talking about the future, that it was somehow very rude to be talking about the future, but for some reason, I couldn't stop. And somehow Jack Anaciello seemed genuinely interested. His eyes were locked on mine. He was nodding attentively. But he wasn't all there.

When I finished, he took my right hand and clasped it between both of his, like a politician, and thanked me for coming. I told him how sorry I was once again, how wonderful Amanda was. I told him that all of the beautiful things about her were true. He thanked me. His eyes were watering. So were mine. I walked away.

I walked into the kitchen, picked up a plastic cup, and poured myself a glass of wine. Then I headed out back for another cigarette. There were at least twenty people out there already, puffing away. The deck was packed. People were standing in twos and threes, inhaling and exhaling, mumbling to one another.

I saw M.J. and Nancy standing on the lawn. Both were blowing smoke, ashing into a stagnant birdbath. M.J. looked terrible, pink and puffed up and wrung out, like she'd been weeping for weeks. She saw me and waved, left Nancy, and walked over. I raised a hand and said hello and stepped off of the deck onto the lawn. M.J. gave me a long hug and told me how happy she was to see me. I found this surprising. I didn't really know what to say.

She asked me if I needed a place to stay, mentioning that a bunch of people were splitting rooms at the TraveLodge over on the Redwood Highway. I told her I was okay, that I was staying at Horvak's place. She said the name rang a bell. I told her that he went to C.U. She nodded. There was a silence. I looked out across the lawn. There was a red-winged blackbird perched on the rim of the birdbath. Nancy wasn't standing there anymore.

"This all feels unreal to me," I said.

"I can't believe she did it," M.J. said.

"I don't think anybody can."

"I knew she had her problems, but everyone has problems. I didn't see this. How could I not see this?"

"Nobody did."

I took a drag of my cigarette, blew a cloud of smoke at the sky, and watched it disappear.

10.

Later that afternoon, all of Amanda's friends went over to Kathy McCormack's house. Kathy was a friend of Amanda's from childhood. Her family lived in a beautiful house on a wooded lot on Morning Sun Avenue in Mill Valley. Wells and I walked in together. The whole place was decked out in white Christmas lights. Everyone was drinking. Bottles and cans everywhere. Kathy greeted us, introduced herself, offered us beers. I took one, thanked her, opened it, and walked outside for another cigarette. I hadn't stopped smoking since I left the church.

The people on the back porch appeared to be intoxicated. There was a joint going around. Laughter and coughing. It almost seemed like a party.

"Mandy would want it to be a celebration," I heard someone say. "She wouldn't want everyone to stand around moping. She wouldn't want it to be sad."

It was nearly 5:00 p.m., and already the sun was down. It was December 23. The days are short that time of year. Amanda had killed herself the day before the winter solstice. Somehow that made sense. I finished my beer, smoked two more ciga-rettes, and made some sporadic small talk on the deck with a guy I didn't know, some neo-hippie from Petaluma with a mangy beard. He was wearing a fur-lined hat with earflaps.

"It's a strange day," he said.

"Yeah," I said.

"Strange energy," he said.

"Really strange," I agreed.

"At least we got decent weather," he said.

"Yeah," I said.

"Amanda brought us good weather," he said.

A few seconds later, I stuffed my cigarette butt inside an empty beer can and walked back inside.

People were starting to get outwardly drunk in the living room. The talking was getting louder and less coherent. The room was filling up with false confidence. I stood around in silence for a minute or two, feeling terribly awkward, and then I decided to leave. I had determined that it was safe to leave. I'd been biding my time, and now it was safe to leave. I could claim a long day and an early flight in the morning. I could walk out without having to lie. I'd done my duty. I'd done the right things, said the right things, gone to the right places. All things considered, everything had turned out fine.

I caught Wells in the kitchen and told him I was on my way out. I asked him if he needed a ride back to the East Bay. He told me no thanks, he was going to stick around and catch a ride later. We shook hands by the stove and shared another man-hug. He programmed my contact information into his cell phone and told me he'd call me. I wished him well and went off looking for M.J. and Nancy.

I found them upstairs in Kathy's room. I knocked twice, lightly, and stuck my head in the door. The two of them were sitting on the bed, locked in heavy conversation. There was a bottle of red wine on the nightstand. Their eyes were red from crying, and their teeth were blue from the wine.

"Hey," I said. "I just wanted to say good-bye."

"Fencer," Nancy said, slurring a little and patting the mattress. "Come sit down."

11.

I walked over and sat down on the end of the bed, and Nancy told me the story: how Amanda had missed her period in June, the summer that we were apart, the summer before I broke up with her. How she had debated about what to do. How she had decided to have the abortion. How she had decided not to tell me. How she'd freaked out, afraid it would scare me away. How she'd had the operation in the city, at a clinic near the Embarcadero. How Nancy had driven her there, was with her the entire time. How there were protesters lining the sidewalks as they went inside, picketers screaming at them, telling them that they were baby killers, murderers, how they would rot in hell for eternity on account of their sins. How it wasn't something I should feel responsible for. How I couldn't have known. How Amanda didn't want me to have to deal with it, how she just wanted it to be over and done with, how she swore Nancy to absolute secrecy.

The news hit me strangely. My reaction was decidedly minimal. I didn't move. I didn't speak. There was a barely detectable feeling in my belly—a weakness, a twinge. But not much more.

"But with everything that's happened," said Nancy, "I feel like it's important to come clean."

"It helps things make a little more sense," said M.J., "but it doesn't solve anything. Not by any means."

"Absolutely," said Nancy. "I'm not trying to say that this is the *reason* she killed herself. Not at all."

"Oh, no," I said. The words fell out of my mouth weakly.

Nancy crawled across the bed and gave me a hug. I didn't hug her back.

"Do her parents know?" I said.

"No," said M.J. "I don't think so."

"We were just talking about whether we should tell them," Nancy said. "I don't know if it would be worth it. They've already been through so much."

"But if it helps them find some kind of closure," said M.J., "maybe it would be a good thing."

"I think I'd wait on that," I said, running a hand through my hair.

"I would obviously tell them that you had no idea," Nancy said.

"I think we should wait on that."

"It's not anything we would do anytime soon," said M.J.

Nancy sniffled, reached for her glass, took a sip of her wine.

I rose to my feet and told M.J. and Nancy that I'd really appreciate it if they didn't say anything. I told them I needed time to think, that I'd like to be the one to make the decision about whether or not to say something, that it was my responsibility. I asked them to keep this information in confidence. They told me they would.

I took a step backward toward the door, not knowing what else to say. There was nothing else to say, really. I didn't want to say anything more, didn't want to debate. I didn't want to coerce, and I didn't want to empathize or discuss.

I just wanted to get the fuck out of there.

Moments later, I walked out of the house, climbed into my rental car, and drove south out of Marin and across the Golden Gate

Bridge, back toward Horvak's place, completely numb. Night had settled in, and the lights of the city were shining in the distance. I rolled my window down and lit up another cigarette, turned on talk radio, and looked out across the bay. The city was alive, glowing like fire beneath the clouds.

The fog was rolling in again.

12.

The Golden Gate Bridge first opened to vehicular traffic at high noon on May 28, 1937. It is approximately 1.7 miles long, and its two towers are 746 feet tall. Channel clearance is approximately 220 feet, and the cables that support the suspended roadway are 36.5 inches in diameter. More people have jumped off of the Golden Gate Bridge to their deaths than any other bridge in the world. It is a magnet for the desperate, arguably the number-one suicide destination on the planet. Depressed people with dramatic flair like to go there on their last legs, ready to cross over into the next dimension.

In 1975, at the Langley Porter Neuropsychiatric Institute in San Francisco, a psychiatrist named David Rosen conducted a study of people who jumped off of the Golden Gate Bridge and accidentally survived. Here is what he discovered:

All these survivors, during and after their jumps, experienced mystical states of consciousness characterized by losing the sense of time and space and by feelings of spiritual rebirth and unity with other human beings, the entire universe, and God. As a result of their intimate encounter with death, some of them had a profound religious conversion; others described a reconfirmation of their previous religious beliefs. One of the survivors denied

any suicide intent altogether. He saw the Golden Gate
Bridge as "golden doors" through which he will pass from
the material world into a new spiritual realm.

In olden times, suicides were viewed as contagious. People who
killed themselves were often buried at crossroads in the dark of
night under large piles of stones. In addition, stakes were sometimes driven through their dead hearts in an effort to prevent the
sickness of their spirits from infecting the living.

Once every twenty minutes or so, somebody commits suicide in
the United States of America.

Approximately once every two weeks, somebody jumps off of the
Golden Gate Bridge.

The
free fall
takes
about
four
seconds.

Those who jump off of the Golden Gate Bridge hit the water
below at a speed of roughly seventy-five miles per hour, with a
force of fifteen thousand pounds per square inch.

In 1993, a guy named Steve Page threw his three-year-old
daughter, Kellie, over the railing of the Golden Gate Bridge. A
few seconds later, he followed her.

In a 1993 poll conducted by the *San Francisco Examiner*, 54 percent of respondents said that they did not want a suicide barrier constructed on the bridge to prevent people from doing things like that. They felt it would mar the bridge. They felt it would obstruct their view. They felt it would impinge upon people's freedoms.

gephyrophobia *n.*
Fear of bridges or of crossing them.

13.

This was the second straight year that I'd lost someone during the holidays. My grandfather had died the year before, on Christmas Eve 1998. My mother's father. We called him Granddad. He was in a hospital bed, alone, when he slipped into The Void. My grandmother had been sitting at his bedside for hours on end. Then, at about 9:00 p.m., she went home to get some rest. Granddad drifted away a couple of hours later, in the dark of night, when nobody was looking.

A month later, each of his grandchildren received roughly $6,000 in ExxonMobil stock. Ticker symbol: XOM.

petroleum *n.*
A thick, flammable, yellow-to-black mixture of gaseous, liquid, and solid hydrocarbons that occurs naturally beneath the earth's surface. Can be separated into fractions including natural gas, gasoline, naphtha, kerosene, fuel and lubricating oils, paraffin wax, and asphalt, and is used as raw material for a wide variety of derivative products.

I was wary of owning an oil stock, worried it would be tantamount to owning wars and pollution. Immediately, I called Horvak out in San Francisco. Horvak was a couple of years older than me and had been working in the financial sector for Charles Schwab. With his assistance, I opened an online brokerage account and cashed out of Exxon with the push of a button. In an instant, all of my oil stock was gone, converted directly into cash. Horvak then informed me that I didn't want to have all that cash sitting around, because cash left to generate meager interest in a savings account would be "dying cash," on account of something called the "rate of inflation."

rate of inflation *n.*
The rate of change of prices (as indicated by a price index) calculated on a monthly or annual basis. Also known as *inflation rate.*

I told Horvak that I didn't want my cash to die. Horvak told me to put my cash in a company called eBay. Ticker symbol: EBAY. Horvak had been tracking eBay and said it was a nice place to start, so in February 1999, I purchased $6,201.47 worth of eBay stock at $21.68 per share.

As of late April 1999, the stock had more than doubled in value. The thing took off like a moon rocket. It was the easiest money I'd ever made. Horvak was out of his mind with excitement at the time, trembling with joy and fantasy. Wall Street was going bananas. Stock prices were taking off, IPOs and record highs in every direction. The tech boom was on. Everyone was an optimist, and nobody could lose.

"You wouldn't believe what's happening out here," Horvak said. "People are just throwing money around. It's stupid. It doesn't make any sense."

Horvak was an animal, day-trading aggressively and making a killing. One day he made $50,000 before lunch. At that point, his portfolio was worth more than a quarter of a million bucks. He'd started out a couple of years earlier with practically nothing, and now he was relatively rich. He was planning on quitting his job in a year. He and his girlfriend, Blair, were going to go travel around the world for a long time, purchasing things.

Blair was a hippie chick with a trust fund.

14.

Inspired by Horvak's success on the open market, I sold all of my eBay shares one afternoon in late April, right before graduation, and started day-trading. The ensuing seven months were an odyssey. Evenings were spent delivering pizzas. Days were spent tracking stocks. I was averaging about four or five hours of sleep per night.

The winning was pretty much relentless. On a typical day, Horvak called me once every hour or so to celebrate. We had brief, ecstatic conversations about numbers and the future. We discussed travel plans and entrepreneurial concepts. I babbled about making an independent feature film. Horvak fantasized about buying a small resort hotel off the coast of Honduras. He sounded like he was on uppers all the time. His mind and his mouth were going a mile a minute. He was betting big, talking about early retirement with some degree of frequency. I think he was closing in on seven figures. My portfolio was growing rapidly as well, albeit on a much smaller scale. The simplicity of the arrangement was nothing short of mind-blowing. It seemed like the easiest thing in the world.

On an average day, I usually took a sizable nap after market close, if my adrenaline levels weren't too high. Then, at about 9:00 p.m., I'd drive over to Fatty Jay's for the late shift.

Fatty Jay's was the name of the pizza establishment that I worked for.

I was just out of college, with a bachelor of fine arts degree in avant-garde filmmaking. All it had gotten me so far was Fatty Jay's and day-trading.

avant-garde *n.*
A group active in the invention and application of new techniques in a given field, especially in the arts.

adj.
Of, relating to, or being part of an innovative group, especially one in the arts: *avant-garde painters; an avant-garde theater piece.*

With my stocks performing well, I could have cashed out and quit the pizza job, no problem. I could have taken my profits and hit the road. I thought about it several times, but I could never bring myself to go through with it. Chalk it up to indecision. At that point, the end of the boom was nowhere in sight. I didn't want to cash out too soon and risk missing out on further profits. At the same time, the stock numbers seemed unreal to me. I didn't trust them entirely. My money was totally intangible. I couldn't wrap my head around it.

Horvak warned me continually that the entire enterprise could come crashing down at any second. We discussed this fact ad nauseam. We were desperate to be wise, advising each other to employ a conservative approach to rabid enthusiasm. We pondered the history of the markets and encouraged each other to stay with our jobs until we got off the ride. Quitting, we felt, might jinx us. It was better, we felt, to keep working hard, lest we anger the financial gods.

The longest I ever rode one stock was seventy-two hours. Some days I'd ride three or four stocks in a single session. My typical routine had me buying at open and cashing out sometime after midday. My goal was always a 2 percent return. If I made 5 percent, I automatically cashed out, no matter what time it was. That was the discipline. At the end of my run, I calculated the capital gains tax, set it aside in my money market account per Horvak's strict instructions, and threw the rest back into the market the following morning. It was easy.

Naturally, my good fortune astonished me; it rattled me to the point of superstition. I didn't talk about it very much, convinced that the market would crash if I said something. Horvak was my only real confidant. I remember telling him one day that I'd never felt luckier in my whole life. I told him that, for the first time ever, I found myself wondering if someone or something was actually watching over me.

"Maybe it's my granddad," I said, half kidding. "Maybe he's supervising my investment portfolio from the next realm."

Horvak told me that he liked day-trading better than weed.

15.

A week or so after Amanda's funeral, the year 2000 arrived. Y2K. For months, the world had been hearing about imminent danger, that Y2K was a disaster waiting to happen, that critical mainframe computer systems were sure to crash on New Year's Day, that the global economy was in grave and utter peril. Kingpins in the federal government were urging calmness, advising citizens to exercise caution and restraint. In the weeks leading up to the big day, the more gullible elements of society had busied themselves by stocking up on food and water, batteries and duct tape, in preparation for the chaos.

But in the end, of course, nothing much happened. Not a goddamn thing. It was total bullshit, start to finish. A dark and mysterious lie. And it was no big surprise.

The millennial celebrations of New Year's Eve were completely misleading as well. A marketing scam, if you ask me. There was money to be made. People were buying. Everyone was in on the act, celebrating the big moment as if it were the real thing, lighting off firecrackers, waving their hands in the air, pretending to be awed. In truth, however, the twenty-first century wouldn't *actually* begin until 2001. New Year's Day 2001 would technically qualify as the first day of the third millennium, because a millennium doesn't *actually* begin until the one thousandth year of the previous millennium is *over with,* the same way a decade doesn't end until the end of the tenth year. A matter of plain common sense. Yet for some reason, human beings felt compelled to celebrate the start of the next millennium a year early. We just couldn't wait.

An arbitrary new millennium had dawned.

16.

All throughout the holidays, I'd been feeling pretty listless, generally disinterested in any kind of socializing. San Francisco was particularly bad. It was followed by my family's sojourn down to Louisiana to visit our extended clan for Christmas. From Louisiana, we headed back to Indianapolis, the place where I'd grown up, and there we endured the rest of our vacation in a state of relative harmony. I wound up spending most of my time in my old bedroom, reading and watching television. I found myself particularly captivated by a book on Warren Buffett, the world's greatest stock market investor. At the time, Buffett was America's second-richest man. His net worth topped out at approximately $36 billion, an amount of money that well exceeded the gross national product of several small nations, like, for instance, Estonia.

The population of Estonia: 1.4 million human beings.

> **gross national product** *n.* (*abbr.* GNP)
> The total market value of all the goods and services
> produced by a nation during a specified period.

Warren Buffett was born on August 30, 1930, during the Great Depression. As a child, he demonstrated a prodigious mastery of numbers and a precocious entrepreneurial streak. At the age of six, he was purchasing six-packs of Coca-Cola from his grandfather's grocery store for twenty-five cents and reselling them for thirty cents. From there, he expanded his enterprises, buying various items and then turning them around for a handsome profit.

By the time he'd graduated from high school, Buffett had earned more than ten grand—roughly the equivalent of $100,000 in modern dollars, when you factor in the rate of inflation.

In 1988, Buffett began purchasing Coca-Cola stock (ticker symbol: KO) in massive quantities, quickly becoming the company's largest shareholder. At the time, the shares were worth about $10.96 apiece. Five years later, they were worth $74.50. By the end of the 1990s, Buffet's stake in the company was valued at around $13 billion.

His profits were enormous.

The ingredients found in a can of Coca-Cola are: carbonated water, high-fructose corn syrup, caramel color, phosphoric acid, natural flavors, and caffeine.

A $10,000 investment in Buffett's insurance and investment holding company, Berkshire Hathaway, Inc., back in 1965 was worth roughly $50 million in the year 2000.

Despite his massive wealth, Warren Buffett continues to live in his home state of Nebraska, in the same gray stucco house he purchased in Omaha for less than $32,000 in the 1950s.

As a youngster, he was rejected by Harvard Business School.

His nickname? The Oracle of Omaha.

17.

Amanda's ashes had been scattered into San Francisco Bay, not too far from the Golden Gate Bridge, on Christmas Day, a few days before the dawn of an arbitrary new millennium. I sold all of my stock three days later, on December 28, 1999. Horvak was stunned when I gave him the news.

"How could you do this?" he said. "How could you bail? How could you puss out before we even get into Q2? We were just getting started."

"I could die any day now," I said.

Horvak said, "What?"

I went on to tell Horvak that Amanda's death had made me rethink some things. I told him I was tired, that I needed rest, that I needed a break from money and trading. I told him I wanted to reevaluate my position in life. I told him I wanted to try to figure out what I thought about things.

"This whole experience has made me realize that I don't really know what I think about things," I explained. "I don't really know what anything *means*."

"Nobody does," said Horvak. "That's the whole point."

My holdings at the time of liquidation totaled roughly $45,000, after taxes.

Relatively speaking, I'd made a *killing*.

• • •

Shortly after cashing out, I wrote a large check to an organization called San Francisco Suicide Prevention. Amanda's parents
had requested that, in lieu of flowers, all donations be sent there
in her name.

I sent a donation there in her name.

I often worried that I hadn't sent enough.

Sometimes I felt as though I should have sent *everything*.

A couple of days later, in a fit of fiscal nervousness, I took
$5,400 and dumped it right back into the New York Stock
Exchange, for safekeeping.

I bought ninety shares of Coca-Cola at $59.18 per share.

I then gave my sisters, Lorraine and Anne, $2,500 cash. I handed
them each twenty-five one-hundred-dollar bills and swore them to
absolute secrecy. Lorraine, my older sister, asked me if I was dealing drugs. I told her yes. Anne, my younger sister, asked me if she
had to pay me back. I told her no.

Shortly thereafter, I found myself researching the history of the
stock market, because I realized that I didn't have any true understanding of what it actually meant. Along the way, I wound up
learning that the American Stock Exchange had once been called
the "Curb Exchange," a fact that amused me greatly. I felt there was
something flawless about the terminology, something wickedly
funny and savagely true. It inspired visions of drug deals, prostitution, and rampant capitalism, all in one fell swoop. It was poetry.

From there, I continued my investigation, an oddly feverish
pursuit that wound up leading me into a broader understanding
of the global economy. What I found, by and large, tended to be
riveting and deeply disturbing—not that this was any big surprise.

I ingested a surreal assortment of sobering facts and figures, most of which were difficult to actually comprehend. I learned, for example, that there are approximately 500 million people in Asia, Africa, and Latin America who are living in what the World Bank refers to as "absolute poverty"; that every thirty seconds, 200 people die of hunger; that for the price of one Patriot missile, a school full of hungry children could eat lunch every day for five years; that half of the world's human beings are struggling to survive on the equivalent of two dollars per day and that half of that half are struggling to survive on the equivalent of one dollar per day; that 1.5 billion people in the world don't have access to clean drinking water; that approximately one fifth of America's food goes to waste every year—the equivalent of about 130 pounds per person; and that the amount of food wasted annually by Americans could feed 49 million hungry people.

Eventually, I wore myself out. I put the books down.

I sat back in my chair and looked at the television.

Jeopardy! was on.

I was a twenty-two-year-old American with $22,500 in my checking account.

I had no idea what I was doing with my life.

My ex-girlfriend had killed herself, and she had once been pregnant with my child.

Had she gone through with the pregnancy, our kid would have been starting preschool soon.

18.

Another person I read about over the holidays: Siddhartha Gautama. A fairly obvious thing to do in the wake of a trauma, perhaps. But nevertheless, there I was.

I took comfort in the fact that Gautama was an actual man. He was born into a caste of warrior aristocrats sometime around the year 560 B.C., in the Himalayan foothills of what is now Nepal. He enjoyed a sheltered childhood in a pleasure-filled palace, oblivious to the miseries of society. He partied a lot and enjoyed the company of several concubines.

Though the specifics of his life history are admittedly cloudy, most religious scholars seem to agree that Siddhartha had excelled in sports and the martial arts, while also enjoying a comprehensive education in literature, religion, philosophy, and agriculture management. He married a cousin of his at the age of sixteen. Her name was Yashodhara, and she bore him children.

Eventually, however, despite all of this comfort and stimulation, Siddhartha became restless. His charmed existence wasn't enough to satisfy him. He tired of his palace, his concubines, his family. He tired of his parties. He tired of his trust fund. He had it all, yet he was deeply unhappy.

One night, against the wishes of his father, Siddhartha snuck out of the palace and wandered into the streets. Here is what he saw:

1.) A sick man

2.) A poor man

3.) A beggar

4.) A corpse

Shortly thereafter, Siddhartha freaked out, essentially. He abandoned his former way of life and dedicated himself to solving the riddle of suffering endemic in all human beings. He even abandoned his wife and family. Naked and alone, he set out into the countryside in search of true enlightenment. He became a wandering ascetic.

Naturally, his life in those days was pretty bleak. He stumbled around, starving and nude, mumbling to himself. He slept on a bed of thorns in the jungle. He held his breath until he passed out, hoping to unlock the mysteries of existence. He went on like this for about six years.

In the end, the experiment failed. Without any food in his belly, Siddhartha couldn't really think straight. Eventually, he came to believe that a life of complete denial wasn't a good idea, and neither was a life of total indulgence. The trick, he realized, was to live a life of balance. There was, he realized, a Middle Way.

Pleased with his newfound knowledge, Siddhartha went and sat in the shade of a large pipal tree for a round of intensive meditation. While sitting there, he had a series of incredible epiphanies. He became enlightened.

In the midst of this epiphanic trance, Siddhartha managed to reduce human existence to Four Noble Truths. Those Four Noble Truths are:

1.) All humans suffer.

2.) All human suffering is caused by human desire,

particularly the desire that impermanent things be permanent.

3.) Human suffering can be ended by ending human desire.

4.) Desire can be ended by following the "Eightfold Noble Path": right understanding, right thought, right speech, right action, right livelihood, right effort, right mindfulness, and right concentration.

Siddhartha went on to spend the rest of his life teaching the Four Noble Truths and the Eightfold Noble Path to anyone who would listen. He died at the age of eighty. His devotees generally believe that he passed into a state of nirvana at the moment of his death.

nirvana *n.*

1.) *Often cap:*

> a. *Buddhism:* The ineffable ultimate in which one has attained disinterested wisdom and compassion.
>
> b. *Hinduism:* Emancipation from ignorance and the extinction of all attachment.

2.) An ideal condition of rest, harmony, stability, or joy.

These days, Siddhartha is commonly referred to by his nickname: Buddha.

19.

It was only a matter of time before my parents and I wound up having "The Conversation" again. It happened on a Tuesday afternoon, a couple of days after the dawn of the new millennium. We were sitting in the kitchen, eating lunch. My sisters were off at the shopping mall, exchanging Christmas gifts, and my parents took it upon themselves to inquire about my plans for the future, my thoughts on steady income, an agenda, a career. It was here that I broke the news about the sale of my Exxon stock and my subsequent astronomical success on the open market. At that point, the ride was over. I figured I had nothing to lose. I came clean, told them everything. My parents were flabbergasted, to put it mildly. My mother asked me if it was legal. My father, though he tried not to show it, was fairly impressed.

"Well, *shit,*" he said.

Naturally, they were curious about what I was going to do next. I told them that I wasn't sure, that my only real plan at the moment was to head back to Boulder and reevaluate my options. I told them that I didn't have the mind to be making any big decisions for a while, and for the moment, that was enough to end the inquiry. They didn't press me any further. In truth, they'd been good about that since Amanda's death. They hadn't really pressed me much.

Toward the end of The Conversation, I yawned and rubbed my eyes. My mother made a face and told me that I looked like

I needed some rest. I nodded in agreement. I hadn't been sleeping well. I'd been waking up frequently in the middle of the night, staring at the ceiling. All I could think about was Amanda waking up in the middle of the night, staring at the ceiling. I thought about Amanda tiptoeing down the stairs. I thought about Amanda at the abortion clinic. I thought about Amanda and me, watching those fireworks on that hillside in Marin.

I thought about Amanda sitting there behind the wheel, lost and broken with the engine running, waiting in the dead of night.

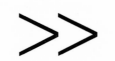

20.

Late April, the arbitrary year 2000. Four months after Amanda's death. Winter had melted into spring in methodical fashion. Twelve weeks flew by in the blink of an eye.

This was when the bubble burst and the dot-com boom met its brutal, inglorious end. In one shocking week, the stock market indexes all dropped dramatically. Carnage on Wall Street. Bloodletting. Dying IPOs. Hyperventilation. Investors worldwide were in a massive panic. Horvak called me up to tell me he had lost more than $90,000 in a three-hour span of time.

"I think it's going to rebound," he said. "I'm going to make some adjustments, restrategize, and decide how to ride it out." His voice was cracking.

After the holidays, I'd gone back to Boulder with the intention of quitting my job and taking it easy for a while, but it didn't wind up working out that way. When push came to shove, I couldn't go through with it. I realized that I didn't want to quit my job, at least not right away. I realized that I didn't know how to take it easy for a while. Sitting around contemplating didn't seem like a good idea. I'd tried it a few times. It didn't work out too well.

In consequence, I had continued to deliver pizza throughout the winter and spring. The work routine kept me busy, and it was simple and predictable. The people opened their front doors and handed me cash; I handed them food and smiled. They said thank you; I told them they were welcome. Then they shut the door. Then I walked away. It was a gestalt exercise, essentially. You wound up getting a little vignette of their world, a snapshot of their life. If your eyes were open, you'd see it: a bass guitar, red-checkered curtains, the smell of Windex, *Architectural Digest,* a Jack Russell terrier, three Frisbees, a Big Bertha driver, a poster of Charles Mingus in a silver frame on the wall, a yellow pack of American Spirits, and a cactus on the windowsill.

You could learn pretty much everything you needed to know about someone based on that information.

Personally, I was beginning to think that this was an excellent way to interact with people. Insofar as human exchanges go, it seemed pretty tough to top. Provided I showed up on time and they tipped me, everyone walked away satisfied and unharmed.

But then, nothing much was risked in this arrangement. And risk, I'd heard, was everything. That was what the mental health experts were always saying.

"Without risk," they'd say, "you cannot get The Magic."

The Magic.

Another fact worth mentioning: I didn't feel much like having sex just then. My interest in meeting pretty girls was essentially nonexistent, which was odd. Normally, I existed in a constant state of wanting to have sex with pretty girls. But now I really didn't. I seemed to have lost my taste for the thrill of the hunt. I didn't really care about getting laid. Getting laid was dangerous. I wasn't in the mood.

At the same time, I kept thinking about actually being in love. In the wake of Amanda's suicide, it had struck me that I'd never actually been in love. While it was true that I'd loved Amanda, it was clear to me now that I'd never actually *been* in love with her.

It was never whole, never fully functional or mature—not on my part, anyway. It was young love, fleeting and unpredictable, sometimes even dumb. It lacked the depth of understanding and selflessness of real love. It wasn't the genuine article, it wasn't the real thing. If it had been real love, then the relationship wouldn't have ended the way that it did—and the blame for that circumstance lay wholly with me. The fact of the matter was, I'd never been in love before. Didn't have what it took. Didn't have the guts. I wasn't able to manage it with Amanda, and I hadn't been able to manage it with anyone else. I hadn't realized that before, but I realized that now. People fell in love every day, all over the world, and I didn't know how to do it. I didn't understand what it meant, and I didn't know how it was done.

This worried me.

21.

In mid-May, I finally made my exit from Fatty Jay's. After much deliberation, I decided to ditch Boulder and go traveling for a spell. The timing seemed right for an adventure. I figured I would willfully disorient myself in hopes that it might help me to discover some kind of valuable new perspective.

A few weeks earlier, I'd purchased a ticket to Cancún, Mexico, where I would be attending the wedding of my good friends A.B. and Jenny. They were getting hitched on the beach in Playa del Carmen, a picturesque village on the Mayan Riviera. A.B. was four years older than I was, a friend I'd made during college, and he had asked me to be a groomsman. Naturally, I'd accepted.

Cancún, I had decided, seemed like a logical starting point for my wanderings.

After the wedding, I planned to fly to Havana, Cuba.

After that, I didn't know what I was going to do.

It was up in the air.

My mentor at Fatty Jay's was a guy named Jim Hogan. Hogan was the owner and general manager. He was a large man in his midforties, twice divorced, misogynistic, and bitter. He had a potbelly and a mullet. He didn't flinch when I told him I was quitting. He was used to this kind of thing. The pizza business tends to see a lot of turnover.

Hogan knew all about my recent travails, all about Amanda

and the funeral and the aborted child. I'd told him the whole story one night after closing up shop. We were in the walk-in freezer at 3:00 a.m., shivering and smoking pot. At that point, he was the only person I had confided in.

A few days before my departure, Hogan insisted on taking me out for drinks at the Bust Stop, a strip club at the north end of Boulder, one of his favorite local hangouts. He was adamant about it.

"You need some naked girls in your life," he reasoned. "You've had a shitty run of luck with chicks. No reason for it. No good explanation. Sometimes you just need to go out and say 'fuck it.'"

One of Hogan's ex-wives was a stripper. Her stage name was Evangeline. Her real name was Margaret. She had divorced him in 1984. Packed up her things and left, with very little explanation.

In 1989, she died in a boating accident in Tampa Bay.

II.

Point Break is one of my all-time favorite films. I believe it to be one of the funniest films ever made, on par with the comedies of Charlie Chaplin, Buster Keaton, the Marx Brothers, Preston Sturges, Billy Wilder, Blake Edwards, Woody Allen, Harold Ramis, John Hughes, and Wes Anderson. It's a distinguished member of a movie subgenre that I refer to as the "accidental comedy."

Accidental comedy is self-explanatory: It occurs when non-comedies wind up being accidentally hysterical. Action-dramas like *Point Break* lend themselves well to this phenomenon. *Top Gun* (1986; Tony Scott, director) is another fine example of accidental comedy.

Point Break. Twentieth Century Fox, 1991. James Cameron, executive producer. Peter Abrams and Robert L. Levy, producers. Rick King and Michael Rauch, co-producers. Donald Peterman, cinematographer. Howard E. Smith and Bert Lovitt, editors. Peter Jamison, production designer. Pamela Marcotte, art director. Linda Spheeris, set decorator. W. Peter Iliff, screenwriter. Based on a story by W. Peter Iliff and Rick King. Directed by Kathryn Bigelow. Rated R.

Synopsis:
Keanu Reeves stars as Johnny Utah, a rookie FBI agent working undercover to bring down a team of bohemian

bank robbers. Patrick Swayze plays Bodhi (short for Bodhisattva), the charismatic leader of the elusive bandits, a self-professed adrenaline junkie who spends most of his free time engaged in a wide variety of dangerous activities, including (but not limited to) extreme surfing and skydiving. Spouting Zen-like maritime philosophy with the swaggering charm of a California stoner, Bodhi quickly establishes a complicated bond with Special Agent Utah, leading him into a world and way of life that are more dangerous and alluring than the virtuous young lawman had ever dreamt possible.

Here are a few of Bodhi's most memorable lines in *Point Break:*

"If you want the ultimate, you've gotta be willing to pay the ultimate price. It's not tragic to die doing what you love."

"Johnny has his own demons. Don't you, Johnny?"

"Just feel what the wave is doing. Then accept its energy, get in synch, and charge with it."

"Fear causes hesitation, and hesitation will cause your worst fears to come true."

"We can exist on a different plane. We can make our own rules. Why be a servant to the law, when you can be its master?"

"This was never about the money for us. It
was about us against the system—that system
that kills the human spirit. We stand for
something. To those dead souls inching along
the freeways in their metal coffins, we show
them that the human spirit is still alive."

"Life sure has a sick sense of humor, doesn't
it?"

I was pretty sure life itself was an accidental comedy.

Back when I was in film school, I had decided that I would one day
like to become the first man to direct an *intentional* accidental
comedy. My plan was to write a psychological action-adventure
along the lines of *Point Break,* something unconsciously vapid and
stunningly self-serious, something numb to its own rubber heart.
I even had a title in mind.

I wanted to call it *The Grandeur of Delusions.*

delusions of grandeur *n.*
A delusion (common in paranoia) that you are much greater
and more powerful and influential than you really are.

2.

Playa del Carmen was a good move. It was nice to be someplace warm, nice to be in the company of friends. It was like summer camp, with booze. It was a reunion in paradise. I felt rejuvenated for the first time in months. I felt *alive*. My spirits were high.

One afternoon while walking around town, I even went so far as to arrange for A.B., myself, and the rest of the groomsmen to go skydiving on the day of the wedding. I did it on impulse, convinced that it would be an appropriate thing to do on the morning of one's nuptials and a good way for me to spend some of my money.

It could therefore be argued that I equated marriage with spending lots of money and plummeting through the earth's atmosphere at terminal velocity.

terminal velocity *n.*
The constant maximum velocity reached by a body falling
through the atmosphere under the attraction of gravity.

The magnitude of terminal velocity depends upon the weight of the falling body. Heavy objects tend to fall faster than lighter objects, as air resistance is directly proportional to the plummeting body's velocity squared.

A.B. was a small guy. He weighed about 145 pounds.
I weighed 175.

A typical skydiver plummets through the earth's atmosphere at a rate of about 120 miles per hour.

According to the *Guinness Book of World Records,* the highest speed ever reached by a plummeting skydiver was 325.67 miles per hour. The record was set by Frenchman Michael Brooke at the Millennium Speed Skydiving Competition over Gap, France, on September 19, 1999.

parachute *n.*
1.) An apparatus used to retard free fall from an aircraft, consisting of a light, usually hemispherical canopy attached by cords to a harness and worn or stored folded until deployed in descent.
2.) Any of various similar unpowered devices that are used for retarding free-speeding or free-falling motion.

Another interesting fact: Shortly after I arranged for A.B. and his groomsmen to go skydiving, I learned that Jenny and her bridesmaids had arranged to go scuba diving that very same morning. While the groom and his groomsmen would be ten thousand feet above sea level, preparing to plummet through the earth's atmosphere at terminal velocity, Jenny and her brides- maids would be fifty feet under, submerged in the crystalline waters just off of Isla Mujeres.

3.

There were no passenger seats on the aircraft. There were no tray tables and no upright positions. There were no stewardesses and no adornments—just a cockpit chair, a throttle, and some gadgets. The cabin was spare and empty, and nobody was talking.

The pilot was a large, unruly Mexican man with a large, unruly mustache. He appeared totally confident in the functioning of the aircraft. He was dressed casually in a T-shirt and shorts. His T-shirt read SUPERVIVENCIA? NO PROBLEMA! Above those words, there was a cartoon drawing of a smiling shark.

I did not know what *Supervivencia* meant. I found this bothersome.

I was seated on the floor of the aircraft, without a seat belt. My knees were up against my chest, and I was hugging them tightly. A.B. was a few feet away, in the back of the aircraft. He was hugging his knees too.

A.B. and I had elected to jump first. The other three groomsmen were on the beach below. They were standing in sand, watching the aircraft ascend, waiting their turn in quiet agony. All three had agreed to go skydiving with varying amounts of reluctance. They were doing it because A.B. was doing it. There had to be solidarity among the groom and his groomsmen on the day of the wedding, just as there had to be solidarity among the bride and her maids. Everyone understood this.

If all went well, A.B. and I would be landing on the beach in a matter of moments, triumphant.

If all did not go well, A.B. and I would die in a tragic sky-diving accident on the Mayan Riviera. It would be the kind of story that caught fire on the AP wire. A horrifying tale, submitted for public consumption. *Inside Edition* would almost certainly run a story on us.

Jenny would be interviewed, backlit and weeping.

My parents would be interviewed, ashen and defeated.

4.

The altimeter needle hit 10,000. The pilot
turned around and gave the divemasters a hand signal.

My divemaster, Alejandro, had just finished fastening himself
to my back with an elaborate system of clips and harnesses.

My palms were raining sweat, and my stomach was in knots.
My mind was racing. I felt medicated. Also, I was deeply concerned that I might urinate and/or defecate in my jumpsuit while
plummeting through the earth's atmosphere at terminal velocity.
I feared that my fear would be so immense that my bladder and
bowels would spontaneously release.

Note: I feared my fear.

Note: I refrained from articulating my fear of my fear to
Alejandro for fear of upsetting his concentration.

In a futile attempt to cool my nerves, I looked over at A.B.,
gave a thumbs-up, and forced a smile. It was the fakest smile I
had ever sent into the universe. It was the smile of a child who
was secretly urinating in a public swimming pool. A.B. faked a
smile in return. He shouted something at me, but I couldn't
make out what he was saying amid the engine's roar. I smiled
again and nodded.

Alejandro placed his mouth inches from my ear and issued
the following declaration:

"I am going to open the door now."

I understood him perfectly and said nothing. Alejandro
repeated his declaration. I nodded and gave another thumbs-up.

Alejandro reached over and unlocked the latch on the Cessna's small side door. The door flew open, and a blast of cold air rushed into the cabin with enormous force. My heart leapt. The sound was tremendous. I was now facing the open door and the empty sky. I slid my goggles over my eyes.

Alejandro positioned himself behind me. He put his mouth up to my ear once again and shouted the following command:

"Step out onto the wing."

Remarkably, I inched toward the edge. There didn't seem to be any other choice. Alejandro was behind me, pushing gently. The ozone layer was whipping against my face. A.B was getting married that day. It was a special occasion. People went sky-diving all the time. It was all perfectly safe. There was nothing to worry about. The important thing to do was to just have fun. The hardest part was jumping. The rest would be easy. Alejandro had a chute, a backup chute, and an AAD (automatic activation device), which would deploy the chute automatically at an altitude of three thousand feet in the event that he somehow slipped into unconsciousness during our descent. The system was reportedly foolproof.

Now I was at the threshold. The bar attached to the wing, where my feet were to be placed, was right there in front of me. Below the wing, there was nothing. Below nothing, there was earth. Below the earth, there was more nothing.

I had to step out onto that wing. I had to step into that nothing.

I placed my feet on the wing. It was the most unnatural moment of my entire life.

My feet were now on the wing of an aircraft that was flying at a cruising altitude of approximately ten thousand feet.

Alejandro asked me if I was ready. I said nothing. Perhaps I nodded.

The next thing I knew, we were dropping, flipping, spinning out of control, a mad rush of air. I didn't know which way was up. I no longer heard the plane. I was disoriented, didn't know where I was. I was tumbling out of control, plummeting toward earth at terminal velocity, and then, suddenly, *vwoompth,* I flattened out. My belly was facing the earth, my arms and legs were outstretched. I had achieved some kind of equilibrium. I was flying. I could see my arms, my hands. I could see wisps of white clouds in the distance. I heard Alejandro let out a battle cry. He was still with me. He had righted us with his expertise.

I looked down. I could see everything. Playa del Carmen. Las Palapas, the resort we were staying at. The Gulf of Mexico, bleeding blue to turquoise as it neared the shore. Hotels tucked among the trees. The beach looked like a long line of cocaine. Inland there was nothing but green.

I didn't feel Alejandro pull the rip cord. I felt only an enormous tug on my harness when the parachute opened and grabbed the atmosphere. We rushed to what felt like a sudden stop. The next thing I knew, everything was silent. The chaos was over. My chute had engaged. My chute was working. I was alive. I was not going to die. I was floating toward earth at a gentle rate of speed, no longer plummeting. Parachute technology had succeeded. Alejandro was manning the toggles, steering us earthward. I didn't have to do anything. I was hanging at twenty-five hundred feet. Provided the elaborate system of clips and harness held fast, I would be arriving on the sandy beach below in a matter of moments, physically intact, completely uninjured.

I looked down, liberated. I thought I could see my friends. I had not soiled my jumpsuit, and I was not dead.

Also, it had just occurred to me that I was laughing hysterically, like a child.

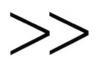

5.

The wedding went off without a hitch. A.B. and Jenny were married in a beautiful seaside ceremony at sunset. A small Mexican priest presided. A mariachi band played over the sound of crashing surf. Margaritas were served.

Two days later, I found myself alone, at the Aeropuerto José Martí in Havana, Cuba. I was relieved, having made it through customs without getting my passport stamped. A gloomy, bespectacled gentleman had handled the transaction. He was in his middle thirties, and the crown of his head was oily and bald. Just to be safe, I'd asked him politely in Spanish to refrain from stamping my passport, aware that getting one's passport stamped was inadvisable in Cuba, where traveling was a direct violation of U.S. trade law. The man said nothing to me in response. He looked at my passport quickly and handed it back to me without a word. When I thanked him for his assistance, he yawned and buzzed me through the security door.

There were guards in green fatigues in the baggage claim area, stone-faced men wielding firearms. They were directing a spastic squad of black cocker spaniels sniffing for bombs and drugs. I'd never seen cocker spaniels doing this kind of work before.

My bag was waiting for me when I arrived at the conveyor belt. I picked it up and walked outside into a swarming horde of taxi drivers. They were all talking to me at once, trying to win my business. It was disorienting. In the end, I negotiated transport with a rail-thin, silver-haired gentleman for the flat rate of US$20. According to my guidebooks, this constituted a fairly reasonable deal.

Next thing I knew, I was sitting in the backseat of his taxi, cutting through the countryside on my way to Havana. The terrain was tropical and unfamiliar. There were tenement building carcasses, laundry hanging from their crumbling balconies. There was a stoic farmer steering a bull-pulled plow through an upturned field. There were dilapidated schools and uniformed children giggling in the littered schoolyards. There was a city bus, impossibly full, arms and faces hanging hot out of the open windows. There were three people on a motorcycle and six in a '57 Chevy. There were weathered men smoking cigars on the sides of the road, trying to flag rides with smiles.

Nobody was wearing sunglasses.

It was illegal for me to be there.

Within minutes, we entered the city. My driver motioned to a bus station on our right and said something in Spanish that I couldn't understand. We passed the Plaza de la Revolución. My driver told me in broken English that the large stone monument in its center stood, like the airport, in honor of José Martí. We made a left turn and wove through the neighborhoods. There were strange faces in the narrow streets. The buildings were Spanish colonial, old and falling down. Children playing stickball on the pavement. Old men smoking on the balconies above. Vintage cars rattling by. Golden era Cadillacs. Buicks and Fords. I rolled down my window and lit up a cigarette. I felt like I was in a time warp.

This was good.

6.

Later that night, I found myself seated at a table in a nightclub. On the advice of my hotel concierge, I had wandered over to a place called the Oasis, on the Paseo de Martí. The Oasis consisted of a long, loud room. There was an eight-piece band on a small stage, and the dance floor was packed with salsa dancers. I was drinking my third mojito. There were girls everywhere. Most were prostitutes, most were dressed in skimpy outfits, and most were very young—teenagers and girls in their early twenties.

Here's how you make a mojito:

Ingredients:

3 fresh mint sprigs
2 tbsp. lime juice
Dash of simple syrup
Club soda, chilled
1.5 oz. light rum

Mixing Instructions:

In a tall, thin glass, muddle mint leaves with simple syrup. Add ice, rum, and lime juice. Top with soda and stir. Garnish with fresh mint. Serves one.

According to article 302, law no. 62, of something called the Cuban Penal Code, prostitution in and of itself was not illegal in Cuba. However, acts *related* to prostitution—such as the exploitation of prostitutes by others—were forbidden by law. Those caught engaging in such ancillary activities—pimps, for instance—faced prison sentences of four to ten years.

sentence *n.*
1.) A grammatical unit that is syntactically independent and has a subject that is expressed or, as in imperative sentences, understood, and a predicate that contains at least one finite verb.
2.) *Law:*
   a. A court judgment, especially a judicial decision of the punishment to be inflicted on one adjudged guilty.
   b. The penalty meted out.
3.) *Archaic:* A maxim.
4.) *Obsolete:* An opinion, especially one given formally after deliberation.

The sexual energy in the Oasis was overwhelming. I could practically smell it.

People were emitting pheromones in there.

pheromone *n.*
A chemical secreted by an animal, especially an insect, that influences the behavior or development of others of the same species, often functioning as an attractant of the opposite sex.

To my left, in the corner, a pair of tourists was getting it on. They appeared to have zero inhibitions. The guy was sitting in a chair, and his girlfriend had mounted him, fully clothed. She was kissing him with tongue and writhing in his lap. Maybe they were French. The French, from what I'd heard, have few reservations about engaging in public displays of affection. They lack American self-consciousness and puritanical attitudes toward sex.

The Puritans were a group of hard-core English Protestants from way back in the sixteenth and seventeenth centuries who, generally speaking, considered pleasure and luxury to be deeply offensive.

I couldn't stop smoking cigarettes.

In the classic film comedy *National Lampoon's European Vacation* (1985; Amy Heckerling, director), bumbling middle-American father Clark Griswold (Chevy Chase) and his dysfunctional family win an all-expenses-paid trip to Europe. While dining in a Parisian restaurant, they encounter a young honeymooning couple from the United States. Deeply in love, the newlyweds are taking full advantage of the social freedoms afforded by France's lax attitude toward public displays of affection, freely engaging in aggressive physical intimacy while waiting for their food, oblivious to fellow restaurant patrons, including (but not limited to) the Griswold family, seated at a nearby table.

It is at this point in the movie that the following exchange takes place between Clark Griswold and his impressionable teenage son, Rusty (Jason Lively):

RUSTY

Dad, I think he's gonna pork her.

                              CLARK
He's not gonna pork her, Rusty. Just eat, okay?

                              RUSTY
I think he is, Dad.

                              CLARK
He may pork her, Rusty. Just eat, okay?

I had just ordered my fourth mojito from a voluptuous waitress with a large brown mole on her cheek.

The French couple in the corner was oblivious to the waitress, the band, and all fellow patrons.

I was pretty sure he was going to pork her.

I hadn't porked anyone in a long time.

I had never porked a prostitute before.

7.

My fourth mojito arrived. I lit another cigarette.
Across the room I saw a beautiful girl. She was sitting on the lap
of a middle-aged man who appeared to be of middle-American
descent. The man looked fifty. The girl couldn't have been a day
older than twenty. She was wearing red velour pants and a
matching halter top. She had shoulder-length hair, and the guy
beneath her was a geek in glasses who looked like your average,
weed-whacking next-door neighbor in Illinois. They had zero
visible rapport. It was a business arrangement, plain and simple.
The weed-whacking geek had paid the beautiful girl to sit on his
lap for a while.

Later, he would pork her.

A song ended. The band members talked among themselves and
tuned their instruments. The girl took the man by the hand and
led him onto the dance floor, smiling. He tried to decline, but she
insisted. She shook her hips, snapped her fingers, and smiled.
The man shrugged, snapped his fingers, and tried to laugh it off.
He was clearly self-conscious and, I noticed for the first time,
perspiring heavily. Sweat was visible on his forehead, illuminated
by the glowing stage lights.

I was convinced he was the kind of guy who had twice been
arrested for masturbating in his automobile near a suburban elementary school.

The music began. The man was awkward. He looked like he was in a conga line on a cruise ship. He had no business dancing. It should have been illegal for him to dance. The girl, on the other hand, was a wonderful dancer. She moved with natural grace and was wonderful to watch. She was young and beautiful and had sex with men twice her age in order to make a living. She was impoverished and desperate, subjecting herself to physical violence and potentially fatal venereal diseases on a nightly basis, for cash.

She was killing herself, essentially.

I finished my mojito. I lit another cigarette. I ordered another drink.

I told myself that I must save the young, beautiful prostitute from the arrhythmic weed-whacking geek, because I was there and he was the death of her, and I could *see* it.

Just then two prostitutes walked over and sat down next to me in a solicitous manner. They were young and ugly and asked to bum cigarettes. I pretended I was deaf. They continued talking to me, using hand motions. I pretended to use sign language. Then I handed them four Camels. Then they asked me for a light. I gave them an entire book of matches and a twenty-dollar bill. They looked at each other, spoke rapidly in Spanish, and laughed. I pretended not to notice.

Admittedly, I was feeling pretty strange.

The prostitutes tried once more to strike up a conversation. I didn't respond. A minute or two later, they gave up entirely. They rolled their eyes, shrugged their shoulders, and rose. They said something in Spanish and walked away with their twenty bucks and their four smokes.

God bless you, I said to myself, though I didn't really know why.

• • •

The song ended. The crowd cheered. The beautiful prostitute and the weed-whacking geek walked back over to their table. The geek sat down, and the girl said something to him, pointing toward the back of the club. The geek nodded and smiled, and the girl walked toward the back of the club, toward the bar. I rose and followed her, making efforts to appear casual. It occurred to me that I was drunk. The girl hung a left into the bathroom. I found a place at the bar and stood there, waiting.

A few minutes later, the girl exited the bathroom. Without a moment's hesitation, I walked up to her and told her that I would like her to come with me. I told her that I would pay her. The girl said something in Spanish that I didn't understand. She pointed toward the weed-whacking geek. I turned around and looked in his direction. He was on the other side of the dance floor, obstructed by salsa dancers. He could not see me. I turned back to the girl, pulled a wad of cash out of my waist belt, and handed her a fifty-dollar bill. She took it and said, "One more." I handed her one more.

She smiled, grabbed me by the arm, and led me past a bouncer out the back door of the club.

8.

Her name was Pamela. That's what she told me, anyway. She had light brown hair and dark brown eyes. If she had been a foot taller, she could have been a model. She spoke better English than I had originally thought. Coupled with my rudimentary understanding of Spanish, we were able to communicate with relative effectiveness. Pamela told me she had been living in Havana for six years. She liked Madonna and *Baywatch* and dreamt of being a pop star. She seemed relaxed and happy, completely at ease with our arrangement.

I, on the other hand, was feeling pretty edgy. I'd been feeling pretty edgy ever since we got to my room. We walked in the door, and all of a sudden I didn't know what to do. My buzz faded and my humanitarian confidence went with it, and I had no alcohol on my person with which to bolster it. Flustered, I said a few salutatory words and offered Pamela a seat on my bed. She sat. I walked over to the nightstand and picked up a bottle of water. It was the only thing I had to drink. I poured us each a glass. No ice. She thanked me. We drank. There was silence. It was awkward. I could hear myself swallowing. I didn't know what to say. I kept drinking. I finished my glass of water and stood there. I kept drinking, even though my glass was empty. Pamela smiled. I smiled back and asked her how she was doing. She told me she was doing fine and asked me how I was doing. I told her I was doing fine and asked her once again how she was doing. She didn't say anything, and neither did I. I looked at her, and she looked at me.

The poor girl is dying, I told myself.

I will not have sex with her, I told myself.

Pamela got up and set her glass down on the nightstand. Without a word, she walked over to me, moved in, and gave me a light kiss on the lips. I closed my eyes and offered no resistance. She pulled away slowly, biting my bottom lip.

"You want to fuck?" she said.

conflict *n.*

1.) A state of open, often prolonged fighting; a battle or war.

2.) A state of disharmony between incompatible or antithetical persons, ideas, or interests; a clash.

3.) *Psychology:* A psychic struggle, often unconscious, resulting from the opposition or simultaneous functioning of mutually exclusive impulses, desires, or tendencies.

4.) Opposition between characters or forces in a work of drama or fiction, especially opposition that motivates or shapes the action of the plot.

conflicted, conflicting, conflicts *v. intr.*

To be in or come into opposition; differ.

Archaic: To engage in warfare.

"Shower," I said to her, stepping back. "How about a shower?"

"¿Cómo?" she said.

"You should use my shower," I said.

I pointed to the bathroom and said the word *baño.* I pantomimed the act of showering and made water noises with my mouth. Pamela nodded and began stripping immediately. She took off her halter top and walked into the bathroom. The girl was all business. I turned away, walked over to the nightstand,

and poured myself another glass of water. I sat on the edge of the bed and listened as the shower turned on. I took a deep breath and looked at my water glass. I massaged the inside corners of my eyes with thumb and forefinger.

Pamela called out to me.

"Wayne," she said. It sounded like "when."

"Yeah?"

"Come here. *Venga.*"

I walked over to the bathroom door slowly. I could hear the water hitting the bottom of the tub in uneven slaps.

"You all right?" I said. "You need anything?"

"Come in," she said.

"No, no. I'm going to stay out here. You go ahead."

"Come in. Is good."

"I'll be here when you get out."

"Come in, Wayne."

I stuck my head in the door. Pamela was on other side of the glass, naked under the showerhead. She looked at me and motioned with her forefinger.

"Come in," she said.

"I'm not getting in."

"You need bath."

"Tomorrow morning. *Mañana.*"

Pamela made a face. "*¿Que es la problema?*" she said. "You no like?"

"No, no. Not at all. I like just fine."

"Come in."

She smiled at me and motioned again. I looked at myself in the mirror above the sink. I looked pretty ravaged.

"Look," said Pamela. She was pointing at my feet.

I looked down. My feet were dirty. I'd been wearing flip-flops, wandering the streets and clubs of Havana for fourteen solid hours.

I looked at myself in the mirror again. "Shit," I said.

I stripped and got into the shower. Pamela giggled and stepped to the side. I stood under the water and let it run over my head, my body. Pamela started soaping my back. I lifted my hands to my face, wiped the water away from my eyes, and turned around to face her. She pressed up against me and gave me a kiss. It tasted like soap and cigarettes.

Pamela and I were kissing. We had been kissing for a couple of minutes when I suddenly experienced a moment of realization. I had a drastic change of heart and pulled away in a rapid burst of motion. My feet squeaked on the floor of the tub, and I nearly slipped and fell. I grabbed hold of the handrail and attempted to gather myself. I was standing there, naked, wet, and erect. I started rambling to Pamela.

I told her that I wanted her to know that she was a fine human being. I told her that I didn't consider her a subhuman because she was a hooker and that I didn't want to harm her. I told her that she was subjecting herself to grave danger, night in and night out, and I wanted to do whatever I could to help her. I was slurring.

Pamela laughed at me. She laughed really hard.

"You crazy, Wayne," she said. "I no understand you."

I asked her how old she was.

"How old?" said Pamela.

"*Sí,*" I said. "*¿Cuántos años?*"

The great soul singer Sam Cooke wrote a hit single called "Only Sixteen" back in 1959. The first verse went like this:

She was only sixteen, only sixteen
I loved her so

But she was too young to fall in love
And I was too young to know

Pamela was the same age as my little sister.

Sam Cooke died on December 11, 1964, at the Hacienda Motel
in Los Angeles, California, at the age of thirty-three. The tale is
tragic and controversial. Apparently, Cooke was in his room with
a young woman, preparing to have sex. They had a dispute and
the woman fled, taking most of Cooke's clothes with her. Cooke
went after her, half naked, wearing only a sport coat and shoes.
A little while later, the manager of the hotel, a woman named
Bertha Franklin, shot him in the chest with a .22 caliber revolver.
She claimed that Sam Cooke had attacked her.

 The coroner's office later ruled that Cooke's death was a jus-
tifiable homicide.

I was showering with a sixteen-year-old Havana prostitute in
room 404 of the Hotel Ambos Mundos.

 I told myself that I must stay calm.

According to the Cuban Penal Code, the official age of consent
in Cuba is sixteen.

Prostitution is illegal in the United States of America, except if
you're in Nevada.

 You can do pretty much anything you want to in the state of
Nevada.

I set the bar of soap down on the little ledge. Pamela picked up
a small plastic bottle of shampoo, and we took turns washing

each other's hair. Then we rinsed. Then I turned the shower off, and we toweled off.

I put on a pair of boxer shorts. Pamela stood there, comfortably naked. I gave her a pair of my boxer shorts and a T-shirt. She put them on uncertainly. We climbed into bed. She asked me once again if I would like to fuck. I told her no thanks. This confused her. She asked me if she should stay. Yes, I told her, please stay. She asked me if I would continue to pay her. Yes, I told her, I'll pay you. With that, I reached up and turned off the bedside lamp. We lay there on our backs, two feet apart, listening to the sounds of cars, voices, and laughter echoing up from the Calle Obispo. And eventually, we fell asleep.

10.

Ernest Hemingway is a major icon in Cuba. In Havana, it is particularly noticeable. All over town, there are reminders of him—in bars and hotels, in restaurants and kiosks. Hemingway had lived in and around the city for much of his adult life, and Castro was reportedly a fan. In the years since taking power, the dictator seemed to have co-opted the American writer as one of his own.

Hemingway's history in Cuba dates back to the middle part of the twentieth century. In 1940, shortly after marrying his third wife, Martha Gellhorn, he purchased a fifteen-acre estate in the village of San Francisco de Paula, located approximately fifteen miles from downtown Havana. The property was called La Finca Vigía, or The Lookout Farm. It would be Hemingway's principal residence for the next two decades.

In 1953, Hemingway was awarded the Pulitzer Prize for his novella *The Old Man and the Sea.* The next year, he received the Nobel Prize in Literature.

In 1959, Castro came to power in a violent uprising. Cuba was in a state of unrest, so Hemingway and his fourth wife, Mary Welsh, left the *finca* and moved to Ketchum, Idaho.

It was around this time that Hemingway began to go seriously batty. Depression, persecution mania, obsession, phobia, and delusions conspired to take his mind. He couldn't really sleep, and he couldn't really write. He was talking and acting like a crazy man. As the months went by, his condition became worse and worse. His friends and family members began to fear for his life.

In November 1960, on the recommendation of a prominent New York psychiatrist, Hemingway was sent to the famed Mayo Clinic in Rochester, Minnesota, where, at the behest of a team of expert physicians, he underwent extensive electroconvulsive therapy.

electroconvulsive therapy n. (abbr. ECT)
Administration of electric current to the brain through electrodes placed on the head in order to induce seizure activity in the brain, used in the treatment of certain mental disorders, especially severe depression. Also called electroshock, electroshock therapy.

Though still not free of all of his delusions, Hemingway was released from the Mayo Clinic in January of 1961. His doctors cited his strong desire to return to work as their rationale for setting him loose. They felt he was on the rebound.

They were wrong.

Back at home in Ketchum, Hemingway's condition deteriorated quickly. In April of 1961, he tried to take his own life no fewer than three times. Once, he even went so far as to try to walk into the whirring propellers of a stationary airplane.

In the wake of these attempts, Hemingway was taken back to the Mayo Clinic, where, over the course of the next two months, he was subjected to further electric shock treatments.

In late June, Hemingway's doctors deemed him fit to be

freed once again. Mary came and picked him up, and together the two of them went back to Idaho.

Two days later, in the early-morning hours of July 2, 1961, Ernest Hemingway killed himself successfully.

Mary was in bed at the time. She heard the shot, raced downstairs, and found her husband dead in the front entryway. He was wearing a red robe, his head was blown apart, and his brains were on the ceiling. There was a high-powered rifle between his legs. He was sixty-one years old.

Ernest Hemingway's father, Clarence, offed himself too. So did his sister, Ursula, and his brother, Leicester.

In 1996, Ernest Hemingway's eldest granddaughter, Margaux, committed suicide in her apartment in Santa Monica, California. She took an overdose of the barbiturate Klonopin, becoming the fifth family member in four generations to kill herself successfully.

11.

The morning after we met, Pamela and I ate breakfast in the café on the rooftop of the Ambos Mundos. The skies were gray, and the air was stifling. The food was terrible— soggy and stale. I had lukewarm coffee and a piece of dry toast. It was the only thing I felt I could hold down. Pamela had a banana. Laughing, she pretended to perform fellatio on it. Yawning, I pretended not to notice.

There were two guys in Hawaiian shirts eating at a nearby table, talking American English. They were wearing shades, and they had briefcases. I was pretty sure they were CIA.

From there, Pamela and I set out into town. We walked along the Plaza de Armas, browsing at books and staring at people. I suggested we take a cab to San Francisco de Paula to check out the Finca Vigía. My hangover was vicious, and I felt like getting out of the city. Pamela told me she'd never been to the Finca before. That settled it. An enriching experience for everyone involved. We walked over to the Canal de Entrada and hailed a cab. Our driver was the nervous sort, a spindly little hombre in a black clip-on necktie. He swung us by Pamela's apartment in the Vedado district on our way out of town. She ran inside, changed clothes, packed a suitcase, and off we went.

La Finca Vigía wasn't as big as I thought it would be. It was a run-down, whitewashed Spanish affair with tall windows and high ceilings. The front steps were crumbling, the paint was peeling, and the foliage was overgrown. The windows were wide-open, and the place was crawling with employees and guards. Every time you took a photograph, they charged you five bucks. It was a tremendous crock of shit.

Pamela seemed to be enjoying herself, for the most part. Her confusion over the fact that we weren't having sex had subsided a bit. I had made zero mention of my psychosexual neuroses, particularly as they pertained to my recent entanglements with abortion, heartbreak, suicide, compound interest, and The Afterlife. And Pamela, to her credit, didn't press for any answers. For one hundred dollars a day, she was willing to live with mystery.

All things considered, I found her to be pretty good company. She had a sweet disposition and seemed to have a good sense of humor. All day long, I watched her interact with others, and she almost always got them laughing. She had a funny, squeaky voice and great facial expressions. And she looked good smoking a cigarette.

In addition to being my travel companion, Pamela was also my translator. Generally speaking, Cubans talked too fast for me to understand anything of substance. My ears picked up bits and pieces, but mostly their rapid-fire delivery left me in the dark. Furthermore, my conversational abilities were severely limited. Even when I did understand what people were saying, the best I was able to come up with in response were simple phrases and platitudes, most of which were useful only in restaurants, airports, and train stations. In normal exchanges, nine times out of ten, I wound up feeling two-dimensional and utterly brainless. With Pamela around, I was able to express myself with some degree of depth and effectiveness. She was, in other words, the conduit through which I demonstrated my personality.

Though aged forty years, the Finca had gone untouched since Hemingway hightailed it to Idaho to begin his hellish descent into the abyss. The place looked lived-in. Eyeglasses resting atop a stack of books on a side table. Half-empty bottles of booze. Cocktail glasses. Magazines. It was as if the man himself might show up back at home any minute now.

Large busts of wild game were hanging everywhere, monuments to Hemingway's formidable skill at killing animals with rifles. The vacant eyes and the vacant expressions made me uneasy. Until recently, dead animals had never really affected me like this. Now, for some reason, I couldn't stand the sight of them.

And I couldn't really eat them, either. This was a new development too. It had started shortly after Amanda's funeral. I was down in Louisiana, standing in my grandmother's kitchen watching my aunt Lucy disembowel the Christmas turkey. I looked at that turkey and its innards, and suddenly, out of nowhere, something inside of me snapped. I walked out of the house in a light sweat, hunched over in the backyard, and nearly vomited. From that moment forward, I stopped eating meat.

carnophobia *n.*
Fear of meat.

12.

Hemingway's closet was the strangest part of the tour. The hanging coats, the hanging pants, and the big, empty shoes. The empty shoes did something to me. I stared at them awhile. They solidified the fact that he had actually existed. The rest of the place just looked like some maniac hunter's secluded island getaway. Then you got a load of the empty shoes, and it hit you.

A long path led from the main house down to the swimming pool. The swimming pool was drained dry and huge, twelve feet deep at the deep end, maybe deeper. To the right of it were four wooden headstones, each one inscribed with a name: Black, Negrita, Linda, and Neron. The burial site of Hemingway's favorite dogs.

"I'm surprised he didn't have their heads stuffed and mounted," I said to Pamela.

"*¿Cómo?*" she said.

taxidermy *n.*
The art or operation of preparing, stuffing, and mounting the skins of dead animals for exhibition in a lifelike state.

Not too far from the pool stood Hemingway's old fishing boat, *Pilar*. The woman on guard knew all about the boat. She even let me take a picture of it, free of charge. I liked this woman. She had a nice smile. She gave us a bit of background on the boat, all of which Pamela relayed to me in broken English.

The woman finished by telling us that we should check out Cojímar, a nearby seaside village where Hemingway used to dock the boat. Apparently, his old ship captain, Gregorio Fuentes, still lived there. Fuentes, she told us, was the man upon whom Santiago, the lead character in *The Old Man and the Sea,* had been modeled.

According to the woman, he was now over one hundred years old. And he accepted visitors.

On hearing this, my interest was piqued.

"We can go visit him?" I said to her.

Pamela translated.

"*Sí, sí,*" said the woman. "Visit."

The gears in my mind started turning immediately. I started daydreaming. I imagined the Old Man and me sitting by the seashore, smoking cigars and drinking rum from goblets made of whalebone. I imagined the Old Man, seated in a rocking chair, looking out wistfully upon the rippling sea. I would be seated at his feet. The golden light of the setting sun would be shining upon our faces.

Old Man, I would say to him. *Tell me the wisdom of the ages.*

All right, the Old Man would kindly reply.

13.

Our cabdriver knew the way. It took us about thirty minutes to get there. We drove through the countryside to the coast. I chain-smoked the entire way, as did Pamela. Our cabdriver smoked too.

Cojímar looked like a ghost town. Hardly anyone in the streets. No cars. One cyclist, blond, wearing obnoxious neon spandex. A German tourist, perhaps. There was a large, decrepit governmental-type building to our left. It looked like an old courthouse, crumbling and abandoned. The lawn out front was littered with trash. The rest of town seemed to consist of small shacks lined up side by side in a vaguely suburban and symmetrical manner.

Our cabdriver got Fuentes's exact address from a bartender at La Terraza, a tavern in town. The house was up a hill, not too far away. It was a one-story affair, just like all the others. For some reason, I found this surprising. I expected the Old Man to be venerated. I expected him to be living like royalty. Anybody who made it to one hundred deserved to be living like royalty, in my opinion.

I knocked on the door, and a man answered. He looked about forty. In perfect English, he introduced himself as Rafael, Don Gregorio's great-grandson. He smiled and invited us inside. We stepped into a small, quiet sitting room. Rafael excused himself and walked toward the back of the house and returned pushing a wheelchair containing the Old Man. On seeing him, my heart jumped and my breath went shallow. The Old

Man was ancient, speechless, and small. His skin was utterly ravaged from age and sun. His nose was bulbous and covered in gin blossoms. He had no teeth. He probably weighed 120 pounds. Everything was shriveled, dying, deteriorated—except for the eyes. The eyes remained lucid and blue.

Pamela said hello, introduced both of us. The Old Man just sat there in his wheelchair, staring blankly in our direction. He said nothing at all and made very little acknowledgment of our presence. I felt completely idiotic.

Rafael, sensing my discomfort, stepped in and did all of the talking. His delivery was fluid. He seemed to have a routine.

After a brief introductory speech, he walked out of the room and returned with some artifacts. One of Hemingway's old deep-sea fishing rods. Gregorio's old fishing knife. A photo album. He regaled us with stories of Herculean drinking binges and implored his great-grandfather to show us the multiple scars on the palms of his hands, accrued over the decades from a multitude of hooks, knives, and fishing lines.

The Old Man turned his hands upside down, and we examined his scars.

Part of the tour.

We didn't stay long. It didn't seem appropriate. The Old Man was old and tired and didn't need to be bothered like this. After about ten minutes of small talk, I made motions to leave, asking Rafael to snap a photograph of Pamela and me with Gregorio before we hit the road. He snapped three shots.

Before we left, he hit us up for cash, explaining that he and his great-grandfather accepted whatever donations visitors might be able to offer as a token of appreciation for the Old Man's time. I gave him fifty bucks.

Rafael then asked Pamela to give his great-grandfather a kiss on the cheek.

"My great-grandfather loves three things," he said to me. "Rum, cigars, and beautiful women."

I tried to laugh. Rafael made his request to Pamela in Spanish. It was so base, even I could understand it. Pamela complied without a second thought, kissing the Old Man on his sunbeaten cheek.

No mention was made of the fact that, for a fee, she would have gladly screwed his brains out.

14.

The following day, we rented a car and drove out to Viñales, a picturesque village a half day's drive from Havana. We stayed for two nights at a big pink hotel called the Hotel Los Jazmines. It overlooked the Viñales Valley and had a big blue swimming pool. Pamela loved it. She loved swimming pools. We swam in the pool for hours on end and drank fruity drinks in the sun. On the morning of the second day, we went horseback riding through Viñales National Park. It was beautiful. The red earth valley floor, the *mogotes,* the lush greenery. Pamela loved that, too. She loved horses.

From there, we drove back to Havana and checked back into the Hotel Ambos Mundos. It was a nice hotel, a good place to stay. Hemingway had written a lot of *For Whom the Bell Tolls* there, in a sea-facing room on the fifth floor. The facade and the interior had been restored with historical accuracy. You walked in the door, and you felt like it was 1934. I liked that.

On my last night in Cuba, we went up to the rooftop bar for dinner and some *Cuba libres.* It was nearing dusk. Our waiter brought us a round of drinks, and the house band started playing. Havana lay below. The Caribbean in the distance. With the sun going down, it was pretty romantic. And Pamela looked beautiful. She was wearing a red dress I'd bought for her in town that day for ten bucks, with red lipstick and red shoes to match.

She looked like something straight out of the 1950s.

Pamela's eyes, I noticed, were a little glazed over. She was on her third *Cuba libre* of the evening and her fifth drink of the day. Everywhere we went, she wanted another cocktail. And she rarely ate. Every time we sat down to a meal, she hardly touched her food. I'd ask her why, and she'd say she was full. She said she didn't want to be *gordo* and filled her cheeks up with air and made a face. Her body was her livelihood. She smoked a pack a day.

She should've been in high school.

A breeze blew over the rooftop. It smelled like the ocean. I lit another cigarette and looked at Pamela.

I told her that she looked like a Cuban Betty Boop, but she didn't understand me.

Two drinks later, Pamela asked me about my life in the States. She wanted to know what it was like, what the people were like. She was convinced it was a wonderland. It seemed as though she wanted me to tell her that the whole country was like one big episode of *Baywatch,* that everyone was beautiful and tan, running around in bathing suits, driving around in SUVs and sports cars, rich beyond imagination.

I tried to explain to her the fallacy of movies and television, but her understanding of English and my understanding of Spanish didn't allow for much more than a basic exchange of ideas. Language barriers are hell on theoretical discussions.

"America has problems, too," I said.

Pamela frowned.

I thought of this thing Mother Teresa once said: "Loneliness is the poverty of the West." I repeated it to Pamela. She nodded. She knew who Mother Teresa was. She said she understood. Maybe she did. Maybe she didn't.

Loneliness is the poverty of the West.

It was a heavy thing to say, but it made sense to me at the time. I was a little bit drunk at the moment. I was feeling kind of sad.

Pamela asked me once again about my family. She wanted to know if my parents were living. I told her yes. I told her all about my parents, where they lived, what they looked like, what they did.

"I miss my parents," I said. *"Me gusta mis padres."* I was getting sentimental.

Pamela nodded.

"My mother is worried sick right now," I said. "She didn't want me to come to Cuba."

Pamela told me she didn't have a mother. Her mother had died many years ago. Brain cancer got her when she was twenty-eight.

"Mi mamá es mi estrella," Pamela said, looking at the sky.

Here's how you make a *Cuba libre:*

Ingredients:

2 oz. white rum
1 oz. lime juice
Coca-Cola

Mixing Instructions:

Pour lime juice over ice cubes in a tall glass. Add rum.
Top with cola. Stir and serve.

It wasn't long before my tongue slipped. The rum took over, and I started giving Pamela unsolicited advice about her future— something I'd been itching to do ever since the moment we met.

"This is dangerous, what you do," I said. "You know that, don't you?"

Yes, she told me.

"You're young," I said. "You've got a whole lifetime ahead of you."

I won't have much of a life if I'm starving, she replied.

"What does your father think of this? He can't be happy about it."

Let's not talk about my father, she said.

She mentioned that he lived in Pinar del Río, that they saw each other now and again. But not too often.

Then the band kicked in with a slow number. Pamela rose, asked me to dance, snapped her fingers, and told me she was tired of talking. There was hardly anyone else up there on the rooftop, just one other table full of fifty-something European tourists. It sounded like they were speaking Italian. Nobody was dancing.

I tried to beg off, but Pamela insisted. She took me by the hand and led me out onto the tile floor. The band members smiled, happy to be playing for someone.

"Yo no comprendo bailar," I said. "It isn't my thing. I'm no good."

"Is okay," she said. *"Es bueno."*

We slow-danced. Left-foot, right-foot circles, nice and easy, nothing complicated, just like junior high. I was holding Pamela's right hand with my left hand. My other hand was around her waist. Her other hand was up behind my neck.

"See?" she said. "Is good."

And it was good. Dancing was a good idea. Our conversations were going nowhere. Talk was cheap. I was leaving Cuba the next day. She was stuck there. I had no business lecturing her. The best I could do was wish her luck and give her the rest of the cash in my waist belt. That right there was the cold, sad truth.

"You take care of yourself," I said to her.

Pamela looked up at me and told me that maybe one day, if things changed, she would come and visit me in the United States. Yes, I told her, please come visit me. She asked me if I would take her to New York City and California. Yes, I told her, of course I would. Anywhere she wanted to go. New York. California. The desert. The West.

The sun was down. I would be gone in fourteen hours. That would be that. I'd never see her again, in all likelihood. She wasn't allowed to leave Cuba, and I wouldn't be going back there anytime soon. There were too many other places to go, places I'd never been before. Places that weren't forbidden by the U.S. government.

I tried to convince myself that I shouldn't be too sad. People came, people went. Life was a transient affair. This kind of thing happened all the time. People met. People parted. People smiled. People showered together. People never saw one another again. People made their own separate ways toward The Void. That was life. That was death. That was the way it went. You'd think I would've been more used to it by now.

I told myself that it was important to look on the bright side. Pamela and I had had a nice time together. We'd spent almost ninety-six hours together. I'd made a new friend in Cuba. I'd paid her one hundred dollars a day, or roughly four dollars an hour, to hang out with me. Nevertheless, it seemed as though we'd forged some kind of meaningful bond that transcended all financial considerations.

The music rolled to a close. The slow number ended. The dance was over. Pamela looked up at me and smiled. Then she hiccupped lightly and put her head on my shoulder. For the first time since I'd met her, she actually seemed sixteen.

III.

My dad's mother was named Rita. My sisters
and I called her Mimi. At the time she was living in a nursing
home, on account of the fact that she had lost her mind.

Alzheimer's disease *n.*
A disease marked by the loss of cognitive ability, generally
over a period of ten to fifteen years, and associated with the
development of abnormal tissues and protein deposits in the
cerebral cortex.

My dad's father was named Frank. My sisters and I called
him Pops. He ran a local butcher shop with his brothers for
forty years before dying in 1995, of a heart attack. It was his
fourth.

myocardial infarction *n.*
Destruction of heart tissue resulting from obstruction of the
blood supply to the heart muscle.

My dad had two younger brothers. First there was Uncle
Wally, the dentist. He lived and worked in Morgan City,
Louisiana, where he was born and raised. His wife, Katherine,
was from Lafayette, and together they had three children:
Melissa, Wally Jr., and Mary-Beth.

Then there was my dad's youngest brother, Uncle Brian.

Uncle Brian was mentally disabled. He was thirty-six years old and had the faculties of a third grader.

Uncle Brian had been at home with Mimi the day she'd lost her mind. He was sitting in the living room, watching television, when he heard a noise. He walked into the kitchen and found Mimi collapsed on the cold tile floor. He summoned the neighbors, and the neighbors called 911. An ambulance arrived and took her to the hospital.

According to the doctors, something in her head just snapped.

Apparently, that kind of thing just happens sometimes. Sometimes people's heads just snap.

dementia *n.*

1.) Deterioration of intellectual faculties, such as memory, concentration, and judgment, resulting from an organic disease or a disorder of the brain. It is sometimes accompanied by emotional disturbance and personality changes.

2.) Madness; insanity. See synonyms at *insanity.*

As a result of his mother's inability to care for him, Uncle Brian now lived in the town of Thibodaux, in a home for mentally disabled people. He worked at a local nursery and watered trees for a living. The nursery gave him plenty of vacation time. Every year he spent three weeks with my uncle Wally and aunt Katherine down the road in Morgan City and three weeks in Indianapolis with my mom and dad.

Getting him from Louisiana to Indiana always presented a certain logistical challenge. Airplanes weren't an option; flying would have terrified him. Trains were somewhat more agreeable but not advisable over such long distances. Travel by automobile was therefore the only truly practical method of transport.

I had been plotting my next move when I called my parents to let them know I had made it out of Cuba alive and was safe and sound in Cancún. At the time, I was thinking of going to northern India.

"You're unemployed," my dad said. "Get your ass to Louisiana, pick up your uncle, and drive him up to Indiana."

I said, "All right."

Judging by the tone of his voice, there wasn't much room for debate.

Under normal circumstances, my dad made the trip, but at that particular time, business obligations had him bound. He had to be in Phoenix that week to attend a business conference. Uncle Wally was in pretty much the same boat. He had his dental practice to attend to, and summer was his high season. The kids would soon be getting out of school, and he was working twelve-hour days, cleaning teeth. He had a backlog of appointments.

With this in mind, the job fell naturally to me. I flew out of Mexico the following morning on a direct flight to New Orleans. My itinerary was completely mapped out. I would be spending a couple of days with Uncle Wally and Aunt Katherine and family in Morgan City, and from there, Uncle Brian and I would set out northward in a rental car, straight up the belly of America on our way to Indianapolis.

2.

Doctors had ascertained that Uncle Brian wasn't afflicted with Down syndrome or fragile X, the two most common chromosomal causes of mental retardation. As a result, the process of identifying the roots of his condition had always been in large part speculative. It could've been genetic. It could've been something else.

My family tended to blame his condition on a lack of oxygen at birth. This line of thinking was logical and may very well have been accurate, but there was little substantial proof to back it up. For the most part, it was just the blanket explanation we used as a shorthand way of talking about his misfortune. It provided us with a brief yet satisfactory method of defining it for the sympathetic and curious, while at the same time allowing us to avoid the sad and scary issue of simple dark luck.

People, generally speaking, don't like to hear about simple dark luck.

The brain requires lots of oxygen in order to function properly.

At the end of the day, there was no clear answer as to why Uncle Brian was how he was. The source of his affliction was a mystery.

Uncle Brian's physical presence was large. Standing five feet seven inches tall and weighing in at a robust 235 pounds, he was blessed with preternatural strength and uncommon coordination.

He was a freakishly good natural athlete, all things considered. He had strong legs, a huge barrel chest, forearms like Popeye's, the neck of a heavyweight champion, and a head that looked like it was carved from a large block of granite.

He was a particularly good bowler, having won three gold medals in the sport during the preceding five years at the Louisiana Special Olympics. With absolutely no formal training and a technique that would make any traditionalist shudder, he managed to consistently achieve scores in the 150 range, slinging the ball down the lane with incredible force, glaring inattention to detail, and utterly shocking precision.

As Uncle Wally liked to say, "The dadgum sumbitch bowls strikes by accident."

Also worth noting is the fact that Uncle Brian's voice was shockingly loud. He had a booming, unaffected baritone that for the most part knew only one volume. The man hollered everything he said. If you asked him how he was doing, for instance, he would invariably shout the following:

"DOIN' OKAY! DOIN' ALL RIGHTY!"

It was practically guaranteed.

In addition, he had a habit of repeating everything he heard on the radio and on television.

And sometimes, just for the hell of it, he repeated what people said to him in conversation.

3.

Uncle Brian and I were in Madison, Mississippi, just north of Jackson. At Uncle Brian's request, we had stopped off for lunch at a local Pizza Hut. Our conversation regarding when and where to eat had taken place in the car a couple of hours earlier. It went like this:

ME: Uncle Brian, you hungry?

BRIAN: *(No response.)*

ME: Uncle Brian?

BRIAN: HUH?

ME: I asked you if you're hungry.

BRIAN: I'M HUNGRY!

ME: Where do you want to stop for lunch?

BRIAN: I WANNA EAT LUNCH, WAYNE!

ME: But *where* do you want to eat lunch?

BRIAN: UH . . .

ME: You got a favorite restaurant?

BRIAN: YEAH.

ME: What is it?

BRIAN: I DUNNOW.

ME: Come on. You know. Think of where you like to eat. What's your favorite place? What's your favorite food?

BRIAN: PIZZA HUT!

ME: You want to eat at Pizza Hut?

BRIAN: YEAH.

ME: You feel like pizza?

BRIAN: I FEEL LIKE A PIZZA!

ME: Okay then. We'll find a Pizza Hut.

BRIAN: I WANNA EAT A PIZZA HUT, WAYNE!

ME: We're gonna stop. Just a few miles.

BRIAN: I LIKE PIZZA HUT!

ME: Okay. We're on our way.

The Pizza Hut in Madison, Mississippi, had an all-you-can-eat lunch buffet. For the incredible price of $7.99, a human being was allowed to enter the restaurant and eat as much food as he was capable of consuming.

This was dangerous.

Uncle Brian's passion for food was extraordinary. He had trouble knowing when to stop eating. It was part of his condition. Left unchecked, the man would eat himself to the point of violent gastric upset. I had been reminded of this fact ad nauseam in the forty-eight hours leading up to our departure.

ad nauseam *adv.*
To a disgusting or ridiculous degree; to the point of nausea.

"Don't let him overeat," my dad said.

"Watch him like a hawk," said Uncle Wally.

"If you're not careful, he'll do some serious damage," my dad said.

"If you let him go, he'll eat himself right into the hospital," said Uncle Wally.

"Okay," I said.

• • •

Uncle Brian was on his sixth and final slice, devouring it with remarkable zeal. When he was finished, I would have to perform the unenviable task of cutting him off. I'd have to find a way to get him out of there somehow.

We hadn't spoken a word since we sat down with our food. Uncle Brian rarely spoke while eating—another rule of thumb with him. Not until his plate was *completely* clean would he consider engaging in any kind of conversation. He wouldn't leave even a single crumb on his plate, or even the tiniest puddle of grease. Everything had to go.

There was an infamous story that Uncle Wally liked to tell involving an all-you-can-eat buffet at a Popeyes fried chicken restaurant many years earlier. It was Uncle Brian's first trip to an all-you-can-eat buffet. The place was packed. Uncle Brian was left to eat at his leisure. He sat there wolfing down fried chicken, biscuits, and gravy for the better part of an hour. He went hog wild. He ate and ate and ate.

Then he turned his head to the left and blew chow all over the floor.

The restaurant cleared out as if it were on fire.

It was my singular mission to prevent all such calamities from reoccurring on my watch.

4.

Road trips reminded me of Amanda. Driving up the interstate, watching the country fly by, I couldn't help but think of her. The two of us had taken a road trip together over spring break, back when we were dating. We drove out to Vegas, and then we made our way to the Grand Canyon and Sedona. This was right after I'd gotten my Jeep. We drove around the Southwest for ten days. No agenda. It was the best time we ever had. Amanda loved to travel, loved to be on the road. She was good at conversation. Good at silence. She never seemed to get tired. And she always insisted that we stop at mom-and-pop restaurants along the way. It was a thing with her. No franchises. No superstores. Nothing familiar. Everything had to be local. All commercial transactions, save gasoline, had to be conducted in a noncorporate environment. Truck-stop diners. Greasy spoons. Local motels. She felt it made the travel experience more authentic. I always liked that about her.

And if something came up along the way that interested her—no matter what it was—she always made sure that we stopped and checked it out. Time wasn't an issue. Itineraries meant nothing. Safety was a secondary concern. She was always reading road signs, thumbing through guidebooks, desperate to make sure that we didn't miss anything. Spontaneity was of critical importance. Landmarks mattered too. She made me stop at the Hoover Dam. She made me drive by a whorehouse. She made me take her out to this enormous crater in the middle of the desert. It took us two hours to get there. We paid twenty dollars each, ascended a mammoth concrete staircase, stood at the lip, and looked down. It was nothing but a giant hole.

I was nonplussed.

Amanda's enthusiasm, on the other hand, was completely undiminished.

Later in the trip, she made me take her to a ghost town in the wilds of Arizona.

"Come on," she pleaded. "We have to do it. We have to see it. Please, please, please."

"Why do you want to see a ghost town? It's a hundred miles out of our way."

"Because if we don't go see it," she said to me, "how will we know that it's there?"

5.

Uncle Brian and I were dressed in full caving gear—wading pants, rubber boots, helmets with headlamps, and so forth. I had paid a premium fee for a private, two-hour exploratory trip through undeveloped sections of Marengo Cave.

Approximately 4.6 miles in length, Marengo Cave is the most visited show cave in the state of Indiana. It was first discovered by a fifteen-year-old girl named Blanche Hiestand and her eleven-year-old little brother, Orris, back in 1883. According to lore, Blanche and Orris had hiked up a hillside one afternoon, reaching a grove of trees surrounding a large, mysterious depression. Together they walked down into the mysterious depression, where, to their astonishment, they discovered a gaping hole.

Our guide was a redneck gentleman named Stewart. Stewart was built like a tank. He had a rust-colored handlebar mustache and shoulder-length blond hair. From what I could tell, he spent an enormous amount of his time wandering around in the subterranean darkness. At the outset of our adventure, I asked him if he ever got scared down there.

"Hey, Stewart," I said. "Do you ever get scared down there?"
"I know this place like the back of my dick," he said.

Thirty minutes into the tour, everything was copacetic. So far, so good. We were wandering along a path through a dark, narrow corridor. The walls of the cave were dripping with water. Uncle Brian seemed to be enjoying himself. He'd been a little on the quiet side, but that was to be expected. He'd entered a new realm, I told myself, a brand-new environment. It was pure sensory overload. I was introducing him to whole new worlds.

"Uncle Brian," I said. "How're you doing, buddy?"

"DOIN' OKAY! DOIN' ALL RIGHTY!"

Within twenty minutes, we were down in the bowels of the cave, wading hip-deep through cold water. Stewart had been talking nonstop from the get-go, inundating us with cave history, cave lore, and various other types of general cave information. We'd heard all about stalactites, stalagmites, helictites, flowstone, draperies, cave popcorn, and rimstone dams. It seemed to me that the guy really knew his stuff. His passion for the subject knew no bounds.

"Look up there," he said, shining his headlamp at the ceiling. "Hot damn."

I looked up there. The ceiling was covered in something.

"Jesus," I said. "What?"

"Bats," said Stewart. "Tons of 'em."

"Jesus," I said.

"JESUS!" said Uncle Brian, echoing.

The ceiling was alive with hundreds of tiny bats, all of them hanging upside down. To me they looked like inverted field mice.

"Bats are the only mammals that can truly fly," Stewart informed us. "Some can glide—take flying foxes, for example—but bats are the only ones that flap their wings and really make it happen."

"They look kind of like inverted field mice," I said.

"They ain't field mice," Stewart said.

"I don't doubt it," I said.

"I KNOW THIS PLACE LIKE THE BACK OF MY DICK!" said Uncle Brian.

Stewart laughed. I explained to him that Uncle Brian had a habit of repeating people.

Stewart then made a deft segue into a detailed explanation of how bats use their extraordinary sense of hearing to navigate flight and hunt prey.

"Most mammals use their eyes," he said. "But bats, they use their ears. Built-in sonar. Technical name is *echolocation*. Freaky little critters, if you ask me. But smarter than most people might think."

echolocation *n.* (in both senses also called *echo ranging*)

1.) A sensory system in certain animals, such as bats and dolphins, in which usually high-pitched sounds are emitted and their echoes interpreted to determine the direction and distance of objects.

2.) *Electronics:* A process for determining the location of objects by emitting sound waves and analyzing the waves reflected back to the sender by the object.

Stewart led us out of the water and around a corner. We followed him to a small opening in the side of the cave wall, where he explained that we would be crawling on our bellies, army-style, for a distance of about 150 feet.

"The space ain't huge," he said. "But I done it enough times to guarantee you there's plenty of room to get through. Your friend here's a big boy, but he shouldn't have any problems. I seen fellas twice his size make their way just fine."

"Uncle Brian," I said, "you think you can handle this?"

"HUH?"

"Are you all righty?"

"I'M ALL RIGHTY!"

"Okay," I said to Stewart. "I think he's doing fine."

Stewart nodded, cleared his throat, and spit into the blackness.

I went in first. Uncle Brian followed me. Stewart brought up the rear. Propped up on my elbows, I shimmied my way forward. The air was dank inside the narrow passageway. I was in the guts of the earth, more than fifty feet underground. It was a world of utter darkness. Sunlight couldn't reach me down there. My headlamp was my only salvation. Without it, I couldn't see an inch in front of my face.

I shimmied my way forward.

Fifty feet into the tunnel, I heard a terrible noise behind me. It sounded like a goat giving birth.

"Uncle Brian?" I said. "You okay?"

"MMMEEWWWWOOOOOOOOOOO!"

I couldn't turn around. The width of the passage didn't allow for it.

"Uncle Brian? You all righty?"

The bellowing petered out into a series of labored, husky breathing sounds.

"Sir!" Stewart called out behind me. "I think your friend here is having some kind of a reaction! I think we're gonna have to get him out of here! He don't seem to be liking this much! Whatcha say we back it on up?"

"What's happening back there?"

"I don't know, sir! He's flippin' out pretty good!"

"Uncle Brian," I said. "You okay?"

"MMMEEWWWWOOOOOOOOOO!"

"Uncle Brian, we're getting out of here right now, okay? You just listen to Stewart, and we'll be out of here in two seconds."

"Brian," said Stewart, "I'm gonna need you to back it up here, partner. You feel my hand on your foot? You just follow me this direction, we'll get you out."

"I WANNA GET OUTTA HERE! I DON'T LIKE THIS, WAYNE!"

Uncle Brian made a series of strange barking noises. It appeared he was having trouble breathing.

"Let's get him outta here, Stewart!" I said.

"You gotta get him to move! He ain't movin'!"

"Then you're gonna have to pull him!"

I backed up until I could feel my foot on Uncle Brian's helmet. He grabbed on to my ankle and squeezed it for dear life. I felt for his shoulder with my boot and started to give him a light push. My heart was thundering in my chest.

"Come on now, Uncle Brian. You gotta help us out, buddy. You gotta back it up if you want to get outta here."

"I WANNA GET OUT OF HERE!"

"I know you do. That's what we're gonna do. You just gotta help us move; otherwise, we can't go anywhere."

"WAYNE," he said, "I WANT MY MOMMA!"

I felt like someone had just hit me in the chest with a red-hot sledgehammer.

claustrophobia *n.*
An abnormal fear of being in narrow or enclosed spaces.

separation anxiety *n.*

A form of anxiety originally caused by separation from a significant nurturing figure (as a mother) and duplicated later in life usually by sudden and involuntary exposure to novel and potentially threatening situations.

6.

Daylight. A late spring breeze. An ambulance.
Three paramedics.

Uncle Brian was lying in the grass, wearing an oxygen mask. The paramedics were checking his vital signs.

It had taken Stewart and me more than two hours to coax him out of Marengo Cave.

The paramedics informed me that my uncle had suffered a mild anxiety attack brought on by an episode of acute claustrophobia. They suggested that perhaps it would be a good idea to take him to the emergency room for a full checkup.

Fear washed over me.

If my dad were to find out that I'd sent my uncle to the emergency room, I'd be a dead man.

I pulled two of the paramedics off to the side.

"Listen," I told them. "It's been a really rough month. He doesn't do too well in hospital environments. His dad died a little while ago, and his mother just went into a nursing home with Alzheimer's. She collapsed right in front of him, 911, the whole bit. I think if he was wheeled into an emergency room in an ambulance right now, it might really be the straw that breaks the camel's back. We're just a few hours from home. I've seen this kind of thing happen before. He usually bounces back if you let him find a comfort zone. If you don't mind, I'd really just like to hit the road."

The two paramedics nodded. The other one finished taking Uncle Brian's blood pressure.

"It's dropping," he said. "He's evening out pretty good."

They talked among themselves and decided to let us go on our way. Mercy.

"You're going to want to stop off and let him clean himself up," one of them said to me. "I think he had himself an accident, if you know what I mean."

I knew what he meant.

"And, for future reference, you might want to think twice before you take him into a cave or any kind of dark, physically restrictive space. I don't think he's really wired for it, if you know what I mean."

I knew what he meant.

As a general rule, Uncle Brian didn't take showers. He took only baths. He didn't like standing under a showerhead. He didn't like to get pelted with water. It made him nervous. I was well aware of this fact.

I pulled off the road and rented a room at a nearby budget motel. I drew Uncle Brian a hot bath and told him to clean himself up. While he was bathing, I threw his dirty clothes away and laid a clean outfit on the bed.

A few minutes later, I heard my uncle singing on the other side of the door. This was a great relief. I took this to mean he was returning to normalcy. He often sang while bathing.

I walked up to the bathroom door and knocked twice.

"Uncle Brian? You doing okay in there?"

"DOIN' OKAY! DOIN' ALL RIGHTY!"

Good, I said to myself. He sounded like himself. Sounded healthy. Stabilized. Normal. Perhaps his short-term memory was such that he wouldn't even recall the cave. Maybe it was all behind him now. Maybe that was his gift, maybe that was the silver lining of his tragic condition: He was incapable of dwelling on things.

On the other hand, the events of the morning could have been the most searing memory of his entire lifetime. For all I knew, the experience had damaged the fundamental nature of his essential being. I could have been the man responsible for robbing him of his innocence, for introducing him to the deepest, most primal fear he'd ever known. If that were the case, it was reasonable to assume he'd spill the beans at some point, in which case he'd probably tell my dad. He tended to confide in my dad when something was seriously the matter.

If my dad were to find out that I had taken my uncle spelunking, I was a dead man.

With the benefit of hindsight, subjecting Uncle Brian to a two-hour tour of the subterranean darkness had been a monumentally poor decision on my part.

But my intentions had been good.

I sat on the bed and turned on the television.

Eminem was on MTV, rapping at the camera. He was furious about something.

Critics often referred to Eminem's music as "incendiary." His critically acclaimed new album, *The Marshall Mathers LP,* had vaulted him into the highest reaches of the cultural lexicon.

lexicon *n., pl.* **lexicons** or **lexica**

1.) A dictionary.

2.) A stock of terms used in a particular profession, subject, or style; a vocabulary: *the lexicon of surrealist art.*

3.) *Linguistics:* The morphemes of a language considered as a group.

Eminem sometimes referred to himself as Slim Shady. That was his other nickname, his other alter ego.

I didn't have a nickname or an alter ego.

I'd never done anything critically acclaimed or incendiary in my whole life.

This made me furious.

Uncle Brian walked out of the bathroom stark naked. I handed him his clothes and told him to get dressed. He saw Eminem on the television. He sang a little bit, dancing along to MTV as he got dressed. Uncle Brian liked to sing along and dance. Didn't matter what he was listening to. Didn't matter if he was naked.

I didn't like to dance.

On occasion, while driving in my car, I would sing along at the top of my lungs.

I studied Uncle Brian's face, his body language, his demeanor. He looked normal. Movement was fluid. Posture was good. He appeared to be showing no visible signs of trauma.

Still, I figured it probably wouldn't be such a bad idea to ask him to keep quiet about our adventures. I figured if I made my request in a circuitous manner, staying away from terms like "cave" and "paramedics," I'd be able to avoid stirring up any unpleasant memories while at the same time doing whatever I could to get my point across.

As he dressed, I casually asked him if he remembered "the morning."

"YEAH," he replied. "I REMEMBER THE MORNING."

I couldn't tell if he really did.

I then asked him if he could keep a secret.

"I CAN KEEP A SECRET!" he replied.

I wasn't sure if he really could.

I promised him that if he didn't say a word about the cave trip to my parents, I would take him to Pizza Hut while we were in Indianapolis.

"If you do a good job of keeping this secret," I told him, "I'll take you to Pizza Hut as much as you want."

"I WANT A PIZZA HUT!" he said.

"Uncle Brian," I said, "listen to me now. I absolutely promise you that if you keep this secret—if you don't tell my dad or my mom or Uncle Wally or Aunt Katherine or anyone else about what happened this morning—I will take you to Pizza Hut no fewer than three times next week. We'll get pizza every day if you want. But you've got to keep a secret. You can't talk about what happened this morning; otherwise, you won't get any pizza."

"YOU'LL TAKE ME TO THE PIZZA HUT?"

"Yes. But only if you keep the secret."

"I WANNA KEEP THE SECRET!"

"Scout's honor?" I said, raising the first two fingers of my right hand.

"ALL RIGHTY!" said Uncle Brian.

He raised his left hand and gave me the middle finger, kind of.

7.

We pulled into my parents' driveway at dusk.
The sky was purple and pink. The tulips in the garden were in bloom. Uncle Brian was out of his mind with excitement. I'd just informed him that his brother was inside waiting for him, with food. He jumped out of the car and raced in through the front door while I removed our bags from the trunk.

My mom was in the kitchen, stirring a pot, when I walked in. We hugged. It was good to see her. She told me I looked thin. I told her about the food in Cuba. She asked me about the road trip. I told her it went fine, that everything went fine. She asked me how Uncle Brian had done. I told her he'd done fine, that everything went fine.

"That's good," she said. "Your father and I were a little concerned."

"He loves to ride in a car," I said.

"Yes," said my mother. "Yes, he certainly does."

Here there was a silence. My mother looked at me for a moment before asking me how I was feeling. She wanted to know how things had been going all spring, how I'd been feeling about life, about work, about Amanda.

"We haven't talked about it all that much," she said. "I feel like I should be asking you about it, checking in on you, but you know that I don't want to pry. That wasn't an easy thing to go through, Wayne, and I'm just wondering . . . how you're doing."

I shrugged and told her that everything was fine, that I was feeling fine.

"There isn't much to say about it," I said. "It's not that I'm avoiding anything, it's just that the whole situation tends to defy any kind of analysis. It is what it is, and that's it. There isn't much else to discuss. So in light of that fact, I'm just trying to get on with things, trying not to think about it too much, trying not to obsess. That's pretty much the extent of it."

I shrugged my shoulders again and dug my hands inside my pockets, and then I glanced up to my left. I could see Uncle Brian through the window above the sink. He was out back on the deck with my dad and my little sister, standing by the grill, bouncing around on the balls of his feet, hollering at the top of his lungs, making wild, emphatic gestures with his hands. The window was closed, and I couldn't make out what he was saying. To the best of my knowledge, neither could my dad. Judging by the look on his face, he was having a hard time deciphering. When Uncle Brian got excited like that, he tended to be incoherent.

This was good.

"My goodness," my mom said. "The guy's got a voice, doesn't he?"

"I just spent twenty hours in a car with him."

"I wonder what he's talking about," she said. "He looks like he's about to burst a vessel."

"God only knows," I said.

Halfway through dinner, the other shoe dropped.

"So," my dad said to me, "what's this Brian keeps saying about an ambulance?"

"A what?" I said, setting my fork down.

"Well, I can't be sure, but I think he was telling me about an ambulance and the two of you walking around in some cave."

I looked over at Uncle Brian. He was locked into his plate of food, oblivious. I felt my face turning red.

"Oh," I said. "We stopped off this morning at these caves in southern Indiana and went on a little tour. Nothing major. Just wanted to get out of the car and stretch our legs a little bit."

I was a terrible liar. When confronted, I tended to falter. It wasn't even worth the effort.

"You went into a cave?" my dad said.

I nodded, kind of.

"You mean underground?" my mom said.

"It was a short tour," I said.

My dad looked at my mom. My mom looked at my dad.

"And what's this about an ambulance?" my dad said.

I picked up my fork and took a bite of food, so as to appear casual. With my mouth full, I explained that Uncle Brian had "a slight panic attack." I highlighted the fact that we had evacuated him immediately and called an ambulance "as a precautionary measure."

"I didn't want to take any chances," I continued. "I felt it was the responsible thing to do."

"You didn't want to take any chances?" my dad said.

"What do you mean 'a precautionary measure'?" my mom said. "What made you think he'd need an ambulance?"

"The responsible thing to do?" my dad said. "What's so responsible about taking him into a goddamn cave?"

Anne giggled.

I explained that Uncle Brian had been hyperventilating slightly. My father tensed up on hearing the word "hyperventilating." With this in mind, I quickly changed my rhetoric in an attempt to defuse a potentially combustible conversation.

"It was a slight oxygen issue," I said. "I didn't want to take any chances."

"A slight oxygen issue?" my dad said. "What in the hell do you mean 'a slight oxygen issue'?"

My choice of words wasn't having the calming effect I had hoped it would.

"There's no such thing as a slight oxygen issue," my mother said.

"He was breathing a little funny," I said. "Wheezing a little bit. I wanted to make sure he was okay. He got a little freaked out in the dark."

"What in the hell were you doing taking him down into a cave, Wayne?" my dad said.

"I don't know. I thought it'd be fun."

"Jesus."

"Who paid for this ambulance?" my mom said.

"Nobody."

"What do you mean 'nobody'?"

"I mean they never asked for anything. They gave him a little oxygen and checked his blood pressure. That was it. They never asked me for anything. We were in a really small town."

"Hundreds of miles from quality medical care," my dad said. "You had no business being there."

"Brian," my mother said. "Brian, sweetheart. How are you feeling? You doin' okay, honey?"

No response.

"Brian," my dad said. "Listen up, pal. Listen to your brother. You doin' all righty?"

"I'M DOIN' ALL RIGHTY," Uncle Brian said. His mouth was full of food. His eyes were glued to his plate.

"See?" I said. "He's normal. Full appetite. It was really no big deal."

"What about you?" my mother said. "What's wrong with you? Why haven't you touched your steak?"

"I told you, I'm not eating meat anymore."

"What do you mean you're not eating meat anymore?" my dad said.

"I mean I've lost interest."

"What do you mean 'lost interest'?"

"I mean I lost my taste for it."

"Jesus."

"It's fine, Joe," my mom said. "It's his choice. If he doesn't want to eat steak, that's his business."

"That's a good piece of steak," my dad said.

"Then you eat it," I said.

My dad jabbed my steak with his fork and lifted it off of my plate.

My mom turned her attention to Uncle Brian.

"Brian," she said, "what happened this morning? Tell us about the cave, honey."

No response.

"Brian, honey. Listen to me for a second. What happened in the cave this morning?"

Uncle Brian stopped eating. He dropped his fork and grabbed the edge of the table.

"I DON'T WANNA GO IN A CAVE, ELAINE! NO WAY!"

"You might not want to use that word," I said.

"We're not taking you anywhere," my dad said. "Calm down. We're just asking what happened, buddy."

"I DON'T LIKE IT IN THE CAVE, JOE! NO WAY!"

He gripped the table. His shoulders rose.

"It's okay, sweetheart," my mom said. "We're not going anywhere. Don't you worry. You're gonna stay right here with us, okay?"

My dad turned to me. "We told you to be conservative with him," he said. "We told you to take it easy, don't let him overeat, and come straight home. You should know better than that, stopping off in the middle of nowhere at some goddamn hole in the ground. There's no telling what could've happened to him."

"It was a safe tour," I said.

"Like hell it was."

Eventually, Uncle Brian calmed down. My mother gave him some more mashed potatoes. The rest of us watched in silence as he cleaned his plate completely. I thought for a moment that the worst of it was over. I thought I was out of the woods. But it wasn't meant to be.

Shortly after finishing his meal, Uncle Brian took a moment to mention that he had "PISSED HIS PANTS" that morning.

My chin dropped to my chest. My little sister choked on her water, spitting it onto her plate. My mother was across the kitchen, standing over by the sink, opening another bottle of wine. She turned around, jaw agape. My dad sat up straighter and glared at me.

"What's he talking about, Wayne?" he said.

"I PISSED MY PANTS, JOE!"

I massaged my eyeballs with thumb and forefinger.

"What in the hell is this, Wayne? What in the hell happened here? What aren't you telling us?"

I tried to remain calm. I tried to remain casual. I explained, to the best of my ability, that Uncle Brian had had a small "urinary episode" as a result of his slight oxygen issue and that I had taken care of the problem immediately, as a precautionary measure. Furthermore, I assured everyone that Uncle Brian had bathed immediately at a nearby motel.

"And then we hit the road and came straight home," I said. "No more stopping. No more side trips. No more accidents. End of story."

"Jesus Christ," my dad said.

"JESUS CHRIST!" said Uncle Brian.

There was a long, uncomfortable period of contemplation as the facts of the case started to register and congeal.

"Listen," I said. "I'm sorry. I didn't mean any harm. I actually thought it might be fun for him. It was a complete accident, nothing more."

"I HAD AN ACCIDENT!" said Uncle Brian.

My mother walked over to the table with the bottle of wine.

8.

A week in Indiana was plenty. Uncle Brian's underground panic attack had gotten me off on the wrong foot. My parents were all over me from the start. On the second day of my stay, they sat me down for another round of The Conversation, eager to hear me explain my direction in life. Something about my aura had them uneasy. I seemed quiet, they told me. Distant and detached. They wanted to know what all of my wandering would amount to. They wanted to know why I seemed so intent on blowing through all of the money I'd been so lucky to make. They wanted to know how I'd been dealing with bereavement. They wanted to know if I'd given any thought to what they liked to call my "trajectory."

> **trajectory** *n., pl.* **trajectories**
> 1.) The path of a projectile or other moving body through space.
> 2.) A chosen or taken course: *"What died with [the assassinated leaders] was a moral trajectory, a style of aspiration"* (Lance Morrow).
> 3.) *Mathematics:* A curve that cuts all of a given family of curves or surfaces at the same angle.

I told them I didn't have much in the way of a conscious trajectory. I'd never been much for planning.

"How am I supposed to know what I'm going to be doing a

year from now?" I said to them. "How am I supposed to know what I'm going to be doing a *day* from now? I can't plan that far ahead. Hell, I can't even plan five minutes from now. It's impossible. Anything could happen."

"You don't have to *know*," my mom said. "You just have to have some idea. Of course the future is uncertain, but you have to be willing to step forward. It's an act of faith."

"What is this aversion you have to planning?" my dad said. "It's a necessity of life, son. We all have to make plans."

"It's not an aversion to planning," my mom said. "It's an aversion to *commitment*."

"Commitment," I said, "implies feeling strongly enough about something that you're *willing* to commit. That right there is the issue. I just haven't decided what I'm committed to yet."

"Well, the sooner the better, I'd imagine," my dad said.

"Some people's vocations come to them at a young age," I replied. "Those are the prodigies. Lightning hasn't struck for me yet."

"Sometimes you have to jump in feet first, son," my dad said. "Lightning doesn't strike unless you fly a kite."

"Exactly," said my mother. "You can't run forever, Wayne."

"You think that's what this is?" I said. "You think I'm running from something?"

My parents kind of looked at me. Then they kind of shrugged.

That night I had a dream about Amanda, the first and only dream I'd had about her since she'd died. It was pleasant. We were in Havana, down by the water, walking along the Malecón, looking at Communists. Amanda was pushing a stroller. We had a baby daughter. We were calling her Amanda Jr. because we couldn't agree upon a proper name. We were going back and forth about what to call her. I wanted to name her May Valentine. Amanda wanted to name her either Fiona or Stella.

At some point along the way, Pamela showed up. I looked to my left and there she was, standing on the rocks below the parapet, wearing the red dress I'd bought her. She was barefooted, holding her red high-heeled shoes in one hand. I was terrified that the tide was going to roll in and crush her. I called out to her in a panic.

Pamela! I said. *Pamela! Get off the rocks! Get away from the water! It's me! Wayne!*

But she couldn't hear me.

10.

The very next day, I made a sweeping decision about my immediate future. I decided to hike the Appalachian Trail for a while. It was something I'd actually pondered before but never too seriously.

I was bowling with Uncle Brian when the notion returned to me, hitting me like a minor epiphany. This time it was serious. I suddenly realized that a summer spent wandering the wilds of Appalachia would satisfy all of my mental and environmental requirements and then some. I wanted the quiet, I wanted the nature, and I wanted the solitude—but I also wanted motion. I wanted variation of landscape from day to day. I wanted to meet strange people. I wanted the potential for interaction with large, untamed mammals. I wanted to rip myself away from the myriad mindless distractions I'd learned to lean on over the years. I wanted another dramatic reduction of familiar stimuli.

I also wanted exercise. Vitality. Physical health. And I wanted to quit smoking. I wanted pink lungs. I wanted to quit committing casual, gradual suicide. That sounded like a decent idea.

Out in the wilderness, existence would define itself on wholly different terms. The trail was immense and unforgiving, running from Springer Mountain, Georgia, to Mt. Katahdin, Maine, a distance of approximately 2,168 miles. It traveled through fourteen states, eight national forests, and six national parks. Generally speaking, the trail itself was about two feet wide. And it was open only to foot travel. No wheels allowed.

Hiking it would be a mental and physical challenge like nothing I'd ever experienced before. It would force me to live without comforts and vices. It would clean me out, purify me. It would force me to confront myself. Perhaps it would strip me of a few illusions. I felt it was exactly the right thing to do.

Normally, individuals who walk long distances on the Appalachian Trail start trekking in March or April, near the beginning of springtime. I would be starting in June, at summer's onset, in the South.

Normally, long-distance hikers do some training beforehand. They lift weights. They run. They stretch. They hike. I, on the other hand, hadn't trained at all. My physical conditioning was average at best. My youth was really the only thing I had going for me. My beanpole legs, tired heart, and young, black lungs would be forced to endure a baptism by fire.

Not surprisingly, my parents' response when I announced my intentions was lukewarm at best. At that point, they'd already given me their opinions on my existence. I knew what they thought I should be doing with my time, more or less. Wandering the wilds of Appalachia clearly wasn't what they had in mind. But to their credit, they made no real effort to stop me.

"You want to do what?" my father said.

"Where?" said my mother.

"I'm going to walk north," I said.

On one level, I like to think that they were impressed with my willingness to endure such hardship voluntarily. And the fact that the trip was going to cost a relative pittance (about $500 a month) didn't hurt either, helping to placate their growing concerns over my penchant for financial myopia.

Beyond that, though, news of my impending foray into the

wilderness did little to allay their concerns about my (woeful) lack of trajectory, my (apparent) deep-seated fear of commitment, and my resultant tendency to (as they perceived it) run away from all things associated with real life.

Real life.

11.

In the days leading up to my journey, I busied myself by stocking up on supplies—boots, a tent, a backpack, a knife. The decision to hike had officially been made, and my excitement was rising. I was ravenous for information and wanted to know everything. I purchased a wide assortment of guidebooks and read through each one with great intensity. By virtue of this process, I found myself inundated with information about a guy named Benton MacKaye, the man primarily responsible for the existence of the Appalachian Trail. His story was deeply intriguing.

MacKaye was born in 1879 and raised in a town called Shirley Center, Massachusetts. He received a master's degree in forestry from Harvard University in 1905 and went on to work for various government institutions, including the U.S. Forestry Service, the U.S. Geological Survey, the Indian Service, and the Tennessee Valley Authority.

In 1915, he married a woman named Jesse Belle Hardy Stubbs, a prominent suffragist. Her nickname was Betty. Together they lived an intellectual and politically active life.

Sadly, Betty was plagued by mental illness. Throughout her life, she suffered intermittent bouts of severe depression. She went nuts in 1918, for example, suffering a full-blown mental collapse. Only with the tireless support of family and friends was she able to manage a functional recovery.

Unfortunately, however, the recovery didn't last. Three years later, it happened again. Betty descended into a fit of terrible darkness in New York City. Deeply concerned, Benton arranged for her to stay at the country residence of his friend Mable Irwin, a Universalist minister and a lecturer on eugenics, hoping the retreat would aid his wife's recuperation.

eugenics *n.* (used with a sing. verb)
The study of hereditary improvement of the human race by controlled selective breeding.

With Mable Irwin's assistance, Benton escorted Betty to Grand Central Terminal, where they were to catch a train to Oscawana, a small town north of the Big Apple.

While Benton was standing in line to buy tickets, Mable and Betty walked off to the ladies' room. Suddenly and without warning, Betty bolted. She pulled away from Mable, darted into the crowd, and disappeared. Mable was frantic. Together she and Benton searched Grand Central and its surrounding streets, trying to track Betty down. They looked high and low, calling out her name.

A few hours later, Benton reported his wife missing.

A few hours after that, Betty MacKaye's body was pulled from the East River.

According to a report in the *New York Times* on April 19, 1921, Benton MacKaye claimed that Betty "often said she intended to end her life by jumping into the Hudson or East River."

end *v.* **ended, ending, ends** *v. tr.*

1.) To bring to a conclusion.

2.) To form the last or concluding part of: *the song that ended the performance.*

3.) To destroy: *ended our hopes.*

v. intr.

1.) To come to a finish; cease. See synonyms at *complete.*

2.) To arrive at a place, situation, or condition as a result of a course of action. Often used with *up: He ended up as an adviser to the president. The painting ended up being sold for a million dollars.*

3.) To die.

Betty MacKaye's remains were cremated. Benton scattered her ashes near a lily pond on Staten Island during a brief outdoor ceremony. Frogs could be heard singing from the lily pond during the service. From that day forward, Benton MacKaye always cherished the song of springtime frogs. It made him think of the cycle of life. It made him think of the beauty of Betty. It reminded him that winter was followed by spring. It gave him hope on days when he was feeling terribly, impossibly blue.

12.

I left on a Tuesday, first thing in the morning.
My parents and Uncle Brian saw me off in the dawn light.

"Be careful," my mom said. "And call us every time you get to a town. And be sure to let me know if they're holding my packages at the post office."

My mom had agreed to send me boxes of food and supplies at designated towns along the trail. She was terrified that I wasn't going to eat properly, that I'd shrivel up to nothing in the wilderness, collapse into a heap, and be fed upon by predators.

It had been a major concern of hers ever since the day I was born.

Uncle Brian said good-bye next. He gave me a clumsy hug that nearly knocked me to the ground. Then he gave me a high five.

He liked to hug people and give them high fives.

I had a hard time hugging people and telling them that I loved them. Even people in my own family.

I had no problem giving people high fives.

"GOOD-BYE, WAYNE!" Uncle Brian said. "I LOVE YOU!"

"Take it easy, Uncle Brian," I said.

Then I gave him a high five.

I said good-bye to my dad last. He hugged me a little bit more tightly than usual, and when he pulled away, I could see that he had tears in his eyes. The man was half Italian. He had never been good with good-byes.

"Just be careful," he said to me.

"I'll be fine."

"Your mother and I, we worry about you."

"Don't worry," I said. "I'm okay."

"We love you, son."

"Okay."

"You take care of yourself out there."

"I will, Dad. I'll be okay."

With that, I climbed into my rental car and started the engine. I backed out of the driveway and rolled away down the street. Uncle Brian took off after me on foot. This was another habit of his: He liked to take off after people on foot as they drove away in motor vehicles. If you weren't careful, he'd run out into the middle of a busy street in hot pursuit.

Driving away, I watched in the rearview mirror as my dad chased him down, took him by the arm, and led him back up to the house. I honked the horn twice and gave one last wave. And then I made a left onto Gray Road.

13.

Back when I was in college, I'd read Jon Krakauer's *Into the Wild,* a harrowing nonfiction account of the mysterious life and death of Christopher Johnson McCandless. A bookstore employee had recommended it to me one Sunday afternoon, and I wound up reading the entire thing in one sitting.

McCandless was a fascinating character. Raised in a fairly affluent Washington, D.C., suburb, he had excelled as both a student and an athlete throughout his youth. According to friends and family members, he had always seemed like a relatively happy, relatively normal individual.

But then things got weird.

Shortly after graduating from Emory University in Atlanta in 1991, McCandless gave away his entire life savings to charity, abandoned all of his possessions, severed contact with his family, and disappeared without a trace. He blazed out West, ditched his car in the desert, burned all of the cash in his wallet, and went on a vision quest. Along the way, he gave himself a new nickname.

He called himself Alexander Supertramp.

In April 1992, about a year into his vision quest, Alexander Supertramp hitchhiked to Alaska and wandered into the wilderness north of Mt. McKinley, all by himself. He was trying to have a transcendent experience on the planet Earth. He was trying to defy his parents, renounce materialism, have an adventure, and return to nature.

Also, he wanted to know what it felt like to be truly *alive.*

A few months later, an Alaskan moose hunter found Alexander Supertramp's emaciated corpse in a dilapidated school bus in the middle of nowhere.

nowhere *adv.*

1.) Not anywhere.

2.) To no place or result: *protested the ruling but got nowhere.*

n.

1.) A remote or unknown place: *a cabin in the middle of nowhere.*

2.) A state of nonexistence: *an idea that came out of nowhere.*

Nobody was exactly sure how Alexander Supertramp had died in a dilapidated school bus in the middle of nowhere. Some thought he starved to death. Some thought he accidentally poisoned himself. Some thought he had a death wish. Others thought him a fool who simply took asceticism too far and paid for it with his life. They thought he was a young, silly punk who had been needlessly burned by the heat of his own idealism.

I didn't really know what I thought.

14.

A.B. and Jenny met me at the Alamo rental car drop-off at Hartsfield International Airport in Atlanta. They had recently returned home to Charlotte, North Carolina, after a two-week honeymoon in Peru. They were tan, freshly married, glowing, unemployed, and still in travel mode. We'd spoken on the telephone two days earlier, and they'd offered to give me a ride to the trailhead. They even offered to hike the first four days of the trip with me. Naturally, I accepted without hesitation.

Having them along at the beginning turned out to be both a blessing and a curse. I was happy to see them, of course, and happy to have company, but knowing they would soon be leaving filled me with dark and inescapable dread. Furthermore, witnessing their conjugal bliss, their unity and confidence, had me feeling obnoxiously inept. I did my best to maintain an external air of composure and optimism, but it was difficult. My fears of loneliness and the unknown rendered me speechless much of the time. And I didn't have the courage to voice them.

By contrast, A.B. and Jenny were in remarkably high spirits from moment one. They were young and in love, and nothing could stop them. I envied them terribly. The inclement weather didn't really get them down, nor did the physical toil. They took everything in stride. They laughed and smelled the flowers. They threw mud at each other and giggled. They cracked jokes, sang songs. They talked effortlessly and treated each other with unfailing kindness. And at least three times a day, they made a point of telling me how excited they were for me.

"You're in for such an incredible adventure," they kept saying. "We're so excited for you, Fencer. This is going to be the experience of a lifetime."

"I know," I said.

As we trudged over mountainsides those first few days, my thoughts kept drifting back to Benton MacKaye. His story had stuck to me. I couldn't get it off of my mind.

In the wake of his wife's suicide, MacKaye had been utterly devastated. He spent weeks in a bleak state of emotional turmoil, living at his brother Hal's place in Yonkers. Family and friends were there to lend their support, doing whatever they could to buoy his spirits. They sent him heartfelt letters of condolence, urging him not to blame himself for Betty's suicide. They encouraged him to remain strong in the face of adversity. They told him he was numb, that it just hadn't hit him yet. They tried, in whatever ways they could, to get him excited about life again.

Benton's brother James, for instance, wrote a highly practical letter in which he advised his grieving sibling to move forward, to immerse himself in work that meant something to him. "The philosophy of utility fits every occasion," he wrote, "and I am applying the principle in urging you to begin at once to plan for the future—as that is the useful thing to do."

It was a letter that Benton seemingly took to heart. His sense of purpose and immediacy seemed to grow stronger after reading it. He started to become extraordinarily focused.

He was at a crossroads in his existence.

A few months later, he published a groundbreaking proposal in the October 1921 edition of the *Journal of the American Institute of Architects* entitled "An Appalachian Trail: A Project in Regional

Planning." In it, he outlined his vision for a footpath running from the highest reaches of the northern Appalachian Mountains all the way to the highest reaches of the southern Appalachian Mountains. The footpath, as MacKaye envisioned it, would connect work camps, study camps, and farms where human beings worn out from the stresses of urban industrial existence could live, work, and play. According to the proposal, the necessity of such a footpath could be argued for thusly:

> Something has been going on these past few strenuous years which, in the din of war and general upheaval, has been somewhat lost from the public mind. It is the slow quiet development of the recreational camp. It is something neither urban nor rural. It escapes the hecticness of the one, and the loneliness of the other. And it escapes also the common curse of both—the high-powered tension of the economic scramble. All communities face an "economic" problem, but in different ways. The camp faces it through cooperation and mutual helpfulness, the others through competition and mutual fleecing. . . .

> . . . The problem of living is at bottom an economic one. And this alone is bad enough, even in a period of so-called "normalcy." But living has been considerably complicated of late in various ways—by war, by questions of personal liberty, and by "menaces" of one kind or another. There have been created bitter antagonisms. We are undergoing also the bad combination of high prices and unemployment. This situation is worldwide—the result of a worldwide war.

It is no purpose of this little article to indulge in coping with any of these big questions. The nearest we come to such effrontery is to suggest more comfortable seats and more fresh air for those who have to consider them. A great professor once said that "optimism is oxygen." Are we getting all the "oxygen" we might for the big tasks before us?

"Let us wait," we are told, "till we solve this cussed labor problem. Then we'll have the leisure to do great things."

But suppose that while we wait the chance for doing them is passed?

15.

The Appalachian Trail was officially completed on August 14, 1937. After years of hard work, Benton MacKaye's dream of a continuous footpath tracing the ridgecrests of the Appalachian Mountains became a reality. Its successful completion was the end result of MacKaye's fundamental vision and the tireless efforts of many men, most of whom were unpaid volunteers.

Over the years, one of the traditions that evolved on the Appalachian Trail was the adoption of a "trail name," which was a hiker's nickname, essentially. Those who endeavored to stay on the trail for an extended period of time tended to adopt trail names. Generally speaking, it was a symbolic gesture representative of a man's desire to transform himself from what he was into what he wished to be.

Appalachian Trail etiquette dictated that trail names must be given to a person. As a matter of protocol, you weren't allowed to give yourself a trail name—which was good. I agreed with this dictum completely. People who gave themselves nicknames tended to irk me. It had always been my belief that a nickname should be given to a man by someone other than himself. I mentioned this to A.B. and Jenny on the first day of the trip. We were standing beside a rushing creek in a deep ravine, refilling our water bottles. The weather was deteriorating. Storm clouds were rolling in, and the tops of the trees were bending in the wind.

"People who nickname themselves should be quarantined," I said.

"I think it's kind of funny," said Jenny.

"I think it's a sign of mental illness," I said. "Someone else has to name me. Otherwise, I'm not doing it."

Thunder rumbled overhead.

"Why don't you call yourself Wolfgang?" said A.B.

"Wolfgang?" I said.

"Wolfgang," he said.

"Why Wolfgang?" I said.

"I don't know. It just popped into my head."

Jenny laughed.

16.

It rained steadily throughout those first four days. The ground was a muddy soup. The north Georgia forest was pure gloom. My feet were blistered and my back ached. My body wasn't responding well to the rigors of trail life. Neither was my spirit. In a matter of twenty-four hours, I was having second thoughts, filled with doubt and terror, unsure if I could hack it. The thought of quitting crossed my mind on several occasions. I found myself dreaming of escape routes, formulating plans. I had sexual fantasies about cigarettes, which I had given up, cold turkey, the moment I stepped on the trail. My mind raced through strategies and rationales. I concocted excuses and constructed fantastically logical explanations for an abrupt and unceremonious exit.

Ultimately, though, the concept didn't sit well. My pride won out. I couldn't quit. Not yet, anyway. There was too much on the line. If I backed out immediately, my parents would feel justified in their trepidations. It would validate their concerns over my trajectory. More to the point, I feared that quitting would do irreparable damage to my self-confidence. I didn't want to wake up one day down the road, haunted by the fact that I had turned my back on the greatest adventures of my wayward youth. The bottom line was, I had chosen this route. I'd made the call. Now I had to tough it out.

At night in my tent, I would give myself pep talks before going to sleep, in an effort to embolden myself. The pep talks went something like this:

Quit being a pussy, you lame, sheltered, weak, white-bread, suburban piece of shit.

pussy *n., pl.* **pussies**

1.) *Informal:* A cat.

2.) *Botany:* A fuzzy catkin, especially of the pussy willow.

3.) *Vulgar slang:*

    a. The vulva.

    b. Sexual intercourse with a woman.

4.) *Offensive slang:* Used as a disparaging term for a woman.

5.) *Slang:* A man regarded as weak, timid, or unmanly.

17.

A.B., Jenny, and I were forty miles up the trail at a place called Neels Gap, a rest stop of sorts along Highway 19, in a valley between two mountains. I was famished and weary. My body was reeling from the toil of ten-hour days struggling over hill and dale. I wasn't doing too hot mentally, either. But I tried my best to put on a good show.

The three of us bought candy bars and Coca-Colas at the Neels Gap camp store. Then we went outside and sat on our packs in the parking lot and ate. The skies were gray, and it was unseasonably cool. The rain had let up momentarily, and the valley wind smelled of earthworms and mud. A.B. and Jenny would be leaving me within minutes. I was feeling desperately sad.

"How do you feel?" A.B. asked me.

"Fine," I told him.

We talked about the past for a while, about college, about our friends. Then we talked about the future, with a little less certainty. We ate our candy bars and drank our Cokes. We wondered aloud what would become of us.

"It's impossible to say," said Jenny. "I couldn't even begin to predict."

"Me neither," I said.

"We live in the nuclear age," said A.B.

"It's a crapshoot," said Jenny.

"Anything could happen," said A.B.

"That's what I'm afraid of," I said.

"It's not necessarily a bad thing," said A.B.

"Let's hope so," I said.

"This is par for the course," said A.B. "This is what's *supposed* to be happening. We're *supposed* to be confused right now. We're *supposed* to be stupid, wandering around in the trees. The next few years, we take our punches. If the world doesn't explode, maybe we'll get to impose our will on it in 2020."

"Ha," said Jenny.

"I'll drink to that," I said.

"To 2020," said Jenny.

"To the wildly uncertain future," said A.B.

"Let's try not to fuck it up," I said.

"To being mired in the design phase," said Jenny.

"Confused in the blueprint phase," said A.B.

"Lost in space," I said.

"This is only the beginning," said Jenny.

"The beginning of the end," I said.

"Hear, hear," said A.B.

It started to sprinkle a little bit.

We raised our cans of Coke and offered cheers.

blueprint *n.*

1.) A contact print of a drawing or other image rendered as white lines on a blue background, especially such a print of an architectural plan or technical drawing. Also called *cyanotype.*

2.) A mechanical drawing produced by any of various similar photographic processes, such as one that creates blue or black lines on a white background.

3.) A detailed plan of action. See synonyms at *plan*.

4.) A model or prototype.

An hour or so later, I thumbed a ride to the town of Blairsville to get some supplies and stay the night in a cheap motel. The guy who picked me up was a college student named Greg. He was short and friendly, pudgy and vaguely bohemian. He pulled off to the side of the road and waited while I gathered my pack.

A.B. and Jenny had seen me off. They were headed in the opposite direction, back to Amiacola Falls, to pick up their truck. I was headed into the wilderness for an unspecified amount of time, and they were headed back to Charlotte. I was headed into the bush, a bachelor with no prospects, and they were getting ready to move into a well-appointed condominium somewhere near the heart of downtown.

We said good-bye at the side of the road.

"Good luck, Fencer," A.B. said. "Keep your head on straight. And try not to get eaten by a bear."

"Okay," I said.

"And write us letters," Jenny said. "Let us know how you're doing."

I told them I would.

18.

As a young man hiking through the north Georgia forest alone, the movie *Deliverance* was never far from my mind. One way or another, the visions preyed upon me. One way or another, the visions won. The woods haunted me. The rivers haunted me. The faces of the nameless hillbillies haunted me. Ned Beatty's utterly authentic performance haunted me in particular: the look of pure torture . . . the desperate scramble . . . the sound of those awful, pathetic squeals. . . .

It was inevitable.

Deliverance. Warner Brothers, 1972. John Boorman, producer. Vilmos Zsigmond, cinematographer. Tom Priestley, editor. Fred Harpman, art director. Marcel Vercoutere, special effects. Bucky Rous, costume designer. Eric Weissberg, composer. James Dickey, screenwriter. Based on the novel by James Dickey. Directed by John Boorman. Rated R.

Synopsis:
Burt Reynolds stars as Lewis Medlock, a hyper-macho Atlanta yuppie who leads his three buddies—Bobby Trippe (Ned Beatty), Drew Ballinger (Ronny Cox), and Ed Gentry (Jon Voight)—on a weekend canoe trip down north Georgia's soon-to-be-dammed Cahulawassee River. The

trip begins promisingly but soon turns nightmarish, as evil, inexperience, and calamity conspire to catapult Medlock and company into a desperate fight for their yuppie lives. Nominated for three Academy Awards, *Deliverance* is a powerful meditation on the powers of nature and the dangers inherent in masculine ritual.

I think the machines are going to fail, the political systems are going to fail, and a few men are going to take to the hills and start over.
—Lewis Medlock, *Deliverance*

Sometimes you gotta lose yourself before you can find anything.
—Lewis Medlock, *Deliverance*

About halfway through *Deliverance,* Bobby and Ed get separated from Lewis and Drew while navigating a particularly technical stretch of Cahulawassee white water. They reach the landing point ahead of their friends, dock their canoe, and step on shore. There they are greeted by a pair of menacing hillbillies, played with frightening authenticity by screen actors Bill McKinney and Herbert "Cowboy" Coward.

The hillbillies hold Bobby and Ed at gunpoint and force them to walk back into the woods. After a few minutes of uncomfortable, foreboding dialogue, McKinney's character beats and humiliates Bobby, ordering him to remove his pants and underwear. Then, with twisted glee, McKinney's character sodomizes Bobby, mocking him for his portly physical stature and imploring him to "squeal like a pig" with each and every savage thrust.

• • •

This utterly disturbing transaction tends to leave an indelible mark on the minds of all who witness it.

It is widely regarded as the finest hillbilly rape scene ever captured on film.

Deliverance, in the strangest of ways, has managed, over the years, to achieve accidental-comedy status.

I like to think of it as accidental black comedy.

The infamous hillbilly rape scene is the film's defining, unintentionally comic moment.

It is funny in the worst possible way.

In his scintillating 1994 autobiography *My Life* (Hyperion Books), screen legend Burt Reynolds recalls the filming of the infamous hillbilly rape scene in the following manner:

> . . . The day before we shot the scene I noticed McKinney hovering beside Ned and sat down between them. I wanted him to see I was Ned's friend. No different than in the script. Then I asked him how he planned to handle the rape scene. . . .

> . . . Staring straight at Ned, he whispered, "I've always wanted to try that. Always have."

> . . . When it came down to shooting it, Cowboy and McKinney were hands-down brilliant. Scared the shit out of everybody. . . . None of that creepy "Squeal, piggy, piggy" stuff was in the script.

But McKinney, I swear to God, really wanted to hump Ned. And I think he was going to. He had it up and he was going to bang him. It's the first and only time I have ever seen camera operators turn their heads away.

Finally, I couldn't stand it anymore. I ran into the scene, dove on McKinney, and pulled him off.

19.

18 June 2000
Somewhere in the north Georgia hills

Dear A.B. + Jenny,

Every time I hear a twig snap, I whirl around, terrified that a sadistic, boy-crazy hillbilly is going to come bounding out of the underbrush wielding a high-powered rifle.

Aside from that, everything's great.

At the moment, I'm in my tent near the Deep Gap Shelter, writing by the light of my headlamp, nursing incredibly sore joints and a collection of large, pustulant foot blisters. I've taken to covering them in duct tape each morning before I set out—it's the only method I've found that provides anything resembling relief. Been trekking all day long, nonstop, wincing with every step, at a daily pace of about fifteen miles. Overdoing it, certainly, but there really isn't much time for rest. Food supply is limited. If I don't move, I'll starve. Have to get to the next road, the next town, to resupply. That's the way it goes.

Been trying in some strange way to make sense of things out here, with mixed results. Originally figured my time alone in the woods would serve well to clear my head and help me untangle some knots and relax a little bit, but in truth, it's probably made me even more confused than I already was, if that's even possible. So far, the only real thing I've discovered is that when you have this much time to think, your mind tends to fly into overdrive and do a number on you. A week or so in wilderness solitude, and I'm pretty sure I've thought about everything that's ever happened to me in my entire life—every memory, every potentiality, every daydream, every night dream, every pipe dream, you name it. Naturally, this has included excessive time spent thinking about my ex, Amanda, and her tragic exit late last year and all of the requisite psychodrama that the situation tends to entail. Don't mean to be a bummer or a purveyor of dark-hearted miseries, but the plain truth of the matter is that solo time in the woods lends itself to mortality contemplation. The dregs come up when the sun goes down. Been trying to get to the bottom of it, trying to decide what to make of it, trying to put some kind of punctuation mark on the whole heart-crushing experience, but all that I've been able to come up with so far is this: Suicide renders you stupid and afraid. Stupid because you'll never know exactly why they did it. Afraid because you're not 100 percent convinced it was illogical.

Like I said, don't wanna be a downer, nor do I want to give you the wrong impression of where my head is out here in the woods. Generally speaking, aside from a few stretches of savage contemplation, my spirits are relatively high. I'm having fun, in whatever twisted way this kind of self-flagellation is fun. I'm having an adventure. Wandering through the sticks. Popping blisters. Stomping in the mud. Writing crazy letters. Drowning in the rain.

I haven't spoken to another human being since Blairsville, pretty much.

Wound up calling my parents from my motel room while I was there. My mother told me to be very careful, to keep an eye out for large wild animals of a predatory nature. I told her not to worry, told her that I have little fear of large wild animals of a predatory nature. Out here, I told her, I have no need to fear bears, no need to worry about bobcats or angry swarms of killer bees. I've only spent a few short days out here in the underbrush, but it's been plenty enough to teach me that the most frightening animal on the planet is the human being. There's very little doubt about it, if you want my opinion on the matter. Out of all of the animals in God's infinite kingdom, the humans are the only ones who really make me shiver. The humans are the ones who keep me up at night.

Rumor has it the indelible backcountry banjo player from *Deliverance* lives not too far from here, in a woefully remote hamlet called Dillard.

With that in mind, I've decided to do a little dance when I cross over into North Carolina tomorrow. A moral victory, certainly, but a victory nonetheless. My first state line. Dancing has never been my thing, as you well know, but out here in the wilderness, where the rain continues to fall in cold, steady, relentless sheets, celebrating one's minor triumphs is vital to the preservation of one's tenuous sanity.

Yours in Christ,
Wolfgang Fencer

P.S. My beard is ferocious.

20.

A man was walking toward me carrying a hatchet. I didn't break stride. I didn't show fear. It was of critical importance that I not break stride, that I show no fear. If I showed fear, he would almost certainly hack me to pieces. On the other hand, if I moved quickly and quietly, with supreme confidence, he would probably walk right on by. Psychopaths, I told myself, tended to pick victims based on weakness. They were predators. They fed on the weak. They had no interest in tangling with someone who might put up a legitimate fight. They had no interest in killing someone who didn't fear death.

The man with the hatchet smiled and extended a hand.

"Ed Griffin," he said.

"Wayne Fencer," I said.

We shook hands.

Ed Griffin informed me that he was an Appalachian Trail volunteer. He was a local from the town of Franklin, out for the afternoon in the light rain, clearing the trail for people like me, moving rocks and hacking away slippery, exposed roots with his hatchet, just to be nice.

"Rain just won't let up," he said.

"No," I said. "It sure won't."

I told him that it had rained on me steadily, day in and day out, ever since I'd set foot on the trail.

"Shoot," he replied. "That ain't no good."

"No," I said. "It sure isn't."

We talked about the weather for another minute or two before wishing each other well on our way.

I watched as Ed Griffin walked off down the trail with his hatchet, whistling Dixie.

Then I continued on my way, whistling nothing at all.

21.

I imagined worst-case scenarios a lot. It was a habit of mine. An indulgence. I imagined terrible scenarios, for kicks, as I moved among the trees. Blood and guts. Utter horror. Demon clowns. Roadside psychopaths.

I often tried to imagine how I would react if I were involved in a plane crash, for instance. I'd entertain myself for hours, imagining myself sitting in seat 18C, an aisle seat, on a long flight across the Atlantic. Suddenly, the cabin pressure would drop and the plane would do a nosedive and flight attendants would stick to the ceiling and hot coffee would fly everywhere and passengers would scream bloody murder.

I wondered what I would do.

Would I join the chorus? Would I panic? Would I pray? Would I weep? Would I experience a religious conversion? Would time slow down to a supernatural crawl? Would my life really flash before my eyes? Would I, like the survivors of the Golden Gate Bridge, experience a mystical state of consciousness in which I lost all sense of time and space and felt an overriding oneness with humanity, the entire universe, and God? Or would I simply scream bloody murder and soil myself while begging for mercy in the paralyzed recesses of my terrified mind?

I liked to think I would be serene. Serenity was the fantasy. I liked to think that I'd surrender. At that point, there would be no sense fighting it. The End, after all, was The End.

I liked to think that I'd somehow have the presence of mind to reach across the aisle and take the hand of the person next to me, whoever it might be. I liked to think that I'd have the presence of mind to say, *Hey. Listen. Don't worry, my friend. Everything will be all right in the end.* I would squeeze their hand tightly, look them directly in the eye, and give them a smile of great warmth. Then, to top it off, I'd wink. Not a sexual wink or a politician's wink, but rather, a wink of real compassion, a wink of real serenity and real mischief, a wink of confidence and conspiracy. A Frank Sinatra wink. A Cary Grant wink. An Indiana Jones wink. A Morgan Freeman wink.

A wink.

I had convinced myself that in a moment of such utter finality, this kind of rare serenity would be mistaken for something supernaturally comforting. My incredibly calm presence would be mistaken for angelic intervention. The person seated next to me would die thinking that an angel had just descended from heaven. They'd die thinking that an angel had somehow appeared on the airplane at the moment of their untimely and altogether unpleasant demise, that an angel had smiled, winked, and calmly informed them that everything was going to be quite all right on The Other Side.

In so doing, I would conclude my time on planet Earth in a uniquely altruistic manner, having exhibited the kind of unselfishly heroic presence of mind that we all hope to possess in times of massive crisis. The final moments of my life would be spent responding to my very highest instincts. The final moments of my life would be lived for someone other than myself.

A few things that had dawned on me during the course of my adventures:

I lived for myself too much.

I thought about myself too much.

I thought about *everything* too much.

That was what I was doing out there in the wilderness: thinking about everything too much. I was walking through thick forest, day after day, with my mind running out of control. I walked through the mud, in a tunnel of green. I couldn't even see the sky. I was buried by forest, thinking about what I was thinking about. It was what I did for a living. I did it eighteen hours a day.

22.

Ultimately, I came to some vaguely satisfying conclusions.

I decided, for example, that a person's state of mind at the moment of their death probably had something to do with how they would fare in the next realm. It was a Buddhist notion, if I recalled correctly. I was pretty sure I'd read about it somewhere once. I was pretty sure Buddhist monks spent their whole lives training themselves to meditate peacefully at the time of death. I was pretty sure that this was the aim of the whole Buddhist enterprise: To face death with grace. To be mellow when the Reaper came.

When a human being died in a state of utter terror, it probably didn't augur well. That was my feeling.

By contrast, if a human being died in a state of deep bliss and serenity, I tended to believe that they would have a better trip. I had no idea *where* they'd go exactly or how. And in all likelihood, they'd go absolutely nowhere at all. But in the event that there really *was* an afterlife, I tended to believe that the efficient management of one's fear was the essential component of a smooth transition.

Unfortunately, however, this strain of logic was not without its deficiencies. One of the problems inherent in the theory was that a convicted serial killer who died in a state of medicated, delirious bliss would theoretically fare better in the hereafter than, say, an angelic social worker who died in a state of massive dread and panic.

And that wasn't fair.

But then again, life wasn't fair.

And if that was true (which it was), then why should I assume that death was fair?

Death probably wasn't fair either.

Another implication of my logic was that suicide would have to be considered one of the very worst ways to die—if not *the* worst—because people who commit suicide tend to be in terrible mental states at the moment of demise. Sad and delusional to an extreme degree. Utterly hopeless. In excruciating pain. Deeply appalled and frightened by life. Resigned to the bleakest escape.

And if this was true, then the method of suicide a person chose and, more to the point, the *time* a person took to kill herself would also seem to be of vital importance.

Those who shot themselves in the head with high-powered rifles, à la Ernest Hemingway, were probably screwed, unfortunately. They died instantly, pretty much, in a moment of total despair. There was no time to ponder, no time to shift mental states or second-guess. What's done was done. They went out in a flash.

By contrast, those who jumped off the Golden Gate Bridge had a few seconds in which to recognize the approach of their own deaths. They had *time* to experience their conversions. For all we knew, they hit the chilly waters of the Golden Gate Strait in a state of total enlightenment.

23.

But that wasn't right either.

In postjump interviews, nearly all Golden Gate Bridge suicide survivors reported feeling a sense of enormous regret on the way down. In the middle of their respective descents, they realized that their earthly problems were solvable. They didn't want to die anymore. Suicide, they suddenly realized, wasn't such a hot idea after all.

While plummeting, many of them even begged God for a second chance at life on planet Earth.

And maybe, I told myself, *that's exactly what total enlightenment feels like.*

Or maybe it was just total desperation.

24.

Amanda had gone slowly. She'd had plenty of time to turn off the ignition, get out of that car, and go back inside. But she didn't do it. She sat there, determined, and huffed those bad gases. Her mental state didn't change. She didn't reverse course. If she had any second thoughts, she didn't act on them. She stayed sad. She drank some vodka and downed a couple of Percocets. She breathed in. She breathed out. She stayed in that dark place and let it swallow her. She thought about herself, her sadness, her emptiness, her pain. She concentrated on dying.

According to some, I should have been mad at her for that. Mental health experts are always saying that anger is a natural emotional response to suicide, that suicide survivors often experience feelings of incredible anger toward their lost loved ones. They feel abandoned. They feel furious that their loved ones have left them.

Personally, I didn't feel angry. I didn't experience any kind of defining moment of rage.

Amanda, I didn't say. *Amanda, you self-centered bitch!*

Maybe I should have been enraged.

I wasn't enraged.

Amanda had killed herself, and she had aborted our kid without telling me, and I really didn't feel angry about it at all. "Anger" wasn't the proper word. More than anything, I just felt defeated. Defeated and deeply sad. Because there weren't any real reasons. There weren't any second chances. It made me listless to think about it. She'd done what she'd done. And there wasn't a goddamn thing I could do about it.

Obviously, she had agonized over the abortion. Obviously, it must have eaten her up inside. She must have had mental and emotional tangles that nobody really had a feel for. She must have buried them. They must have burned, they must have gnawed at her guts. She must have felt pretty alone.

I wondered what I would've done had I known about it. Maybe I would've paid for the abortion. Maybe I would've tried to stop her. Maybe I would've bitten the bullet and proposed marriage. Maybe it would've brought us closer. Maybe we would've had the child and lived happily ever after. Maybe we would've given it up for adoption. Maybe we would've done a terrible job raising it. Maybe it would've been a mess.

I didn't know what to think about that.

I didn't know how I felt.

Somehow, though, I could imagine how she must have felt in order to get to the point where she was willing to kill herself. Somehow I could actually imagine what it must have been like for her in those final dark hours. I was able to empathize. For some reason, I was able to identify with her.

Or maybe I was numb and my anger just hadn't hit me yet.

My feet were killing me.

The flowers were in bloom.

My unborn child had died in a state of utter serenity, in all likelihood. My kid had had a clean slate, an unstained soul. My kid wasn't even fully developed. My kid was still pure, still innocent, floating blissfully in the amniotic fluid of the womb in a state of heavenly semiconsciousness. My kid, for the most part, was a bunch of congregated cells at the moment of death. My kid wasn't even really a kid yet.

I tried like hell to take comfort in that.

Most likely, Amanda's parents, Jack and Nora Anaciello, would never be completely comfortable ever again. They'd had a daughter for approximately two decades. And then they didn't anymore. Their daughter had chosen to die. She'd ended the life they had given her, and she'd left them behind on planet Earth to deal with her decision.

No matter how much pain I felt, nothing I was going through, nothing I was feeling, could even come close to comparing to the kind of pain those people were feeling.

They were experiencing the queen of all losses.

I was somewhere in North Carolina when I decided that I wasn't going to tell the Anaciellos that I'd gotten their daughter pregnant. I didn't have it in me, and I didn't figure it would help anything. It wouldn't bring their daughter back, and it wouldn't give them any answers. It would just give them questions. It would just give them someone else to miss. It would just give them more pain. They didn't need any more questions, and they didn't need any more pain. And they didn't need anyone else to miss. Amanda was gone. She'd taken her reasons with her.

That was enough.

Maybe it was dead wrong of me to handle it that way.

Maybe it was dead right.

I didn't really know.

Morality, it seemed to me, was subjective and gray, and shit happened, and everybody had a different take.

I didn't know what the answers were.

All I knew was that I'd been walking northward in Appalachia for some reason, trudging over mountains in the rain, fending off mosquitoes and ticks, seeking strange discomfort, asking for more pain. I was trying to formulate a plan. I was talking to myself a mile a minute. I was thinking about what I was thinking about. I was trying to have an experience. I was looking for wisdom with little success.

Existence, from what I could tell, could be ugly and difficult, and much of the time it hurt. In response to difficulty, ugliness, and pain, I had a variety of options at my disposal. On the one hand, I could always go jump off of the Golden Gate Bridge. Or I could go lead a life of quiet desperation. Or I could stand in the belfry and shout epithets into the wind. Or perhaps I could be like Ed Griffin. I could pick up a hatchet, walk out into the dark woods, and spend my time moving slippery rocks and exposed roots so that others wouldn't slip.

25.

Benton MacKaye never remarried. He spent the rest of his life as a bachelor. Even to his closest friends, he was reluctant to talk about his former wife or even mention the fact that he had once been married. He fathered no children in his lifetime but was generally regarded as the father of the Appalachian Trail. His entire existence was devoted to the wilderness. He sought to conserve and protect it, to understand its meaning, and to articulate its relationship to humanity.

He died in his sleep on December 11, 1975, at the ripe old age of ninety-six.

26.

8 July 2000
Hot Springs, NC

Dear Mom + Dad,

I'm in Hot Springs, North Carolina, staying at a dingy youth hostel. Weather's been bad lately, so regardless of the accommodations, I'm glad to be inside. There are some friendly people around, which makes it nice. Just this afternoon, I met a young married couple from Scottsdale, AZ. Chad and Katrina are their names. Chad owns a record store. Katrina is clairvoyant and expert at the art of palmistry. About an hour ago, she gave me a free reading and informed me that my life line is exceptionally long. She told me that I can look forward to an incredibly lengthy existence here on planet Earth. Was happy to hear the news, of course, but at the same time had to wonder if palm readers ever look at someone and say, "I'm sorry, sir, but your life line is incredibly short. You can expect an untimely and altogether unpleasant demise sometime very soon." As far as I can tell, that scenario seems unlikely. Katrina tells me she's well paid back in Scottsdale: $100 an hour, sometimes more. For that kind of money, I imagine people expect good news.

Life on the trail tends to be fairly interesting, as you might expect. A few nights ago, I wound up having a pretty surreal experience while camping on a hillside here in North Carolina. Had just finished pitching my tent on a little plateau when this

guy named Dom walked up with his four young kids and introduced himself. (They were camped nearby, out for a long
weekend.) As it turned out, Dom was a tremendous Civil War
buff, a self-proclaimed expert on the topic. Without any provo-
cation or encouragement whatsoever, he started explaining to
me and his kids that the tents pitched on the hillside were reminiscent of the way a Civil War camp would have looked way
back in the day, albeit on a larger scale. From there, he
launched off into a detailed description of the battle tactics of
the Confederacy, the sad and terrible demise of the plantation-
based agrarian economy, and the fatal errors of Stonewall
Jackson. The division between the North and the South, he let
it be known, was still very much alive and well. He even pre-
dicted that the South would rise again and crush the North
utterly—and sooner rather than later. All I could do was stand
there and nod along. The guy was completely serious.

On a different note, time spent living out-of-doors has
brought me face-to-face with the simple fact that I don't really
know very much about my natural environment. It stuns me to
think that I have so little knowledge of plant life and such a minimal understanding of the animal kingdom. All day long, I find
myself walking around out here, with greenery and wildlife in
every direction, stupefied by the fact that I don't really know
what to call anything. I don't know what anything is named. I
seem to have lost all contact with animals and the land. Machines
and concrete and air-conditioning and gasoline have made it
such that I've never really had to interact with my environment
in a meaningful way. And I suppose that's why I'm out here: I'm
trying to interact with my environment in a meaningful way.

So far, so good. (I think.)

Anyway . . . with that in mind, I'm gonna go ahead and wrap

this one up and get off to sleep. Eyelids are getting heavy and the crickets are chirping and my body needs rest. Gotta make fifteen tough miles tomorrow, heading out of town over mountain terrain. Hopefully, the weather will clear up.

Will be sure to write again soon with more news from the outer limits. If things keep happening the way they have been lately, I'm bound to have plenty of good stories to tell. Give my best to Lorraine and Anne, and take good care. Until next time . . .

Your peripatetic son,
Wayne

27.

The Erwin Motel. Erwin, Tennessee. Room 13.

I'd been there for three days and counting, laid up in bed, spending my time watching television, eating enormous quantities of processed foodstuff. At that point, I'd walked three hundred miles.

Two days before my arrival in town, I had somehow contracted a staph infection in the wilderness. My legs had swollen up to twice their normal size. They had turned puffy and red and itched to an inordinate degree. It was a highly uncomfortable experience.

foodstuff *n.*
A substance that can be used or prepared for use as food.

Shortly after thumbing a ride into Erwin, I visited a licensed physician named Walter Redfield. Redfield was wildly obese, which unsettled me slightly. I'd always had trouble accepting the notion of wildly obese health care professionals. Nevertheless, Dr. Redfield was a nice guy and, from what I could tell, a perfectly competent physician. He gave my legs a thorough examination, diagnosed my condition, and prescribed antibiotics and an appropriate ointment with very little hesitation. Per his instructions, I had been ingesting the antibiotics and applying the prescribed ointment to my legs three times daily. The staph infection appeared to be subsiding.

I had decided that I liked the word "ointment" quite a bit.

Several times during my stay in Erwin, while lying there in bed, watching bad television, I found myself repeating it aloud, over and over again, just to amuse myself.

"Ointment," I kept saying. "Ointment. Ointment. Ointment."

It was mid-July in the arbitrary year 2000.

I hadn't had much contact with human beings lately.

ointment *n.*

A highly viscous or semisolid substance used on the skin as a cosmetic, emollient, or medicament; a salve.

My motel room, I realized, had a certain miraculous quality to it. In there, I had access to a shower, a toilet, a telephone, and cable television, at all times. Before, I had never fully understood the glory of those comforts. Before, I had always taken them for granted.

I didn't want to take anything for granted anymore.

In truth, I could have been back out on the trail, walking northward under the summer sun. Dr. Redfield had advised me that I could recommence hiking immediately, provided I apply my ointment with vigor, but I didn't really want to recommence hiking just then. At that point, I preferred to stay in my motel room, applying my ointment in the cool, conditioned air. The plain truth is, I was kind of tired of walking. The concept wasn't agreeing with me of late. Somewhere along the line, it had lost its luster. Before, I'd been obsessed with the notion of perpetual motion, but lately, I'd been satisfied with doing absolutely nothing at all.

28.

It should also be mentioned that my time in the wild had been a boon to my creative life. Hiking was good for the imagination. I had even managed to conceive a detailed plotline for *The Grandeur of Delusions,* my intentional accidental comedy, while navigating a particularly tough section of Tennessee hill country. Up until that point, I hadn't been able to generate the levels of concentration and acerbity necessary to make the thing fully congeal. Out on the trail, however, everything crystallized in effortless fashion. The film appeared like a diamond in my mind. I envisioned it as a big-budget action picture, rife with stilted dialogue and spectacular violence, with a story line firmly rooted in the aesthetic traditions of guys like George P. Cosmatos and Michael Bay.

The Grandeur of Delusions. DreamWorks SKG, 2002. Steven Spielberg, Jeffrey Katzenberg, and David Geffen, executive producers. Wayne Fencer, producer. Janusz Kaminski, cinematographer. Michael Kahn, editor. George Costello, art director. Maria Rebman Caso, set decorator. Harley Jessup, production designer. Music by John Williams. Wayne Fencer, screenwriter. Based on the novel by Wayne Fencer. Directed by Wayne Fencer. Rated R.

Synopsis:
The year 2142. Malcolm Faltermeyer is a top-level government assassin grieving the mysterious

disappearance of his wife and child, both of whom have vanished into the depths of space while on a holiday trip to the moon. In the wake of the tragedy, Faltermeyer retreats into deep cover, working as a stockbroker at a monolithic Manhattan investment bank. But his return to civilian life is short-lived, as he soon receives a covert order to eliminate Dr. Hansel Baird, a menacing paraplegic genius blessed with tremendous intelligence and powerful clairvoyant abilities. Baird's attempts to gain power over the global population through a cutting-edge mind-control process called "The Fear" are beginning to gain traction, and it is up to Faltermeyer to stop the evil doctor from succeeding in his diabolical quest. What Faltermeyer doesn't know, however, is that his pursuit of Baird will lead him directly to the bottom of his heart's darkest mysteries.

I had once read that the best ideas often come to us in a flood of information, when we least expect it.

I had once read that the best ideas are rarely the product of conscious, calculated thought.

Out on the Appalachian Trail, there were no tissues. There were also very few people. When your nose was running, you plugged one nostril and blew. This procedure is sometimes referred to as a "farmer's blow."

The plotline for *The Grandeur of Delusions* came to me during a farmer's blow. Mucus sailed from my nose into the Appalachian wilderness. And a story was born.

My plan at the time was to write the screenplay and sell it to DreamWorks SKG for seven figures and a cut of the back-end profits. That right there was the fantasy. That right there was my new trajectory, just in case anyone asked.

So, Wayne. Tell me. What is your trajectory these days?

I'm going to write a screenplay about a bereaved assassin hot on the trail of a clairvoyant, paraplegic genius who is hell-bent on subduing the global population with a cutting-edge mind-control process called "The Fear." Then I'm going to sell it to DreamWorks SKG for seven figures and a cut of the back-end profits.

Fantastic!

Thank you.

That's one hell of a trajectory.

Thank you. I tend to agree.

29.

Amanda and I used to go to the movies a lot.
Once a week at least. I was always taking her to the movies. I
remember we went to see a post-run showing of *Before Sunrise,*
the Richard Linklater film, up at the Flatirons Theater a few
months after we started dating. We got into our first real fight
that night. It was a Sunday, and we were hung over and tired.
There had been a house party the night before. Amanda had gotten sick. Now she wanted to stay in and rest and make dinner,
and I wanted to go see the film. It started as a conversation. The
conversation turned into a debate. The debate turned into an
argument. I told Amanda I would go see the movie on my own
and come home afterward and we would make dinner. And if she
didn't want to wait, she could eat on her own and I'd order
something for delivery. That way, I figured, we could both do
what we wanted to do and everyone would be happy.

"I don't want you to go to the movie," Amanda said.

"Why not?" I said.

"Because we always go to movies. We go to movies practically every time we go out."

"So what? I like going to movies."

"Yeah. That's fine. I like movies too. But sometimes we can
do other things."

"Like what?"

"Like talk."

"What do you mean 'talk'?"

"I mean talk. Hang out. I mean we go to the movies and sit in the dark theater and watch the movie, and then we come home. We never hang out and talk, just the two of us."

"We're talking right now."

"That's not what I mean."

"I just want to go see a movie."

"Why can't we just relax and stay home for a night?"

"You're welcome to relax. I said that already."

"I want you to stay here with me."

"I will stay here with you. I'm gonna be here all night. I'm just gonna go see a movie first."

"Well, why can't you just stay here and not see the movie?"

"Because I think that's ridiculous. It's Sunday night, and I wanna go see a movie."

"I don't feel well, Wayne."

"So why don't you just stay home and take a nap, and I'll be back in two hours? We'll make dinner and we'll hang out."

"I'm tired."

"It's not like I'm asking you to strain yourself."

Amanda waved a hand in front of her face and walked out of the room. I followed her down the hall.

"What?" I said.

She stopped and spun around. "All I'm asking you to do," she said, "is stay at home for once and hang out with me in a room with the lights on so we can actually have a conversation."

"We have lots of conversations."

"No, we don't."

"Yes, we do."

"No, we really don't."

"Yes, we really do."

"I think you're being a jerk," she said.

"I think you're overtired. All I'm saying is, if you don't want to go, you don't have to go. I'll be back in two hours. And we'll hang out."

"Why can't you just go another night?"

"Why can't I go tonight?"

It got to the point where we were yelling. I finally caved in and told Amanda I would stay home. Fuck the movie, I said. Let's cook dinner. Then Amanda got pissed off and insisted on going to the movie. I told her no, it's fine, if it means that much to you, we'll stay home. No, she said, we're going to the goddamn movie. She completely reversed field. Demanded that we go. Put her shoes on, grabbed her purse, and wouldn't take no for an answer. It was miserable. I tried to open my mouth to apologize. She walked outside, angry, and slammed the door behind her.

So we went to the show.

The movie wound up being pretty great. Offbeat entertainment. A genuine romance. The stuff of collegiate dreams.

The story was pretty straightforward. An American drifter named Jesse meets a French grad student named Celine. They're on a train in Europe, Hungary to Austria. They get to talking. They wind up spending fourteen hours together in Vienna. They have an incredible, nonstop conversation. Everything is magical. The city is alive. They bare their souls. They connect. They revel. They meet fortune-tellers, actors, benevolent bartenders. They go to a music shop. They drink wine in a park. They have sex under the stars.

The movie ends with the two young lovers saying good-bye at the train station. Standing on the platform in the morning light, they promise to meet again, in the exact same spot, six months later.

Amanda and I sat there in the theater, stunned silent, and watched the credits roll. We didn't leave until the houselights came up.

"I loved it," Amanda said.

"Me too," I said.

We walked back to my apartment in the chill of the night, holding hands. Not a word was said. Upon arriving at my place, we tore each other's clothes off in a frenzy and went directly to bed.

30.

I was surrounded by Christians. There were approximately twenty of them, junior high school kids on a weeklong camping trip. They were led by four college-aged, deeply devout counselors, all of whom, unbelievably, were named Matthew. One of them informed me that they hailed from a Baptist church in Boone, North Carolina.

Strangely enough, I'd seen these people before. We'd crossed paths a couple of days earlier just outside of Grayson Highlands State Park in southern Virginia, famous for its large herds of feral ponies. The Christians had been sitting in a meadow, eating lunch, and I had blown right by them. A friendly wave of my hiking pole. Little to no conversation. Now somehow they'd gotten ahead of me. They must have had wheels . . . vans or a chartered bus. I descended a hillside, emerged into a clearing, and there they were again, sitting Indian-style in the tall grass, eating lunch.

The Four Matthews recognized me and immediately stood to greet me, making their introductions, one by one.

"Matthew," said Matthew #1.

"Matthew," said Matthew #2.

"Matthew," said Matthew #3.

"And Matthew," said Matthew #4.

"Jesus," I said.

Everyone chuckled.

• • •

For some reason, the Four Matthews seemed to be impressed with me. The fact that I'd been wandering around in the wilderness by myself for a while seemed to have earned me a certain level of respect. They were treating me like some kind of exhibit, like some kind of special guest lecturer. They were using my presence as an opportunity to teach their young charges a valuable lesson. They were giving me far more credit than I deserved.

"Wayne here has been at this for more than six weeks," Matthew #1 said, pointing at me. "You guys think about that for a second. You guys chew on that. This guy's out here every day, on his own, hauling all of his own gear in this heat. More than forty days. Solo."

The young Christians groaned.

"Next time you guys think you've got it bad, you chew on that a little bit," Matthew #2 said. "Some people out here are going all the way to Maine. They got six, sometimes seven months lined up. More than two thousand miles. Now, you just imagine that for a second."

One of the young Christian campers asked me if I was going all the way to Maine. He was a smallish boy with buckteeth and glasses.

"How far you goin'?" he said. "You goin' all the way to Maine?"

"I don't know," I said. "I doubt it. I haven't really planned that far ahead yet."

"But it's a possibility?" Matthew #4 said.

"Anything's possible," I said.

"You hear that, guys?" Matthew #1 said. "You hear what Mr. Wayne just said? Anything's possible."

The young Christian children stared at me.

"Your beard ith huge," one of them said. He had a slight lisp and a severe backcountry accent. It made for an odd and unsettling combination.

I nodded and shrugged.

"Are you ever gonna shave it off?" he said.

"I haven't decided."

"How long do you think it'll take you to make it up through Virginia?" said Matthew #3.

"We'll see," I said. "The heat makes it tough to gauge."

There was no response. The campers were silent. I looked at the ground and shifted in my boots.

"Well," I said, "I should probably get going. I've got a ways to go before the day's up."

"Sure thing," said Matthew #3.

"Say," said Matthew #1, "you mind if we say a prayer for you before you take off?"

"A prayer?" I said.

"Yeah," said Matthew #1. "A short blessing to send you off and wish you well on your way."

"Does it matter if I'm a Christian or not?" I said.

An awkward silence.

"Not really," said Matthew #1.

"It doesn't matter," said Matthew #2.

"What's your affiliation, if you don't mind me asking?" said Matthew #3.

"I don't really have one," I said.

"None at all?" said Matthew #2.

"Not really," I said.

"No matter," said Matthew #1. "Just a short prayer. For good luck."

"Yeah," said Matthew #2. "You never know, it might do you some good."

I said okay.

The Christians stood up, held hands, and encircled me. They closed their eyes, bowed their heads, and stood in silent prayer. Birds were singing. The sun was shining. I stood there, blinking. I felt like I should say something.

Matthew #4 cleared his throat and broke the silence. "All right, guys," he said. "How about a little Lord's Prayer for Wayne here?"

The campers bowed their heads and prayed:

> *Our Father, Who art in heaven*
> *Hallowed be Thy Name;*
> *Thy kingdom come,*
> *Thy will be done,*
> *on earth as it is in heaven.*
> *Give us this day our daily bread,*
> *and forgive us our trespasses,*
> *as we forgive those who trespass against us;*
> *and lead us not into temptation,*
> *but deliver us from evil. Amen.*

I was a lapsed Catholic. I knew the Lord's Prayer by heart. It had been recited at every Catholic Mass I'd ever attended during my youth. I'd heard it so many times, in fact, that I could even remember the exchange between priest and congregation that took place right after the Lord's Prayer during a standard Catholic liturgy. It went like this:

PRIEST: Deliver us, Lord, from every evil, and grant us peace in our days. In Your mercy keep us free from sin, and protect us from all anxiety as we wait in joyful hope for the coming of our Savior, Jesus Christ.

CONGREGATION: For the kingdom, the power, and the glory are Yours. Now and forever. Amen.

The Four Matthews and the young Christians finished reciting the Lord's Prayer on my behalf. After a brief moment of silence, Matthew #2 offered up a few supplementary requests to God and/or Jesus, in an effort to further ensure my safe passage into tomorrow.

"Dear Lord Jesus," he said, "we pray that You will shine Your light upon our friend Wayne as he walks among Your splendid creations in this vast and beautiful kingdom that You have given us to enjoy."

"Amen," said everyone.

"Christ Almighty," said Matthew #1, "we hope that You will see fit to bless our brother Wayne here with an abundance of peace and joy as he makes his way forward, not only here on the Appalachian Trail, but also on the trail of life. In Your name, we pray."

"Amen."

"And may we also pray, dear God in heaven," said Matthew #4, "that Your son Wayne be blessed with as much pleasant weather as possible as he marches onward through Virginia and beyond. Should You see fit, I think it's safe to say that a small reprieve from the sweltering summer heat would be greatly appreciated."

Everyone chuckled.

"Amen."

"Dear Lord," said Matthew #3, "in Your profound and holy perfection, please see fit to clean the world of its sins and to keep our brother Wayne safe from harm as he wanders forth in Your honor. Please give him strength to overcome whatever obstacles he may be faced with on his path through life. Whatever grief and sorrow may reside in his heart, whatever pain may rise up from within, please see fit to remind him of Your ever-abiding presence in all things, so that he might proceed with courage and wisdom, free of all fear and all doubt. For this we pray with all our hearts."

"Amen."

The Christians opened their eyes. They looked at me with what appeared to be an air of expectation. I was feeling a little bit odd at the moment, a little bit uncertain of myself. Their attention overwhelmed me. The unnerving earnestness of the prayer circle had me tongue-tied. Nevertheless, it seemed appropriate that I should offer some kind of comment at the end of it all, in response to their extended efforts.

"Thank you," I said. "Thanks very much. I really appreciate it."

"You're welcome," said Matthew #1.

"You're welcome," said Matthew #3.

"You're welcome," said Matthew #4.

"You're welcome," said Matthew #2.

"Thanks," I said again.

The young Christian campers told me that I was welcome.

I nodded and made my way out of the circle slowly. Truth be known, I was feeling pretty uncomfortable.

"God bleth you," said the kid with the backcountry lisp.

"You too," I said.

"God bless you," said the others.

I broke the circle. The smallish boy with buckteeth stuck his hand up as I passed by. I gave him a high five and walked away northward, completely alone, off into the shade of the trees.

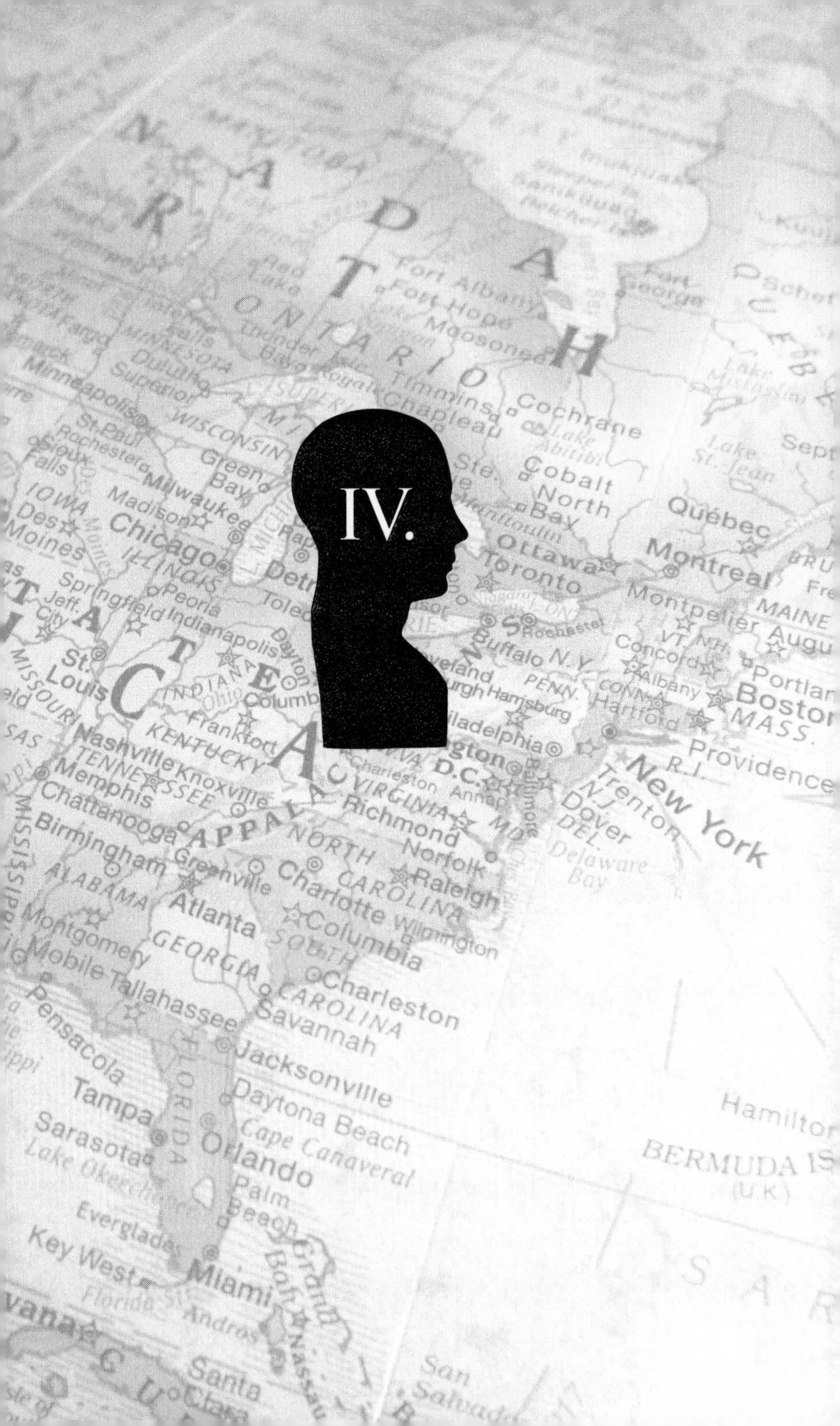
IV.
Fort Albany
Moosonee
Timmins
Chapleau
Cochrane
Cobalt
North Bay
Ottawa
Toronto
Québec
Montreal
Montpelier
Augu
Concord
Albany
Portlan
Boston
MASS.
Hartford
Providence
R.I.
New York
Trenton
Dover
DEL.
Delaware Bay
Buffalo
N.Y.
Harrisburg
PENN.
Philadelphia
Baltimore
D.C.
Richmond
Norfolk
Raleigh
NORTH CAROLINA
Charlotte
Wilmington
Columbia
SOUTH CAROLINA
Charleston
Savannah
Atlanta
GEORGIA
Greenville
Birmingham
ALABAMA
Montgomery
Mobile
Tallahassee
Pensacola
Jacksonville
Daytona Beach
Cape Canaveral
Orlando
Tampa
Sarasota
Everglades
Key West
Miami
Nashville
Knoxville
Memphis
Chattanooga
KENTUCKY
Frankfort
St. Louis
Indianapolis
Chicago
Milwaukee
Madison
Green Bay
WISCONSIN
Minneapolis
St. Paul
Rochester
Sioux Falls
Des Moines
IOWA
Springfield
Peoria
Jeff. City
Duluth
Superior
MINNESOTA
Thunder Bay
Hamilton
BERMUDA IS
(U.K.)
ONTARIO
Lake Abitibi
Lake Mistassini
Lake St. Jean

1.

Late July. New York City. I had arrived by train,
having exited the Appalachian Trail on a whim forty-eight hours
earlier. By that point, I'd traveled nearly six hundred miles on
foot. Six hundred miles seemed like enough. I was tired. I walked
out onto a highway in rural Virginia and thumbed a ride to the
town of Marion. From there, I caught a bus to D.C. In D.C., I
caught the train.

A friend of mine, Morgan Lynch, was living in a tiny one-
bedroom apartment on Grand Street at the time, deep in the
heart of Chinatown. I had arranged to stay with him for a few
days while I assessed my trajectory and contemplated my next
move.

The city was sweltering, as hot or hotter than the Appalachian
Trail. I'd never been there before and hadn't anticipated that
kind of heat. The pavement, the concrete, the bodies, the cars—
all of it conspired to make Manhattan a kind of convection oven.
And the stench was fantastic, particularly near the subway's
many orifices.

I was sweating bullets.

There were a lot of Chinese people around.

So much had happened in so little time.

My train had arrived in the early evening, a couple of hours
before the sun went down. Lynch and I set out on a walk right
off the bat so that I could check out my surroundings and get the

lay of the land. We wandered the city aimlessly for more than two hours, looking at people and things and talking nonstop. On our way home, we happened to pass a dead body. It was lying on the sidewalk at the corner of Houston and Ludlow. An elderly man. I could tell by the spots on his hands. He was laid out on his back, dead as a stump, and he wasn't wearing a wedding ring. A cop was standing there, waving people by, waiting for an ambulance to arrive. The cop had spread a jacket over the dead body's face, but the rest of it was exposed.

"Jesus," I said.

"Welcome to New York," said Lynch.

"Jesus," I said.

"Heart attack," said Lynch. "Heart attack or aneurysm."

"I wonder who he is," I said.

Lynch shrugged. Then he coughed, briefly.

Thunder rumbled overhead, and it started to drizzle a bit.

A taxi driver laid on his horn.

Hordes of pedestrians walked past the dead man, relatively unfazed. They were in a hurry to get out of the rain.

Sirens sounded in the distance.

The summer wind smelled of heat, inclement weather, body odor, concrete, and hot dogs.

2.

Lynch was two years older than me, someone I'd known since the earliest days of my childhood. After graduating high school, he'd gone on to Vanderbilt, where he studied journalism. From there, he'd moved to New York City, where he landed a job at a magazine called *The Bomb*. *The Bomb* catered to the eighteen to thirty-six male audience. Its contents revolved around women, automobiles, weaponry, celebrity, and gadgetry.

That particular week, Lynch was racing against a deadline, hard at work on an article for an upcoming issue. He was writing the third part of a six-installment feature on unusual weaponry and/or methods of torture. The previous month, he'd done a piece about Molotov cocktails. This month it was the Taser.

Here's how you make a Molotov cocktail:

Ingredients:

1 glass bottle
3 cups flammable liquid
1 rag
1 lighter

Mixing Instructions:

Fill glass bottle with flammable liquid. Stuff rag into mouth of bottle. Ignite rag with lighter and throw cocktail at desired target.

Here's the definition of Taser:

Taser *n.*
A trademark used for a high-voltage stun gun.

Tasers look like pistols, essentially. They fire small, dartlike electrical probes a distance of approximately 20 feet at a rate of about 135 feet per second. The probes are connected to the Taser via thin, high-voltage, insulated wire. The probes sink into the flesh or clothing of a human target, delivering a formidable, pulsing electrical charge. The charge cause massive loss of neuromuscular control, thereby stifling the target's ability to perform any kind of aggressive, coordinated action.

Generally speaking, the force of a Taser's charge is plenty enough to knock a large, angry human being flat on his ass. Generally speaking, the charge is nonlethal. Tasers are not considered firearms and are perfectly legal for private use, without permits, throughout most of the USA. (Note: Tasers are restricted from citizen use in Hawaii, Massachusetts, Michigan, New Jersey, New York, Rhode Island, and Wisconsin.)

Advanced Taser M-18L
with Laser Sight

A couple of weeks before my arrival in New York, one of the world's leading Taser manufacturers had sent Lynch a demo Taser in exchange for a plug in the magazine. Lynch and his buddies at the office had been shooting each other with regularity ever since.

This was technically illegal.

3.

My second night in town, I made some
telephone calls to people I hadn't spoken to in a while—my parents, my sisters, some friends. I informed them of my where-
abouts and my decision to leave the trail. Everyone sounded
good, for the most part. They seemed supportive of my decision.
They sounded relieved to hear that I was out of the woods,
immersed in society, associating with other human beings again.

The last person I wound up calling was a guy named Henry
Long, an old friend from film school days. I couldn't reach him
at home in Boulder, so I tried him on his cell phone.

"Hello?" he said.

"Henry," I said. "It's Fencer."

"Fencer," he said. "Where the fuck are you?"

"I'm in New York," I said.

"You're shitting me," he said.

Henry, as it turned out, was in New York as well. It was his
hometown.

The guy was a true character, one of the most interesting
people I'd ever met. His energy level always seemed to be off the
charts, and his life story was one for the record books. Born on
a commune in upstate New York in the mid-1970s, he'd been
adopted by a well-to-do couple from the Upper West Side. Six
months later, his well-to-do parents divorced. Henry's mother,
Jane, got custody. She later discovered she was a lesbian. Henry
was homeschooled until the age of fourteen, at which point he

went on to Stuyvesant High School, where he was deeply anti-social and excelled in the sciences. Somehow he wound up at the University of Colorado, where, like me, he studied avant-garde film. The past few years, he'd been living in Boulder with his girl-friend, Rose, subsisting on a modest stipend given to him by his adopted father, whom he hated terribly and hardly knew.

At the time of my call, Henry was operating in a state of deep emotional turmoil. As it turned out, Rose had left him a few days earlier after five years of dating. The whole thing had happened completely out of the blue. Apparently, she'd been cheating on him, conducting a clandestine affair with a man she had met on the Internet. And then, out of nowhere, she'd flown the coop. While Henry was out running errands, Rose packed her bags and took off for Iowa to be with her new lover until the end of time.

She left Henry a note.

It said good-bye, essentially.

Henry was now at his mother's place on the Upper West Side, attempting to come to terms with the situation. He was wildly upset, talking at a rapid clip, telling me all about Rose and her midwestern Internet lover. He rambled about it at length, spar-ing no detail. And then he delivered even bigger news.

"And to top it all off," he said, "I called my biological mother yesterday."

"You *what*?" I said.

"I did it in a fit yesterday afternoon. We're having lunch together tomorrow. I'm losing my shit. I'm fucking panicked over here."

"What do you mean you called your biological mother?"

"I mean what I said: I contacted my fucking birth mother."

"Just like that?"

"Yeah, just like that."

"How did you find her?"

"She lives in the city. I've known about it for years. Up until now, I haven't wanted to call. But for some reason yesterday afternoon, I said fuck it and picked up the phone."

"And what happened?"

"She said hello."

"And?"

"And we talked."

"About?"

"About nothing. I can't remember. It was quick. I said hello. I told her my name. She was silent. I think she might've been crying. I said that if it would be okay with her, I'd like to meet her. And she agreed. We made a hurried plan. It happened fast. Neither of us could really handle being on the phone for long."

"What's her name?"

"Selma."

"Selma?"

"Yeah."

"Selma what?"

"Selma Hoffman."

"I've never met a Selma before," I said.

"Me neither," said Henry.

"And what about your biological father?"

"He's dead."

"Shit."

"It's no big deal. I've known about it for a long time. He died years ago. Haven't I told you that?"

"No."

"Yeah. He dropped dead back in, like, 1984."

"That sucks."

"Yeah, well, at least he's not alive to torture me."

"So what are you doing now?"

"Sitting over here, drinking vodka."

"Do you want to go out?"

"No."

"Should I come over?"

"No. Jane'll get suspicious."

"She doesn't know about this?"

"Hell no."

"Why not?"

"She'll freak."

"I want to meet her."

"Not a chance."

"Why?"

"I've got enough shit going on right now. I'm not about to start leading people on tours through my alternative home life."

"So what are you going to do all night?"

"Sleep. I just took two Valium. I need to be rested."

"Where'd you get Valium?"

"The medicine cabinet."

"Can I have some?"

"Maybe. I have to check how many are left."

"How do you feel?"

"I feel softheaded. But I felt softheaded before I took anything. I think it's just making it worse."

"So where are you and Selma meeting tomorrow?"

"We're having an early lunch at a place called the Gandhi Café, over on Bleecker."

"The what?"

"The Gandhi Café."

"You're kidding me."

"Don't ask. I'm not the one who picked it."

"The Gandhi Café."

"Yeah."

"That sounds terrible."

"I know."

"That's almost like having a Martin Luther King Café."

"I know."

"Or a JFK Café."

"I know."

"Imagine what it would look like."

"Stills of the Zapruder film on the wall . . ."

"Oswald burgers . . ."

"Magic-bullet milk shakes . . ."

"Warren Commission fajitas . . ."

Henry half laughed. "Warren Commission fajitas," he said. "I'd probably order those."

4.

Henry was a documentarian. He'd been keeping an exhaustive video diary for several years. It was his life's work. He carried a digital video camera on his person at all times and had recorded himself, talking about himself, every single day for the past six years, logging more than one thousand hours of tape.

We had arranged to meet up in Tompkins Square Park after his lunch with Selma. When I arrived, Henry was slouched down on a park bench and appeared shell-shocked. I sat down next to him, and he immediately handed me his camera. I noticed he was drinking a large can of beer wrapped in a brown paper bag.

"Get this on tape," he said. "Interview me."

"Are you sure?"

"No."

"Don't you want to wait?"

"No. It's fresh now."

"How do you turn this thing on?"

"The green button on the left."

I found the green button on the left and pressed it. The camera came alive slowly.

"Where's your buddy Lynch?" Henry said.

"On deadline. He's working on a three-thousand-word article about Tasers."

"Tasers?"

"Yeah."

"Shit."

"I know."

"How come I don't have a job like that?" said Henry.

"I keep asking myself the same question."

I slid a couple of feet to my left and turned the camera on him, zooming in until his head filled up the entire frame. I pressed record, and the red light went on. Henry was looking out across Tompkins Square Park at nothing in particular. I had him in profile. I cleared my throat loudly and began the interrogation.

So, Henry. Tell me: How are you feeling?

Foggy. Numb. Emotional. Detached. Terrified. Relieved. Gastric. Confused.

So you woke up this morning and—

You need to say the date and time.

I do?

Yeah. Here. I'll do it. What's the date today?

July 31st.

Monday, July 31st, the year 2000. 1:47 p.m. Tompkins Square Park. New York, New York.

Okay. You ready?

Yeah. Where were we?

You woke up this morning and—

I didn't wake up. I never went to sleep. I got in bed at eleven last night and closed my eyes, but I never really slept. It was a very superficial kind of rest at best. The Valium screwed me. It had the opposite of its intended effect; the chemicals manifested differently than I thought they would. They made me think *more,* not less. And then things got out of hand in an emotional sense, because it was the middle of the night and my perceptions were skewed.

Meaning what?

Meaning I drove myself crazy. Meaning I laid there under the covers and exaggerated everything half to death, cooking up fantastic, doped-up scenarios of massive calamity, over and over again—scenarios involving some kind of emotional breakdown at the restaurant. I worried that I would sob uncontrollably throughout the lunch. I envisioned myself breaking down at the table, bawling my eyes out, blubbering. Then I saw myself having to be escorted to the men's room by the maître d' while onlookers stared at me, saddened and stunned. And then from there, I envisioned my mood shifting from one of delirious distress to a furious, irrational kind of anger. I saw myself bursting out of the bathroom, purple-faced, with tearstained eyes, screaming at my biological mother, castigating her savagely for abandoning me and blaming her for the multilayered emotional and psychological impact her decision has had on my existence.

Secondly, I worried that I would get physically ill and puke all over the table.

So what time did you get up?

Sunrise. As soon as I saw light come through the windows, I was out of there. I showered, shaved, brushed my teeth, flossed, clipped my nose hairs, plucked my uni-brow, put on deodorant, and so on. And then I spent about an hour trying to figure out what the fuck to wear. That was another disaster— and completely atypical of my normal behavior. Under normal circumstances, I don't give a flying fuck what I look like or what I wear, but this morning it was suddenly a monumental quagmire. I must've put on six different outfits, staring at myself in the mirror. I couldn't decide whether to dress up or dress down. At first I wanted to wear a nice button-down shirt, but then I started worrying that I'd sweat through it in the heat. I was also afraid that it would be too dressy and too inauthentic. I felt it made me look unlike myself, like I was trying too hard to impress, because I rarely wear nice button-down shirts. So then I put on a T-shirt, which is what I normally wear, but that didn't look right either.

What was wrong with it?

It was that T-shirt of mine, the one with the cartoon drawing of the guy standing at a urinal, and then underneath him it says "The Future Is in Your Hand."

(Laughter.) And you felt that would have been inappropriate for a first meeting with your biological mother.

On one level, sure. I mean, it goes without saying that the humor involved is lowbrow and potentially even subconsciously antagonistic. And, of course, for whatever reason, you want to make a good first impression. You don't want your biological mother to think you're *completely* degenerate and crass. But then again, this is the kind of thing I wear without a second thought on an ordinary average day, so part of me was just like, "Fuck *her.* If she can't take a joke, then to hell with her. This is who I am. Why am I so worried about impressing the bitch? She wasn't sufficiently impressed with me from the beginning, so why should I worry about impressing her now?"

So how did you finally settle on your outfit?

(Camera zooms out briefly to reveal Henry's outfit: a short-sleeved, gray collared shirt, khaki pants, and brown leather shoes.)

I finally just said fuck it and gave up. I snapped. Everything I put on seemed like it didn't fit, or it wasn't me, or it looked like shit. Nothing looked good. And this was the last outfit I tried on before I gave up and forced myself to walk out of the fucking apartment. It had to be done. Otherwise, I'd probably still be standing there, wetting my pants over what the fuck to wear. That or I would've shaved my head.

Shaved your head?

(Camera zooms back in.)

Yeah. I stare in the mirror sometimes—it's like this weird old habit of mine. I stand there, staring at myself, trying to figure out what I look like, trying to imagine what I'll look like in the future, with age. And if I do it for too long, I almost always have this really strong, really strange compulsion to shave my head bald.

Weird.

I've come close a few times. I have no idea what it means.

Maybe it means you want to be a monk.

Maybe it means I want to be a skinhead.

(Laughter.) Okay. So back to your day. You're out of your apartment early, you head out into the city—

I head out into the city and get breakfast at an old restaurant in the neighborhood. I read two newspapers and two awful entertainment magazines, cover to cover. That took up a couple of hours. I must've pounded six cups of coffee. I got so wired that I had to go for a walk. I kept telling myself to externalize things, you know? To get my mind on other people, other things, the flowers, the trees, so that I could quit having that goddamn conversation with myself.

What goddamn conversation with yourself?

The one I'd been having all night and all morning. The giant anxiety-riddled conversation about what my mother was going to look like, act like, be like. The giant anxiety-riddled conversation about everything that might go, should go, could go wrong, either by my doing or hers. I just felt I needed to put my attention on things other than myself, because at that point, it was clear—at least with respect to this particular circumstance—that I didn't have the first fucking clue what to say to myself when I talked to myself. So I figured it was better not to say anything at all.

That's an interesting way of putting it.

What?

"I didn't know what to say to myself when I talked to myself."

That's how it felt to me. That's how it still feels to me. Lately, I've been confronted with the notion that I pretty much suck at the whole fucking process. When push comes to shove, I have no idea what to say to myself when I talk to myself. I'm not too bright, when it comes right down to it. And if that's true, and if it's also true that most human problems are pretty much self-created, it can make for a fairly shitty realization.

I think you're being a little too hard on yourself. Most people in your shoes would probably be the same way.

"Most people" are irrelevant in this context. So what if the majority would fumble? That doesn't make it necessary or right. And it should also be said that some people *wouldn't* fumble. They wouldn't freak out. They would deal with their discomfort and handle the situation with relative aplomb.

Relative aplomb.

Yeah. Relative aplomb.

Pun intended?

No.

I think you're doing an okay job of handling yourself, all things considered.

I'm drinking a forty-ounce Schlitz at two p.m. on a Monday.

(Laughter.) But at least you have the decency to cover it up with a brown paper bag.

I find no consolation in that.

So. Going backward. You get to the Gandhi Café . . .

Right. I'd say at this point it was about ten or ten thirty or so. I had about two hours to go. I was way ahead of myself, way early. Something important is gonna happen, something that has me nervous, I almost always show up early. I'm like that with the airport, too. It's the weirdest goddamn thing . . . a sickness, almost. Flying makes me a little edgy. Don't like it. Can't stand it. But for some reason, the idea of *missing* a flight is intolerable to me. The thought of it practically sends me off the deep end. Makes no sense. I have to get there early. Have to settle in. Have to walk around, get my bearings, watch the people, eat some food. Airplanes make me nervous to the point of indigestion, but I could wander around a goddamn airport forever, eating overpriced, terrible food.

I like airports too.

We're a breed.

I'd like to be the guy who drives the crippled and the elderly from concourse to concourse in that beeping golf cart.

Right. Exactly. Just the constant flux of people from all walks of life, migrating in every direction, headed somewhere. I can't get enough of that shit.

And why is it that no matter how much I've eaten that day, I show up at the fucking airport and immediately I'm famished?

And your only option is a piece-of-shit nine-dollar hot dog.

(Laughter.) Exactly.

Right.

Okay. So then there you are at the Gandhi Café . . .

Yeah. Ninety minutes early or whatever. I find the place, no problem. Stare in the windows. It's empty, dark. Doesn't even open until noon. I've got time to kill. So I just start walking. No real plan. Walking through the heat. And then it's just too goddamn hot, so I grab another couple of magazines at another newsstand and duck inside another café.

What magazines did you get?

People and *US Weekly.*

Really?

Yeah. At that point, those were the only kinds of magazines I could tolerate. They're like the periodical equivalent of television. I didn't have the head to be reading anything else. My mind would have exploded. The idea was to stop thinking. Or at the very least, distract myself with static. I needed garbage.

Sure.

What better way to murder forty-five minutes?

Right.

And so then noon arrives. Or approaches, I should say. It still wasn't noon yet. I blew through both magazines, got up, left the café, and I was still early. I started making my way back toward the Gandhi, and then I get there and the goddamn place is still closed. So I'm standing out front,

pacing, and my mind starts going. I start thinking up ways
to introduce myself. Will we shake hands? Will we hug?
Will I get the door for her? Will I peck her on the cheek?
Will I bow? Will I curtsy? All that bullshit. Then I worried
that I was going to be standing there, pacing, when she
showed up. And I didn't want that to be her first image of
me, so I walked across the street and waited there instead.
It was a stakeout, essentially.

Jesus.

My nerves were absolutely fried. Every middle-aged woman
that walked by, I was terrified to look at her. Every one of
them was *her* at that point, you know what I mean? Every
time I saw a goddamn skirt, my heart skipped a beat. It got
to the point where I didn't even want to look at anything.
So I just stood there with my hands in my pockets and
stared at my shoes, but that didn't really do me any good
either. Standing still was intolerable too. I felt like I looked
too conspicuous, too obvious, that if my mother saw me
standing there, she would almost certainly know that I was
him, I was her son, and that I was a chickenshit, standing
across the street, staring at my shoes, too scared to stand in
front of the goddamn restaurant like a grown man. So
instead of standing there, I just started walking again,
thinking it would be better if I showed up a few minutes
late, rather than right on time, which was my original plan.
I decided I didn't want to be the first one there. Too much
anxiety involved, too much trouble. I figured it would be
better to let her show up first, and then I'd walk in a few
minutes late, full of apologies. So I just kind of ambled

along with my eyes down, trying to relax myself, trying to keep myself cool.

Waiting for the moment of truth to arrive.

Right.

And so when did you finally get back to the café?

Probably about ten after twelve. The door was open. I walked right in. No hesitation, no second thoughts, no wasted motion, nothing. I made a beeline. I'd been working up to it. That was the plan. Just walk in, be calm, don't think twice, just do it. I assumed Selma would be there, seated at a table in the middle of the crowded restaurant, and she'd wave me over. But then I walked in, sweating like a motherfucker, and the only person in there was this really old guy with hair coming out of his ears, sitting at a window table, eating naan. And then the owner of the place walks up to me, this short Indian guy with a big gut—Gandhi or whatever—and he's offering me a menu, smiling at me, asking if I'd like a table for one. And right then the door opens behind me, and *boom,* I turn around and there she is.

Your mother.

A spitting image of me.

No way!

Dead serious. First time in my whole life I've ever seen

anyone who actually looks like me. I thought I was going to fall over.

Oh my God.

It was nuts.

So what happened? What did you do?

I have no idea. I remember just kind of standing there, and she immediately moved in and gave me this big hug. I don't even think we said anything beyond "hello," and all of a sudden she just plows right into me. And then we're hugging. And then we're still hugging. And then I'm thinking, "Jesus Christ, we're still hugging." And then I realize that I've got tears in my eyes. And I can hear my mother sniffling on my shoulder. And of course there's this Gandhi guy, standing behind us. And he doesn't know *what* the fuck is going on.

Holy shit.

It was bizarre, man. Completely bizarre.

So what'd you have for lunch?

Neither of us ate. We ordered food and didn't touch it. I got some tandoori, she got the vegetable vindaloo. Neither of us touched a thing.

What did you talk about?

Shit. Who knows? Everything happened so fast. At first it felt kind of formal and awkward. Selma started in right away . . . it seemed like she had a speech prepared. She wanted me to understand the circumstances of my birth and why she put me up for adoption and so on. Her tone was weird. It was like she was paranoid I was going to attack her.

I don't find that weird.

She just wanted me to know that I was better off having been adopted. She and my father weren't married. She was actually one of his patients. They were having an affair. She got pregnant with me at nineteen. Didn't have any dough. Didn't have her shit together. She was screwing her gynecologist, a married man. Didn't know what to do. Was young and confused. At odds with her overbearing parents. Susceptible to crackpot ideology. Moved upstate to this commune. Blah, blah, blah.

So wait. Your biological father was your biological mother's gynecologist?

Yeah.

That's fucked up.

Welcome to my world.

Did you know that before?

No. But I don't really find it all that shocking. It sounds about right to me. Consistent with the rest of my existence. So far, I'm relatively unfazed by the news.

And overall the lunch was cordial?

Yeah. It was fine. Once we settled down and Selma got her speech out of the way, we just kind of started shooting the shit. She asked me about my life, where I went to school, and so on. And you want to know something weird?

What?

I started off by telling her about Rose. Right away I just launched into this huge tangent about Rose. Explained the entire fucking relationship, practically . . . just babbling like a monkey, one thing after another. How we'd met in college, how we didn't like each other at first, how in love we were, how we used to go for walks down by the creek, our dog, our favorite restaurant, all that little bullshit. And then I started blabbing about the affair. The Internet. The chat room. Everything. Blah, blah, blah. The whole goddamn soap opera.

Jesus.

Yeah. It was awful. Never in a million years did I think I would tell her about any of that shit. But then I started talking about it, and it was like I couldn't stop myself. Yesterday I almost started talking about it with some kid on the subway. I think I have abandonment issues.

It would make sense.

I think most kids who are adopted have it on some level. That nagging question of why you were given up, why you weren't a wanted child. And then, with Rose leaving me, it's that same kind of thing. And I'm aware of it. That's what makes it so goddamn maddening. And the irony, of course, is that there I was, divulging all of that bile about Rose to the woman who is the source of my abandonment issues in the first place.

And so what was her reaction?

She just sat there with her hands in her lap, kind of nodding along. I think she was kind of stunned that I was getting so personal with her right off the bat. For all I know, it scared the ever-living shit out of her.

Did she have anything to say about it?

No. She just kind of stuttered some questions, offered her sympathies, made a few quasi-philosophical remarks about the healing powers of time, and so forth. The fact that Rose left me for some guy she met on the Internet seemed to really fascinate her. So we talked about that for a little while. And then we just kind of gradually moved on to other things. I knew I'd been talking too much, so I tried to keep my mouth shut and let Selma take over for a while.

So what did she have to say?

You'll never fucking believe this.

What?

She's a filmmaker.

No!

Yeah. She does documentaries. Right now she's working with some human rights organization on a propaganda film for Leonard Peltier. She's trying to get him released from prison.

So she's political.

Heavily.

And what did she say when you told her about your film work?

She freaked. Couldn't believe it. It was a weird moment. She said she wanted to see everything, asking me all about what I'd done, blah, blah, blah. So I told her I'd send her my reel. And then from there, we just kind of talked about our favorite movies for a little while. Which was a nice downshift into triviality.

A regular conversation.

Yeah. I found myself relaxing a little once I got past that introductory bullshit, the background stuff, talking about our pasts and whatnot. After that, it was almost like I was meeting somebody on a friendly level. Talking to her wasn't too difficult, which was a huge relief. She's pretty friendly, pretty smart. Not too crazy. There was definitely a certain similarity there. There was definitely a tangible sense of commonality or connection or whatever.

She's your mother.

Yeah. On one level. But the truth of the matter is, despite all of the buildup, I didn't really find myself having any kind of maternal thoughts or feelings about her. Aside from the way she looked, and the knowledge that I have about her being the woman who produced me, she didn't really *seem* like my mother. She didn't really *feel* like my mother. Jane's my mother, you know?

Sure.

Selma seemed like my friend, or someone I knew from childhood but hadn't seen in years, or maybe like some kind of older sister, or some distant great-aunt I'd never met before, or something like that.

She didn't raise you.

No. She just gave me her DNA, shat me into the world, and sent me on my way.

(Laughter.) Is that how you put it to her in the restaurant?

Exactly. We had a lengthy discussion about how she shat me into the world.

No wonder you didn't eat.

(Laughter.)

So then what? How did it end? What happens next?

It ended kind of naturally. Lunch was over. She had to be somewhere—or at least that's what she said. I told her I had to be somewhere too. We walked outside and said good-bye, great to see you, wonderful to meet you, all that stuff. I gave her my address and phone number in Colorado; she told me to call her whenever I'm in New York. Then I pulled out my camera and knocked on the window of the restaurant and asked Gandhi to snap a photo of us, for the record books. Selma and I sat on a park bench, and he snapped a couple of shots, and then it was good-bye. We hugged again, and then we walked off in opposite directions.

Wow.

Yeah.

So now what?

So now I'm sitting on this goddamn bench, talking like a goddamn maniac, drinking a shitty beer, trying to figure out what it all means.

What does it all mean?

Fuck if I know.

Are you glad you did it?

Sure. Why not? It's a weight off my back. The mystery's dead, in a certain sense. Now I know. I'm sure that counts for something.

It has to.

Let's get the fuck out of here. My foot's falling asleep.

Which one?

The left one.

Okay.

Make sure you push the red button.

Right.

5.

The following day was my birthday, August 1. It was a strange day, a murky day, a day of melancholy and fatigue. I spent the afternoon in the East Village, wandering around. Had some lunch. Bought some clothes at a thrift store. And then that night Lynch and Henry took me out on the town. I was feeling out of sorts. Not quite myself. For the first time in my life, it felt depressing to be celebrating a birthday. I knew that I was still young, but I felt like I was getting old. I got the sense that my life was flying by and I wasn't making any progress.

Lynch and Henry made dinner reservations at the Tribeca Grill. They wanted to take me out to celebrate. I didn't feel like celebrating, but backing out would have been rude. I felt like I had to go and I had to have a good time. It was my birthday, after all. I wasn't allowed to be blue. With that in mind, I decided to get drunk and do my best to forget about it. We ate like kings and drank three bottles of wine at the table. Then there were some tequila shots. Henry bought a round in honor of my birthday, then Lynch bought another round in honor of the first round. By the time dinner ended, we were annihilated. Lynch and Henry were hitting on our waitress, trying to get her to come out with us. I kept talking about women, urging Lynch and Henry to take me to another bar. "Let's go find some women," I kept saying. "Let's go out to another bar."

I hadn't said anything like that in a long time.

• • •

BRAD LISTI

A little while later, Lynch took us to one of his favorite pubs somewhere across town. I forget the name of it. I didn't even bother to look. All I know is that it was dark and crowded and it had a pinball machine inside. Lynch and Henry were wagering money on who could beat the other guy at pinball. They both claimed to be experts.

The place was a madhouse. We walked inside, and it was body to body. Lynch and Henry muscled their way in and made a beeline for the pinball machine in the back. I decided to head up to the bar and buy a round of drinks. Lynch and Henry tried to hand me money, but I fended them off. They'd picked up the tab at dinner. I wanted to buy them a round.

Up at the bar, I noticed two girls standing off to the side, talking to each other. One of them was beautiful. She had long, honey-colored hair, beautiful skin, and feline eyes. I walked right up to her and started talking. Liquid courage. Not a moment of hesitation.

"Ladies," I said. "Sorry I'm late. . . ."

I put my arm around the pretty one. I never did things like that. The girls looked at each other and laughed. Neither of them seemed drunk. I told them how beautiful they were. I told them I'd been in the woods all summer. I was standing there in thrift-store clothes with my big beard. I told them that seeing the two of them on the heels of a summer alone in the wilderness was miraculous, like some kind of magical dream. I was completely full of shit, an absolute moron. I asked them what their names were, where they were from. The pretty girl's name was Felicia. She was from Texas. I forget what the other girl's name was. I think it might have been Eve.

As it turned out, Felicia had a boyfriend. He'd been in the bathroom when I made my initial approach. On returning to the bar, he found me standing there with my arm around his girl. He came up behind us, and I felt someone tap me on the shoulder. I turned around, and there he was, staring at me. He was a big guy, a good-looking guy, an Ivy League guy. Big shoulders. Big jaw. Polished. Groomed. Texan. He looked like he worked out.

I found him offensive.

"Easy there," he said to me. "That's my girlfriend you're hanging on to."

He was talking to me with an authoritative tone, like I was a dog he was trying to train. I told him to relax. Felicia peeled my arm away and introduced him as her boyfriend. I think she said the guy's name was Pete. In truth, I wasn't really listening to her. I was focused on Pete for some reason. I was angry for some reason. Something about Pete didn't agree with me. I told him once again that he needed to relax a little bit. Pete put his hand on my chest, pushed me away lightly, and told me to go get myself another drink. I overreacted and pushed him back. Next thing I knew, we were locked up. Pete put me in a headlock and punched me in the face. I swung back wildly and hit him in the neck. People turned and looked; a crowd fell in around us. He was twice as strong as I was and half as drunk. I tried to push myself free of the headlock. We fell back into the bar and knocked over some glasses. I could hear Felicia and the other girl yelling for help. Pete squeezed my head like a grape and hit me in the face again. Everything went black for a moment. Then I saw stars.

A couple of seconds later, a bouncer arrived. The bouncer was bald and much larger than Pete. He put me in a full nelson and took me outside. And that was it. That was the end of it. Everything happened fast. A matter of seconds. Next thing I knew, I was standing on the sidewalk with a bleeding nose and a cut lip. Cars were going by, and I was trying to explain to the bouncer that I needed to get back inside and get my friends. The bouncer told me to shut the fuck up and hit the road. I tried to bribe him with cash. He stood there with his arms folded. I told him it was my birthday. He threatened to call the cops.

I walked.

I had no idea where I was. I just walked off into the city, dabbing my bloody nose with my new thrift-store shirt, looking for a pay phone. I had tears in my eyes and no real idea where they had come from. I kept on walking, figuring I'd find a phone and call Henry. We'd go someplace else, I'd lick my wounds, and the celebration would continue.

I walked into a corner store and bought a pack of cigarettes and a beer. My face was a mess. Blood everywhere. The guy at the register looked at me like I was crazy. He took my money, put my beer in a bag, and gave me some change and a couple of Kleenex. I went outside and dialed Henry's cell phone number, dabbing my face with the Kleenex. It rang four times. Nobody answered. Henry was drunk at the pinball machine. He couldn't hear the ring. I left a message, then I hung up and tried calling one more time. No answer. So I hung up the phone and started walking again. It was a hot, humid night, and I was sweating through my shirt. I lit a cigarette and drank my beer and kept on walking.

Lynch had given me a key to his place, so I figured I'd head back over there and wait for him to get home. I walked up to a doorman standing outside of a hotel and asked him for directions to Grand Street. He took a look at my face and asked me if I was all right. I told him I was fine. You don't look fine, he said. I told him it was my birthday. The guy stared at me for a couple of seconds. Then he shook his head and pointed to his left and rattled off a bunch of directions.

Somehow I wound up in Union Square. Don't ask me how I got there. The directions the guy gave me were a lost cause. I was too drunk to remember them. I made a few wrong turns and wandered the city streets until I came out into a clearing. I had no idea where I was. I walked out onto the square, and there were some young kids standing around, teenagers smoking cigarettes. I couldn't tell if they were hippies or punks. They looked miserable. I lit a cigarette and walked over to them and asked them where Grand Street was. They looked at their shoes and told me to take the subway downtown to Canal Street. I thanked them and walked away.

The station was dank and empty, and it smelled like urine. I bought a MetroCard at the window from a deliriously tired Puerto Rican girl, and then I walked through the turnstile and found a map on the wall. I studied it until I found my train: the N or the R, downtown to Canal. It wasn't too far.

Down on the platform, it was quiet, just a couple of people here and there. Gangsters. Laborers. Overworked investment bankers. There was a homeless guy sitting off to the side with his back against the wall, a fat black guy with an Afro and a silver beard. He was sitting on the platform, and he had a blanket spread out in front of him. He was selling an odd assortment of dry goods—shoes, socks, watches, books, you name it. Everything was spread out on the blanket. There was a sign in his lap that said WILL SIT ON MY ASS FOR FOOD.

"Hey, brother," he said to me. "Whatcha say, man?"

I said hello.

"Good prices," the guy said. "Everything's low. Come on now, brother. Just takes one."

I walked over to the blanket and looked around. Most everything was garbage. The watches were gaudy. The books were tattered, and most of them I'd never even heard of before. There were a couple of neckties. There was an old-fashioned bottle opener.

For some reason, I found myself staring at a dog-eared paperback copy of *Awaken the Giant Within,* by peak-performance guru Anthony Robbins. I'd heard of it before. I'd seen the infomercials. There was a photograph of the author on the cover. He was smiling at me in Technicolor. Glowing. Happy. Fulfilled. Mocking me. I bent over and picked it up.

"Five dollar," the guy said.

"Five dollars?"

"Five dollar."

I looked back down at the blanket and saw a used teddy bear sitting off to one side, an old brown bear with a pink ribbon around its neck and one eye missing. It was haggard and worn, lying on its side, arms and legs contorted. It looked lonesome as hell.

"How much for the bear?" I said.

"Wilhelmina?" the guy said, pointing.

"Yeah," I said. "That one."

"Ten dollar."

"She's missing an eye."

"Ten dollar."

Behind me I could hear the train coming. I turned around and looked and saw the N come rattling out of the tunnel with its light on.

"Ten bucks, man," the guy said, rocking back and forth. "Ten for Wilhelmina. You get the book, it's fifteen. Come on now, brother. You can't beat that shit."

The train slowed down, rolling to a stop. I picked up Wilhelmina, took a twenty out of my wallet, dropped it on the blanket, and told the guy to keep the change. He picked up the bill and shook my hand.

"Thank you very much," he said. "God bless you, my brother. Thank you very, very much."

"Happy birthday," I said.

Then I turned around and got on the train.

6.

Anthony Robbins was something of an American icon. I'd seen a documentary about him on television before. He was six foot seven, 265 pounds, and wore a size 16 shoe. He was physically fit and remarkably well groomed. His infomercials had long been standard fare on late-night cable television.

Robbins was born on Leap Day, February 29, 1960, and raised in Southern California. At the age of seventeen, he was working as a janitor, earning roughly forty dollars per week. He lived in a tiny studio apartment in Venice Beach. The apartment was so small, he had to wash his dishes in the bathtub. It was a depressing time. Robbins was forty pounds overweight and floundering.

That same year, Robbins attended a seminar by motivational speaker Jim Rohn, and it changed his life forever. He came away inspired. He came away wanting to impact the world. In a moment of delirious ambition, he decided that he wanted to become the president of the United States one day. He then started mapping out the rest of his years on planet Earth in methodical fashion, writing down what he would like to accomplish, in ten-year blocks of time. During his twenties, he decided, he wanted to become the foremost one-on-one practitioner of neuro-linguistic programming (NLP), which, roughly defined, amounts to the study of the structure of subjective experience. During his thirties, Robbins envisioned expanding his practice to groups; during his forties, to entire organizations; and during his fifties, to the government level.

Beyond that, he planned to follow a religious path.

He graduated high school, bypassed college entirely, and started pursuing his dreams with feverish determination.

In the intervening years, Robbins went on to become one of the nation's leading authorities on the psychology of peak performance. He was generally regarded as an expert at the art of personal, professional, and organizational turnaround. He wrote five internationally bestselling books, which were published in fourteen languages. His *Personal Power* audiotapes sold more than thirty-five million copies worldwide. He provided advice and counsel to numerous entertainment legends, Fortune 500 CEOs, championship coaches, championship athletes, high-profile politicians, and internationally famous medical doctors.

In addition, Robbins was the chairman of five private companies and the vice chairman of two others. Together these companies generated revenues of approximately $500 million per year. The businesses included an award-winning 300-acre spa and resort in Fiji; a nutraceutical company; a publishing house devoted to health, fitness, and nutrition; and a toy company that specialized in toys of an educational nature.

Robbins also made significant contributions to the world of psychology and intervention, having cofounded the Robbins-Madanes Center for Strategic Intervention, an organization dedicated to the creation of formalized training tools and programs for the therapeutic community.

In addition, Robbins played a significant role in the inception of the presidential summit for America's Promise, in which systems were designed to provide more than two million mentors for youngsters throughout the United States of America.

Furthermore, Robbins had created the Anthony Robbins Foundation, which, among other things, was responsible for the annual holiday "Basket Brigade," a charitable offering that fed more than one million people in nine countries and provided support to programs in 2,046 schools, 758 penitentiaries, and more than 100,000 health and human service organizations and homeless shelters.

In addition, he was a black belt. He was also a licensed jet helicopter pilot. And he knew how to speed-read.

At that point, he was forty years old.

V.

Los Angeles isn't a typical American city.

It has no center. It has no monorail. It doesn't have much of a subway system. It doesn't stand at attention. Instead, it reclines across the desert, languid and chaotic, a tangle of highways beside the rippling sea. It cooks in perpetual sunlight, under a rapidly deteriorating ozone layer, and waits for people to arrive.

And people arrive.

megalopolis *n.*

1.) A very large city.

2.) A region made up of several large cities and their surrounding areas in sufficient proximity to be considered a single urban complex.

I'd arrived in town two weeks earlier. Flew from New York to Denver, gathered all of my personal effects, and drove eighteen hours straight to the coast without stopping.

Now I was in thick traffic on the I-10, bumper to bumper at high noon. Thousands of human beings, going somewhere. And me, somewhere in the middle, heading east at a crawl, looking for the exit for La Cienega Boulevard. According to the directions I'd been given, the offices for White Light Films were somewhere to the north, in a 1950s-era office building on

Beverly Boulevard. My meeting was scheduled for 1:00 p.m.

The first draft of *The Grandeur of Delusions* was tucked inside my satchel, 118 pages long. I'd completed the draft in five days' time, in a furious and unprecedented burst of creative energy. The week I'd spent in New York seemed to have functioned as some kind of fulcrum. Seeing my friends, wandering the city, the debacle on my birthday—all of it had sent me into a massive state of hyperactivity. Henry's travails in particular had really struck a nerve. The meeting with his biological mother set off fireworks in my mind. The dramatics of the rendezvous, the intense sympathy I felt for everyone involved—it all provided me with a sense of urgency that had previously been lacking.

Upon finishing the script, I immediately started making phone calls, hoping to get my work into the hands of someone who could actually do something with it. Naturally, this was difficult. The only real lead I received came from a guy named Howard Strahan, one of my old film professors at the University of Colorado. Strahan was kind enough to put me in touch with a man named Mitchell Baxter, the president of a small production company called White Light Films. Apparently, the two men knew each other through a friend of a friend. Baxter, in a gesture of goodwill, had agreed to meet with me for thirty minutes to discuss the project and lend me whatever advice and counsel he could.

As a matter of self-amusement, I liked to blame my most recent series of rash decisions on Anthony Robbins. I'd wound up reading *Awaken the Giant Within* while nursing my birthday hangover at Lynch's apartment in Chinatown. The preceding night, needless to say, had been a complete and total disaster. Lynch and Henry had come home from the bar only to find me passed out on the couch, bleeding from my nose and mouth, holding a teddy bear in my arms. They woke me up immediately and demanded a full explanation. I did what I could to give them one.

The next morning, I woke up early, far too hung over to sleep. The apartment was silent and empty. Lynch had already left for work. Henry was gone too. I looked down at the floor and saw the book and the teddy bear sitting there. Memories came back to me in pieces. My head was pounding.

I felt like an idiot. I fished my cigarettes out of my shirt pocket and lit one, then I looked at the bear and the book and laughed. Then I picked up the book, turned to the first page, and started reading. It was done on a lark, more out of curiosity than anything else. I was expecting crackpot schemes, positive thinking, and shameless quackery. But then something funny happened. The words on the pages started making sense to me—far more sense than I thought they would. I sat there entranced for the better part of five hours, and by the end of the day, I had read the entire book, start to finish. Furthermore, I had concocted a brand-new plan for my immediate future.

I could only take this to mean that I was a deeply troubled individual.

Lynch, of course, was completely incredulous. When he got home from work that night, I informed him that I'd just purchased a plane ticket to Denver. I told him about the book, picking it up off of the coffee table and waving it around. I proclaimed its genius, only half kidding, and ruminated about the possibility that the hands of fate had guided me to it. Lynch blanched. A look of terrible concern spread across his face.

"I'm serious," I said to him. "Forget the infomercials. Forget the fact that he looks like a Ken doll on steroids. This book is really good. This guy knows what he's talking about. It's a contemporary rendering of simple logic and ancient wisdoms."

"You poor, sad fool," said Lynch.

"I'm not kidding you," I said. "I wouldn't be surprised one bit if this guy becomes the president of the United States one day. This country could use a good shrink."

"Get well soon," said Lynch.

I bet him a hundred bucks that it would happen sometime within the next twenty years and that, when it did, it would be revolutionary. We shook on it.

I shaved my beard that night.

I boarded a plane to Denver sixteen hours later.

It is in your moments of decision that your destiny is shaped.

—Anthony Robbins

Within a week, I was in Los Angeles.

My first four days in town, I stayed at a ratty old motel on Venice Boulevard. By day, I drove around the city, familiarizing myself with my new environs and searching for suitable accommodations. By night, I worked on *The Grandeur of Delusions,* logging nearly twenty-five pages per session. The story came out of me in a flood.

In the end, I wound up renting a 500-square-foot studio apartment on Rose Avenue in Venice Beach, five blocks from the water. The apartment was tiny but functional. It had a kitchenette with a sink and a decent-size closet. I didn't have to do my dishes in the bathtub, and I was ten pounds underweight.

2.

I parked my car at a meter on Beverly, near the intersection of Edinburgh, on the same side of the street as the White Light office building. There was nearly an hour to kill before the meeting, so I decided to get some food. I walked half a block to the west to a diner called Swingers. There were tables outside, all of which were full. The people at the tables appeared rumpled yet somehow remarkably fashionable, and the waitresses were dressed like cheerleaders. For some reason, I was wearing a coat and tie.

I stepped inside, took a seat at the counter, and set my script in front of me as though it were a place mat. The girl working the counter walked up to me and smiled. She had a nose ring and bright blue eyes, her hair was jet-black and spiked (it could have been a wig), and her arms were covered in tattoos. Her name tag said ZÖE. She handed me silverware, a menu, and a napkin, then asked me what I'd like to drink. I told her I'd like a glass of ice water. She rapped her knuckles on the counter and told me that it was coming right up. I thanked her.

After surveying the menu for a minute or two, I settled on the penne arrabiatta. From there, I began leafing through my screenplay, re-reading critical scenes, checking for spelling errors and typos. Everything, as far as I could tell, was in perfect working order. I felt particularly good about the end of the script, as it involved several quasi-philosophical exchanges between Malcolm Faltermeyer and Hansel Baird. In my opinion,

249

these particular discourses contained some of the film's finest accidental comedy and served well to illuminate its remarkable levels of sustained vapidity. Examples of such exchanges could be found throughout this section of the story, one of which went as follows:

FALTERMEYER

Gig's up, Dr. Baird. You've made your last move. It's done now. It's over with. You want to go down alive, then you surrender peacefully. Go the other road, and things are gonna have to get messy.

BAIRD

Things have been messy for a long time, Malcolm. How quickly you seem to forget. Your obsession with masking the considerable fear in your heart is really starting to amuse me.

FALTERMEYER

Fear doesn't scare me, Doctor. I've stared down the barrel of the worst fear a man can know. The way I see it, fear has nothing on me. And it sure as hell doesn't live in my heart.

I left Swingers at 12:45 p.m., headed back over to the White Light office building, and took the elevator up to the third floor.

I stepped into a fluorescently lit hallway and found my way to a men's room, where I proceeded to wash my hands and talk to myself. I checked my teeth in the mirror, took a deep breath, and adjusted my necktie. I told myself to relax, relax, relax. And then I walked back out into the hall.

The White Light receptionist was an overfriendly young debutante with platinum blond hair. She saw me walk in and set down a copy of *Entertainment Weekly.*

"Wayne Fencer," I told her. "Here for a one o'clock meeting with Mitch Baxter."

"Gloria," she said to me, smiling widely. "One moment please, Wayne."

She glanced at her computer screen, smiled again, and told me to have a seat. I had a seat, trying to decide if her breasts were real. She picked up the telephone, buzzed Baxter's office, and informed him that I'd arrived. Baxter said something in reply, but I was unable to make out what it was. Gloria then turned to me and asked if I would like anything to drink—a bottle of water or a soft drink. I told her that I was just fine, thank you. I settled into my seat, removed my script from my satchel, and pored over it once again, in an effort to appear professional.

Ninety minutes later, Mitchell Baxter finally stepped out into the lobby to greet me. He was wearing blue jeans and a pale yellow oxford.

"Wayne," he said, smiling easily. "Mitch Baxter. Sorry I'm late."

I stood up and shook his outstretched hand.

He was much smaller than I thought he'd be.

3.

Baxter wore eyeglasses with thick black frames and an expensive-looking silver wristwatch. His hair was black, sprinkled with flecks of gray, and his sleeves were rolled up halfway to his elbows. There was something slightly agitated about his demeanor, yet at the same time, he smiled no matter what he said.

The walls of his office were adorned with movie posters, photographs, and a multitude of placards and awards. To my right hung a large color picture of a man standing atop the summit of a snowy mountain. A motivational poster. Below the photo was a caption. It read:

Ambition
Aspire to climb as high as you can dream.

Baxter told me that he had founded White Light in 1987. He had been working as an executive producer for PBS in Washington, D.C., and decided to take his act to Hollywood. He was young, ambitious, and felt there was a lot of money to be made in cable television programming. He felt there was a void in the marketplace.

"I surveyed the landscape," he said to me. "Back then, TV was all sitcoms, all bad acting and canned laughter—*but it was growing like a weed.* There wasn't nearly enough quality programming of an educational or documentary nature, but the opportunity was there. The need was there. And I was convinced that the audience was there. The network base was expanding. There were no guarantees, of course—never are in this business—but I felt strongly enough about it to take the chance. So I grabbed my cojones, rolled the dice, moved out here, and hung a shingle. The rest is history."

In the ensuing thirteen years, White Light had carved out a niche for itself producing one-hour documentary television programs revolving around the great outdoors. *Last Legs,* a twelve-part series on endangered species, had won the studio four Peabody Awards in the early 1990s. Other White Light programs had appeared on a wide variety of channels, including PBS, the Discovery Channel, Animal Planet, and NBC. The company also produced educational programs, which were then sold directly to public school systems throughout the United States.

"But now," said Baxter, "we're looking to expand our operations into the feature film game. We want to parlay what we've done into a whole new realm. You can't stay static in this business. Stasis is death. We're always on the lookout for new talent and new material. We have a nice little thing going right now, but we always want to get better. We've got great relationships with a lot of the major studios, and I think that, given the right project, we'll get a deal done sometime in the next year."

"That's great," I said.

"We're pretty pleased with the way things are going," said Baxter.

"I can imagine," I said.

"We really think the sky's the limit around here," said Baxter.

"Wow," I said.

"It's been a good ride," said Baxter.

"Have you ever considered doing an action movie?" I said.

"As a matter of fact," said Baxter, "I'm working on a deal with CBS right now. They want a Saturday-night two-hour special, something that combines nature and thrills. We just finished pitching them a movie about a killer crocodile, a *Jaws*-on-the-Amazon kind of thing. It's just a matter of getting the numbers right."

"Wow," I said.

I raised my script from my lap and mentioned that I envisioned *The Grandeur of Delusions* as a big-budget action movie.

Baxter nodded and blinked once, slowly.

"Do you mind if I give you some unsolicited fashion advice?" he said, changing the subject.

"Fashion advice?"

"Regarding your suit."

"My suit?"

"Yeah," he said. "This is Hollywood, my friend. You don't have to wear a suit."

I felt myself blushing. "To be honest with you," I said, "I wasn't quite sure what to wear."

"Weddings, funerals, fund-raisers, and awards shows," he said. "Otherwise, it's business casual. And once you make your mark, you can wear whatever the fuck you want."

"Okay," I said. I felt uncomfortable and loosened my tie.

Sensing my discomfort, Baxter segued immediately. He asked me about my background. I told him about my course of study at the University of Colorado. I told him about my trip to Cuba, careful to leave out everything pertaining to Pamela. I talked about Old Havana, Hemingway's Finca, the national park in Viñales. Baxter was particularly captivated by my trip to visit the Old Man. The moment I mentioned it, he shifted in his leather desk chair. His focus intensified.

"My God," he said. "That sounds like a movie right there."

"It was something," I said. "The guy was ancient."

"The Old Man," said Baxter.

"The *Old* Man," I said.

"And what did he say to you?" he said.

"Not much," I said.

"That must have knocked your socks off," he said, smiling.

"It did," I said.

bullshit *n. (vulgar slang)*

1.) Foolish, deceitful, or boastful language.

2.) Something worthless, deceptive, or insincere.

3.) Insolent talk or behavior.

I continued on with an extended anecdote about my time on the Appalachian Trail, hoping it would cement my credibility. I figured it might play to Baxter's seeming affinity for the great outdoors. I started in Georgia and worked forward chronologically. Baxter sat there making finger steeples with his hands, nodding his head, interjecting the words "Jesus" and "fuck" at regular, alternating intervals. I focused on the journey's physical hardships, in an effort to heighten its dramatic effect. I told him about the bugs, the blisters, the parasites, and the staph infection. Baxter squinted at me. I couldn't tell if he was disgusted or captivated.

"You were out there all alone for almost two months?" he said to me.

"Yeah," I said.

"Do you have a screw loose?" said Baxter.

I didn't know quite what to say to that. Baxter appeared somewhat serious.

"That sounds like a goddamned nightmare," he said.

I laughed, kind of.

"At times, it was," I said.

"I'm not a camper," said Baxter. "Gotta have a mattress and a hot shower. Don't mind a day trip in the sticks, but come nightfall, I'm heading straight for the Four-fucking-Seasons."

Ha, he chuckled. Ha-ha-ha-ha.

Ha, I chuckled. Ha-ha-ha-ha.

A wave of fear rippled up my spinal cord.

And then the phone rang.

4.

Mitch Baxter spooked me. He was precisely the kind of animal they warned you about, the one you were told to fear when you came out to Hollywood. There was something mechanical about him, something cold and hidden and passive-aggressive and soulless. I sat in his office for twenty minutes. We talked. Everything was remarkably cordial, but nothing much was said. More important, nothing whatsoever was said about my script. We never really got to it. Baxter never asked me about it. He avoided the topic seamlessly. He smiled and slid through the meeting with impeccable skill. I never really got the chance to bring it up. Then the phone rang, ending everything. Baxter picked up. Said a few words. Put his hand over the receiver. Smiled and claimed it was an urgent call. Told me to leave my script and my contact information with Gloria. He said he would have one of "his people" give it a read. The reader would be writing up a report on it and would mail it to me directly a few days down the road. If it really blew the reviewer away, he told me, we would continue our discussions in earnest. If the reviewer hated it, well, then I'd know that, too. And with that, we stood up and shook hands. I said thank you. Baxter told me to keep sending him scripts as I completed them.

"Keep me in mind," he said. "Always keep me in mind."

"Okay," I said.

I walked out.

• • •

Instead of heading back to the beach, I stuck around Hollywood all afternoon. Drove around awhile. Looked at people. Looked at things. I learned the streets—Fairfax, Sunset, Fountain, La Brea. I had my Thomas Guide laid out on the passenger seat. I drove past Grauman's Chinese Theatre on Hollywood Boulevard, observing the hordes of tourists, sweaty and pink, baking in the sun, taking pictures of inanimate objects, looking at the names of famous dead people on the sidewalks. I thought about getting out of my truck and walking around, but ultimately, walking amid the tourists in the heat didn't really appeal to me. It seemed better in my Jeep.

Later that afternoon, I wound up going to see the latest Woody Allen movie, *Small Time Crooks*. It was playing in the theater at the corner of Crescent Heights and Sunset. I bought a ticket and went inside and sat down in the back row, in the cool, conditioned air. The movie was nothing special. In truth, I hadn't liked a Woody Allen movie in years. Back in the day, they'd been great, but nowadays, the comedy seemed flat. The films functioned as monuments to graceless aging. Woody's character was somehow always hooking up with someone one-third his age. It was pathetic. It made no sense.

What made *Small Time Crooks* even worse was the fact that everyone in the theater was there alone. There were six of us scattered throughout the theater. From the back, I had a view of the entire scene. There was a lady down in the front row, and she was completely off her beam. The Queen Nut. She talked to the screen. She interacted with the story. She laughed hysterically at even the faintest whiff of a joke.

"Oh!" she said, laughing. "Oh my God! Oh, please!"

When she laughed, she sounded like a dying hyena. It

sounded like she was in pain. I wound up paying more attention to her than I did to the movie. I walked out of the theater feeling pretty uneasy.

From there, I drove over to the Whole Foods Market on Santa Monica Boulevard to do some grocery shopping. Whole Foods was a health food store that specialized in food products that hadn't been sprayed with noxious chemicals. It was filling a void in the grocery store marketplace.

I wandered the store for a while, filling my basket with groceries, before venturing over to the cash registers to pay. I looked for the prettiest checkout girl, found her, and walked over to her line. This was common practice for me. I tended to select restaurant tables and checkout lines based on my level of attraction to the waitress or the cashier.

My checkout girl was small and oddly attractive. She had light gray eyes, a little waist, and a big chest. Her hair was short and brown, adorned with barrettes. I was watching her ring up the older gentleman standing in front of me. The older gentleman was tall, thin, and stoop-shouldered, and he appeared to be in his seventies. He was wearing a brown plaid shirt and mustard-colored polyester pants, and for some reason, there was a sheet of floral-print paper towel hanging out of one of his front pockets. In addition, he appeared to be completely incapable of speech. He kept motioning with his hands, pointing at the items on the conveyor belt, trying to communicate with the girl, devoid of all sound. I decided he was probably a mute. Had he been a foreigner, unable to speak English, I figured he would have been mumbling to himself in his native tongue. He would have at least attempted some kind of hybrid brand of communication. But the guy didn't utter a word.

From there the gears of my mind started turning. I started

imagining scenarios. I told myself that it might be funny if I pretended to be mute when it was my turn to check out. I imagined that it would cause the cute cashier to laugh. Perhaps it would charm her. Perhaps she would be flabbergasted by my wit. If I could do it with a completely straight face, the joke would almost certainly work. The girl would giggle, astonished by the savage nature of my understated humor.

Ultimately, though, I opted against it. Couldn't bring myself to do it. Couldn't pretend to be a mute. Didn't have it in me. The thought of the cashier's reaction was simply too much for me. I wouldn't have been able to maintain my composure in the face of it. I wasn't capable of that kind of deadpan performance. I lacked the self-control. I was too enamored of my own joke, and whenever that happened, I was doomed. And so too was the joke itself.

Furthermore, there was always the chance that the young girl at the register wouldn't respond to my brand of humor. There was always the chance that she was politically correct and would therefore find my light mockery of the mute old man to be cruel and offensive. I was aware of the fact that my sense of humor was fairly specific. It didn't seem right to chance it. It was an inappropriate audience at an inappropriate venue.

I watched as the mute old man signed his credit card slip and wandered out of the grocery store and into the streets of Los Angeles. I stepped up to the register, smiled, and said hello to the cashier, trying to keep things ordinary, trying to keep things simple and straightforward. The cashier smiled back at me. Her name tag read ASIA.

"Is your name really Asia?" I said.

"It really is," she said.

By the tone of her voice, I could tell that she had answered this question countless times. By the tone of her voice, I could tell that she didn't really appreciate my choice of phrasing. I feared I had insulted her.

"That's a nice name," I said, trying to recover.

"Thank you," she said.

And that was the most I was able to say. I didn't know what else to say to the girl. I was thinking too hard about what to say to the girl. What I needed to do was to stop thinking about what to say to her and just let the conversation happen—or not—in an organic manner. But I couldn't do that at the moment. I wasn't capable of organic exchanges. My mind was a tangle. And she was too damn cute. And I was feeling too strange.

I was mute.

As I stood there looking at her in silence, it occurred to me that I probably needed to go out on a date. I figured that going out on a date would probably be healthy. I figured that nine out of ten mental health experts would probably advise me to ask this cashier on a date, just to see what would happen.

I figured that Anthony Robbins would probably advise me to be an active dater, to take chances, to wear my heart on my sleeve, to wring life dry of every possible positive experience.

I didn't have the balls to ask the girl out on a date.

balls n. (vulgar slang)

1.)

a. The testicles.

b. Courage, especially when reckless.

c. Great presumptuousness

Asia ran the last of my groceries across the scanner, punched a few keys on the register, and came up with a total of $74.07. I removed my Visa card from my wallet and swiped it through the scanner.

"Credit or debit?" she said.

"Credit," I said.

She pushed a few more buttons. The computer whirred and clicked, and the printer started printing. My groceries were in a chaotic pile at the end of the conveyor belt. It occurred to me that I should have bagged them. I should have helped out. That would have been the nice thing to do, the chivalrous thing, the gentlemanly thing. But I blew it. I was too busy thinking. My imagination had run away with me.

Asia ripped the credit card slip from the printer and slid it my way. I picked up the pen and signed. Yawning, she asked me what kind of bags I would like. Inexplicably, I didn't respond right away. I finished signing, put the pen down, and looked at her. We made eye contact. Her face was expressionless and beautiful.

"What kind of bags?" she said again, pointing at my groceries.

I grinned at her awkwardly and said the word "plastic."

5.

I got a job the next day. Did it on a whim.
I think I was bored. Plus, my financial situation wasn't what it once
had been. I wasn't broke, but I was well on my way. Somewhere
along the line, I had decided that I didn't want to bottom out completely. As fun as it sounded, I didn't want to blow through every
last dime. I figured it was a good idea to keep some cash on hand,
in case of an emergency. That seemed like the sensible thing to do.

With this in mind, I returned to delivering pizzas, despite the
daily protests of my ailing Jeep. I took a job at a place called
Gino's, a high-end pizzeria over on Abbot Kinney Boulevard. I'd
spotted a Help Wanted sign while driving around that morning
and went in later that afternoon. The night manager, Gavin, took
one look at my résumé and hired me on the spot. He skimmed a
short letter of reference written for me by Jim Hogan, my boss at
Fatty Jay's, and that was that. I started the very next night.

Gavin turned out to be a pretty good guy. He'd gotten his
master's degree in creative writing a couple of years earlier, hoping to be an avant-garde poet, but then things had changed suddenly, and now he wanted to be an avant-garde movie star, a poet
of the silver screen. He had a pencil-thin mustache and medium-
long hair. His girlfriend was an actress too. Crystal was her name.
I never got the chance to meet her, but Gavin was convinced that
she was wildly talented. He talked about her constantly, called
her a cross between Chrissie Hynde, Rita Hayworth, and
Jennifer Jason Leigh. I had no idea what that meant, but I went

along with it anyway in the name of professional decorum.

Gino's was a pretty nice place, by far and away the nicest restaurant I'd ever driven for. The food was outstanding. It had even won a few "Best of L.A." awards. Overall, I felt pretty good about the gig. In a lot of ways, it seemed like a natural progression, a logical step into the world of gourmet. My schedule was sane, my customer base tended to be flush with cash, and they usually tipped handsomely for a job well done. As far as I was concerned, it was a fine arrangement for the time being. It would make me profitable, albeit meagerly. It would put me in contact with people. And it would give me something to do.

A couple of days after my hiring, I ran the four-to-ten shift on a Friday night. Business was thriving. I was making my way around all right, and the sunset on the water was spectacular. I was feeling pretty good about things.

After my shift, I drove around awhile. I wheeled through Santa Monica, past the Third Street Promenade, and then I wound my way back down to Venice, watching the people on the sidewalks coming in and out of the bars. A couple of times, I thought about parking and going inside for a drink, but I never did it. Didn't have the guts.

When I got home later that night, there was a message on my answering machine. I pressed the button and listened. It was Lynch.

"Fencer," he said. "It's Lynch. Call me back right away, the second you get this message, doesn't matter what time it is. I've got a golden proposition for you, and we've got to talk about it as soon as possible."

I picked up the phone immediately and called him back, anxious to hear the news. It rang four times, maddeningly, before sending me into voice mail.

6.

First thing the next morning, the phone rang.
It was Lynch. He informed me that he had just experienced a
major career breakthrough. *The Bomb* had assigned him to cover
the Burning Man festival in Nevada. His editor was going to fly
him out West, all expenses paid, to get a firsthand look at the fes-
tivities for a feature article slated to appear in the December
issue. He wanted me to come along "to help collect data on the
periphery." The party was due to start in four days. If I could get
myself to Nevada, the rest of the trip would be free of charge,
covered entirely by the magazine. Naturally, I felt it was an offer
I couldn't refuse.

After hanging up with Lynch, I got on the phone with Gavin, my
boss at Gino's, and told him I needed the week off of work. As luck
would have it, Gavin was a pushover, completely sympathetic to
my cause. I informed him that I had a once-in-a-lifetime opportunity to go to Burning Man and write for a national publication.
That was all it really took. Gavin was a fan of Burning Man, and
he was vaguely familiar with *The Bomb.* He even asked me if the
magazine published any poetry. I told him I wasn't sure. He said
he couldn't guarantee that my job would be there when I returned
but that it probably would. I told him I'd take my chances.

That afternoon, an overnight FedEx parcel arrived from New
York, compliments of Lynch. It contained a voluminous stack of

articles about Burning Man, all of which had been accumulated and photocopied by one of the magazine's trusty interns. "Background research," Lynch called it. Part of our necessary preparations.

I sat on my front porch reading the stuff for the better part of three hours, trying to wrap my head around the impending adventure. Depictions of the event varied from piece to piece. Burning Man was a survival exercise, it was an arts festival, it was an experiment in civic planning. It was an *experiment.* By nature, it defied definition and description. Ultimately, it was something you had to see for yourself.

What happened, essentially, was this: Every year, tens of thousands of human beings converged on the Black Rock Desert for one week near the end of the summer. There they erected a temporary metropolis called Black Rock City. The city was set amid a vast and otherworldly desert landscape notorious for its harsh and unpredictable climate. Temperatures were liable to soar into the triple digits during the day and just as liable to plunge below freezing at night. Rainstorms, violent dust storms, and blistering winds were regular occurrences. In spite of all this, Black Rock City managed to be both modern and cosmopolitan, complete with streets, nightclubs, restaurants, cafés, sporting events, parades, installations, sculptures, lasers, concerts, radio stations, an airport, newspapers, and so on. It included all of the trappings of a modern metropolis while at the same time func-tioning as a wholly original and wildly untamed organism, unique unto itself.

At the heart of the enterprise was a man named Larry Harvey, Burning Man's main creator and, for many years, its principal spokesman and figurehead. Several of the articles Lynch sent me were centered on him. The guy was enormously compelling.

Now in his early fifties, Harvey was a product of the baby boom, born in 1948 and raised on the outskirts of Portland, Oregon. His childhood had been difficult. His mother was a distant woman, unable to show her children the warmth and affection they craved. His father was a cowboy type, semiliterate and fiercely independent, a Freemason who earned his living as a carpenter. He was a decent and honest man with a detectable inner passion, but like his wife, he had great difficulty expressing his deeper feelings. Larry's older brother, Stewart, was a pious boy who had more in common with his parents than he did with his younger brother. As a result, Larry spent much of his youth in a state of profound isolation, taking great solace in the wilderness and spending untold hours locked away in his bedroom, reading books and magazines and cultivating a rich inner fantasy life.

In the late sixties, Larry left home for good. He served briefly in the army and endured some unfulfilling college experiences on the GI bill. A few years later, he settled in the small town of Coquille, Oregon, where he lived with a woman named Janet Lohr. Supported entirely by Janet's elementary school teaching salary, Larry spent much of his time immersed in books, finding refuge in the works of Freud and post-Freudians like Kohut, as well as in the literary offerings of such writers as Shakespeare, Dickens, and Forster.

In the late seventies, Larry and Janet moved south to San Francisco, and their romance faded soon after. Larry, now in his thirties, was suddenly faced with the task of trying to support himself—the first time in his life he had ever done so. A series of odd jobs would follow. He grilled hot dogs at the Farm, San Francisco's legendary punk-rock club. He was a bicycle messenger. He drove a cab.

He paid his rent sometimes.

"I never really wanted a normal job," he once said. "I never could do it very well. The only thing I ever wanted to do was what I absolutely *had* to do. I wanted to realize some kind of vision—I just wasn't sure what it was."

During this period of time, Larry sometimes attended parties thrown by a local sculptor named Mary Graubarger. The parties took place on San Francisco's Baker Beach, a beautiful cove located near the foot of the Golden Gate Bridge, long a favorite spot for Bay Area nudists. Mary and her friends built sculptures using materials that had washed ashore. A giant bonfire was lit and dinner was served. And at the end of the night, the revelers often torched their creations.

At one such gathering in the mid-1980s, Mary and her friends put an old car seat in a hole in the sand. Then they burned it, along with a pile of old clothes. The resulting scene was surreal and cruelly beautiful, reminiscent of a terrible accident. Larry Harvey happened to be standing there at the time, watching it burn with great interest.

The experience made an impression on him.

7.

It is incumbent upon all Burning Man attendees to provide their own food, water, shelter, and fuel. As such, the powers that be at *The Bomb* had agreed to rent Lynch an RV for the week. Unfortunately, however, there were no RVs available in either Reno or San Francisco. On account of the festival's soaring popularity, every recreational vehicle within a three-hundred-mile radius of Black Rock had long since been rented. At the moment, the nearest available RV was located in Las Vegas, four hundred miles south. Vegas had therefore been selected as our official point of rendezvous. Lynch had procured a thirty-foot motor home from what he assured me was a reputable rental establishment about a mile from the Strip. It would serve as our home base for the duration of the mission.

The morning of my departure, there was a knock at the door. A young guy with a buzz cut and a bleached goatee was standing outside, slightly out of breath. He was about my age, and he was holding a large envelope. A local courier. I signed for the delivery, walked back into my apartment, and tore the envelope open. My script was inside, along with a two-page typed critique, or "coverage," as industry parlance would have it. I sat down on my futon and read it.

Here's what it said:

The Grandeur of Delusions tells the story of MALCOLM FALTERMEYER (45), a bereaved assassin who comes out of semiretirement to take on DR. HANSEL BAIRD (65), a clairvoyant, wheelchair-bound scientist with designs on taking over the world via mind control. The story starts out in New York before venturing off into the Los Angeles underworld.

In brief:

- An odd assortment of thinly realized characters shows up.

- An adventure ensues.

- Somehow, against all odds and in total defiance of logic, Faltermeyer saves the day.

The script is unfocused, slightly too long, and suffering terribly from a lack of proper tone. The conflict is poorly conceived, and the dialogue is ridiculously, comically bad.

Hansel Baird, the movie's villain, is more funny than frightening, and his presence as the movie's dark force is decidedly weak. He makes only sporadic appearances throughout the first two acts, muttering incoherent nonsense about the control of (a) information, (b) weather systems, and (c) "the mindscreens of the citizenry." If this was intended as comedy, it worked. If it was intended as authoritarian malevolence, well . . .

At the heart of the screenplay's failure is its total misunderstanding of its own identity. The movie can't decide if it wants to be a full-blown action picture or a psychological tête-à-tête between two troubled men . . . or maybe even a slapstick comedy(?). Some of its most harrowing action sequences are littered with half-brained and ultimately futile attempts at rudimentary philosophy. To say that such nonsense is grating would be as big of an understatement as this writer is capable of making.

In conclusion, the lack of craft and professionalism in *The Grandeur of Delusions* is the screenplay's most resonant "quality." The cast of characters is uniformly two-dimensional and truly *annoying beyond belief.* In a movie such as this—one that requires its audience to believe in and root for a hero of a decidedly wooden nature—it is of paramount importance that said character possess at least a few qualities of an endearing nature. Unfortunately, this is not the case with this script.

This reader suggests a "Strong Pass" on *The Grandeur of Delusions* and its author. What's on the page right now is harebrained garbage and isn't even remotely worth the time and energy that would be needed to fix it.

—J.T.

I set the coverage down on my bed and stared at it for a while. Then I walked over to my stereo. I put the Mantovani Orchestra on at top volume. Track one. "Charmaine." Then I pulled a pack of cigarettes out of my dresser drawer and lit one. Then I started packing.

• • •

A few minutes later, the phone rang. I walked back over to the stereo and turned the volume down. I looked at the caller ID. It was Lynch.

"Fencer," he said. "It's Lynch."

"I know," I said. "Where are you?"

"I'm here. Got to the Luxor about twenty minutes ago."

"How's everything?"

"Everything's good," he said. "It's hot as fuck outside. I left a key for you at the desk."

"Perfect," I said. "I'm packing as we speak."

"Good. Make sure you bring a lot of warm clothes."

"Will do."

"And sunscreen, lip balm, shades. All that stuff. And bring weird shit, too, as much weird shit as possible, whatever you have, whatever you can think of. Super Balls, crayons, bubble gum, temporary tattoos, fake feathers, costumes—you name it, it'll work. We need stuff to barter with. There's no vending out there."

"I know. You told me."

"Right. So whatever we bring, great. Whatever else we need, we'll pick up in Reno."

"Perfect."

"And bring something to burn, too, for when the Man goes down. On Saturday night, everybody hurls something of sup-posed significance into the fire. If you can think of something, bring it."

"I'll see what I can find."

"What's the matter? You sound bummed out."

"Nothing," I said. "I'm just tired."

"Are you feeling lucky?"

"Not really."

"Good. Give me a number for roulette. I'll put twenty bucks on it."

"Nine," I said.

"Nine it is," said Lynch.

I wished him luck. We hung up. I walked over to my bed. The coverage for *The Grandeur of Delusions* was there. I folded it three times and stuffed it inside my backpack. Then I walked back over to the stereo and turned the volume up.

8.

America West flight 355 to Las Vegas, seat 18C. The woman on my right was from Hawaii. She was native and portly. Upon boarding, we had introduced ourselves in a cordial and perfunctory manner. The woman informed me that she was meeting her boyfriend in Vegas, at Bally's. Her boyfriend was from Montana. Somehow they'd been conducting a long-distance love affair for the past three years. He worked for a technology company and traveled to Hawaii once a month. She worked for the Honolulu Chamber of Commerce and rarely traveled. I couldn't remember her name.

We were arcing out over the Pacific, making a giant U-turn.

If the plane were to lurch suddenly in the sky and begin plummeting toward the sea, I was going to reach my hand out and offer it to the woman from Honolulu. I was going to tell her that everything was going to be all right in the end, and then I was going to wink at her.

aviophobia *n.,* also **aviatophobia, pteromerhanophobia**
Fear of flying.

It occurred to me that I probably shouldn't be on an airplane at the moment. Under normal circumstances, I wouldn't have been on an airplane at the moment. Instead, I would've been back in Los Angeles, continuing my rapid assimilation into the

Entertainment Capital of the World. But these were far from normal circumstances.

In an hour, I would be in Vegas. The following morning, Lynch and I would board our recreational vehicle and drive eight hours north to Reno, where we would be meeting up with Horvak and Henry, both of whom, at my suggestion, had become last-minute additions to our operation. Henry was catching a flight from Denver to Reno the following afternoon, and Horvak and his girlfriend, Blair, were driving in from San Francisco. All of us were scheduled to convene at the Super Kmart on the northwest side of Reno at approximately 6:00 p.m., where we would load up on food, water, and various other sundries. We would consolidate our crew into the recreational vehicle, and from there, we would venture off bravely into the heart of the madness.

9.

In the spring and summer of 1986, Larry Harvey was working independently as a landscape gardener, running a small business he called Paradise Regained. As the summer solstice neared, he found himself beset by a strange and undeniable impulse. For reasons he couldn't entirely explain, he wanted to build a large wooden man and burn him all the way to the ground. And so with the help of his friend and colleague Jerry James, Larry Harvey built an eight-foot-tall man out of scrap wood. And on June 21, 1986, they took the wooden man out to Baker Beach, doused him with gasoline, and lit him on fire.

At the time of ignition, there were several people scattered along the beach. When they saw the wooden man go up in flames, they were drawn to it like moths. Larry and Jerry stood in the sand by their flaming creation, dumbfounded by the sudden attention. It was an instant and completely unexpected congregation, spontaneous and wholly unplanned. As the wind blew the flames in one direction, a woman reached out and held the wooden man's unburned hand. Moments later, a young troubadour with a guitar started singing an impromptu song about fire. Larry and Jerry were moved by the experience.

And the Burning Man festival was born.

Four years later, in 1990, the Man stood four stories tall. Hundreds of people showed up at Baker Beach to watch him burn. To the chagrin of the revelers, some cops showed up too.

They informed everyone that burning a four-story wooden man on a public beach was, in fact, a gross violation of the law. It would not be allowed. Larry and his roommate, Dan Miller, stepped forward and made efforts to negotiate. In the end, it was agreed that the Man would be raised but not burned. Larry gave the cops his word, and the cops left the beach.

As a result, the mood among onlookers quickly deteriorated. They had come for a spectacle; now it wasn't happening. They grew restless. Some grew upset. Some argued that they should burn the Man anyway. Some even got violent. When Larry Harvey tried to calm the unruly mob, one guy even went so far as to try to choke him. It was a bad scene.

In response to this outburst, the Man was disassembled and removed from Baker Beach in haste. It was evident that the spectacle had outgrown its venue.

Burning Man had reached a crossroads in its existence.

In the days that followed, plans were laid for the burn to take place over Labor Day weekend in the Black Rock Desert, an otherworldly landscape some three hundred miles to the east of San Francisco, in a remote corner of northwestern Nevada.

The Black Rock Desert's most striking feature is a silt alkaline salt pan called the Black Rock Playa, formerly the home of Pleistocene Lake Lahontan, a body of water that covered about 8,665 square miles of northwestern Nevada about 13,000 years ago.

In prehistoric times, lush vegetation and freshwater were abundant throughout the region. Rivers drained off of the Sierra Nevada Mountains and the Modoc Plateau, suffusing the countryside with life. Camels, horses, saber-toothed tigers, and giant mammoth roamed the region freely.

At present, the playa is dry as a bone. Vegetation is far from lush, and there are no more mammoths or saber-toothed tigers—anywhere. The playa is vast, flat, empty, and ringed by large, rippling mountains. It is one of the largest and most pristine desert valley floors in the United States of America, running about forty miles long and twenty miles wide. It is also the second-largest completely flat topographical region in the Northern Hemisphere.

Approximately ninety participants attended the first desert burning at Black Rock in 1990. The Man was ignited by a guy named David Warren, a retired carnival worker and veteran fire-breather. On account of high winds, Warren suffered facial burns during the proceedings. Otherwise, it was a very peaceful affair.

In 1999, the Man burned for the fourteenth time.

More than 23,000 human beings were on hand for the celebration.

10.

The final approach toward Black Rock City
was made well after midnight, amid howling winds and sideways
rain. Lynch was at the wheel of our recreational vehicle at the
time. The vehicle was aptly named "The Searcher." I was riding
shotgun. Horvak, Blair, and Henry were in back, playing cards
and drinking beer. They'd been playing cards and drinking beer
ever since we'd left the Super K in Reno.

I was half asleep when we rolled into the town of Empire, in
Washoe County, just south of the Black Rock Desert. Lynch
made a noise and tapped me on the shoulder. I opened my eyes
and saw lights in the rain. We were pulling into the parking lot at
the Empire Store, the last place to buy provisions before entering the festival grounds. From the front of the store hung a large
banner beating smartly in the wind. Lynch leaned forward over
the steering wheel and pointed at it.

"What does it say?" he said.

"I can't tell," I said.

I sat up straighter in my seat and squinted. It took me a
minute, but eventually, I was able to make out the words.

The banner said:

WELCOME TO NOWHERE

11.

It was hard to avoid thoughts of the apocalypse out there. The place looked like a giant crater, reminiscent of the aftermath of large asteroids and large, merciless bombs. The desert floor was flat as a board, a fissured surface of bright white alkaline clay, beaten down by winter rain, baked solid by the sun. A large brown mountain chain rose up all around, the lip of the crater. Somewhere in the middle of it all sat Black Rock City, a spirited exercise in organized chaos, laid out in a careful configuration beneath a wild and wholly unpredictable sky.

Back when I was in college, I'd taken a history course that centered on the invention of the atomic bomb. One of the more peculiar things I learned was that the world's first self-sustaining nuclear chain reaction had taken place on a squash court. The reaction occurred on December 2, 1942, at approximately 3:24 p.m. CST. The squash court was located beneath the west stands of Stagg Field, an athletic stadium located on the campus of the University of Chicago. Enrico Fermi, a university physics professor, was the man in charge of the operation. Members of the University of Chicago football team had helped him to assemble his groundbreaking atomic pile. The pile was made of black graphite bricks and covered on three sides by a gray cloth balloon.

This successful reaction signaled the dawn of the atomic age.

At the time, World War II was raging. Hitler's armies were

roaring through Europe, crushing everything. Meanwhile, German physicists were busy trying to initiate and control a nuclear reaction of their own. They were hoping to transform their efforts into the construction of a weapon heretofore unseen, a weapon of tremendous force and unprecedented destructive power.

reaction *n.*

1.)

    a. A response to a stimulus.

    b. The state resulting from such a response.

2.) A reverse or opposing action.

3.)

    a. A tendency to revert to a former state.

    b. Opposition to progress or liberalism; extreme conservatism.

4.) *Chemistry:* A change or transformation in which a substance decomposes, combines with other substances, or interchanges constituents with other substances.

5.) *Physics:*

    a. A nuclear reaction.

    b. An equal and opposite force exerted by a body against a force acting upon it.

6.) The response of cells or tissues to an antigen, as in a test for immunization.

The official mascot of the University of Chicago is the phoenix.

phoenix *n.,* also **phenix**

1.) *Mythology:* A bird in Egyptian mythology that lived in the desert for 500 years and then consumed itself by fire, later to rise renewed from its ashes.

2.) A person or thing of unsurpassed excellence or beauty; a paragon.

3.) *Cap:* A constellation in the Southern Hemisphere near Tucana and Sculptor.

As early as the 1930s, many of the world's leading physicists were worried that Hitler and his henchmen would find a way to build atomic weapons. Enrico Fermi was among them. So was his colleague Leo Szilard, and so was a Hungarian-born physicist named Edward Teller.

Szilard and Teller even went so far as to contact Albert Einstein, the smartest human being of all time. They urged him to warn President Franklin D. Roosevelt of the potential danger of a German superbomb.

Einstein responded. In August of 1939, he wrote a letter to President Roosevelt warning him of the ballistic potentials of nuclear reactions. He informed him of the German pursuit of superweapons and encouraged him to maintain contact with American scientists working to create nuclear chain reactions of their own.

And so the arms race began.

12.

The yellow sun beat down. Clouds swirled.
Winds blew. Waves of white dust drifted through the air, covering everything in a thin, persistent grit.

I was sitting in a lawn chair, smoking a cigarette.

A man in a homemade silver space suit lumbered by, handing out candy. He was trailed by a band of naked ladies playing flutes and recorders, their bare breasts painted to look like sunflowers.

An art car rolled across the desert at five miles an hour, a giant blue whale on wheels, driven by a guy in a pirate suit.

Meanwhile, a white-bearded sixty-year-old man blew bubbles into the breeze. He was completely nude and slathered head to foot in lime green iridescent body paint.

Across the way, three elated drag queens jumped on a trampoline, feather boas flying.

Bells chimed.

Fireworks cracked in the sky.

On July 16, 1945, the first atomic bomb was tested approximately two hundred miles south of Los Alamos, New Mexico, in the middle of nowhere. The test site was code-named "Trinity." It consisted of twenty-four acres of dry desert scrub in the Alamogordo Bombing Range, located in an unforgiving desert landscape called Jornada del Muerto (Journey of the Deadman).

• • •

By that time, Franklin Roosevelt had died, and Harry S. Truman had become president.

On July 25, 1949, a couple of weeks before the nuclear bombings of Hiroshima and Nagasaki, President Truman took a moment to scribble the following entry in his diary:

> We have discovered the most terrible bomb in the history of the world. It may be the fire destruction prophesied in the Euphrates Valley Era, after Noah and his fabulous Ark.
>
> Anyway we "think" we have found the way to cause a disintegration of the atom. An experiment in the New Mexico desert was startling—to put it mildly. Thirteen pounds of the explosive caused the complete disintegration of a steel tower 60 feet high, created a crater 6 feet deep and 1,200 feet in diameter, knocked over a steel tower 1/2 mile away and knocked men down 10,000 yards away. The explosion was visible for more than 200 miles and audible for 40 miles and more.
>
> This weapon is to be used against Japan between now and August 10th. I have told the Sec. of War, Mr. Stimson, to use it so that military objectives and soldiers and sailors are the target and not women and children. Even if the Japs are savages, ruthless, merciless, and fanatic, we as the leader of the world for the common welfare cannot drop that terrible bomb on the old capital or the new.

He and I are in accord. The target will be a purely
military one and we will issue a warning statement
asking the Japs to surrender and save lives. I'm sure
they will not do that, but we will have given them the
chance. It is certainly a good thing for the world that
Hitler's crowd or Stalin's did not discover this atomic
bomb. It seems to be the most terrible thing ever
discovered, but it can be made the most useful.

nucleomituphobia *n.*
Fear of nuclear weapons.

13.

Black Rock City was shaped like a giant horseshoe. There were streets, clearly marked and arranged in a U-shaped grid. The U-shaped streets were named after parts of the human anatomy, in keeping with the festival's theme of "The Body": Feet Street, Knee Lane, Anal Avenue, Sex Drive, Gut Alley, Avenue of the Heart, Throat Road, Brain Boulevard, and Head Way. The straight streets cut through the U-shaped streets at regular intervals. They were named after hours on the clock, starting with 2:00 at one end of the horseshoe and continuing, in half-hour intervals, all the way to 10:00 at the other end.

We lived at 8:30 and Avenue of the Heart. It was a pretty good neighborhood.

In the dead center of the horseshoe's hollow stood the Man, gazing out over Black Rock City from atop a pyramid made of hay bales, a towering four-story monument to hope and finitude.

On Saturday night, shortly after sundown, he would burn.

I entertained myself with the notion that *this* was what would happen if the Big One hit. Maybe if the Big One hits, I told myself, the world's few remaining survivors will convene in the wastelands in the aftermath, giving rise to a bevy of semiutopian, hedonistic shantytowns characterized by outrageous celebration, massively creative explosions of self-expression, a bartering economy, and a nearly obsessive preoccupation with sex, fire, art, and the finite nature of existence. Maybe the world's new leader will be a nonleading leader, an antiauthoritarian bohemian with a penchant for innovative social theory. Maybe Burning Man is a demonstration of how human beings might handle things in the event that we finally succeed at fucking things up for good, which, as far as I can tell, could happen any day now.

Or maybe not.

14.

On our first full day in town, I went for a bike ride with Horvak and Blair in the heat of the afternoon. They had brought five bikes with them from San Francisco, enough for everyone, which turned out to be a good move. Black Rock City was huge, and auto traffic was prohibited (art cars excluded). Bicycles were therefore the most convenient and sensible method of transport available.

The three of us rode out of the city into the emptiness of the open playa. The landscape was extraterrestrial, impossibly vast. Horvak suggested that we ride as fast as we could toward the horizon with our eyes closed, and Blair and I agreed. We picked a direction, spread out, and sped off. The idea was to see how long we could go without looking.

I closed my eyes and pedaled as fast as I could across the desert toward the mountains. My tires ripped against the earth, and my heart was thumping in my chest. Horvak was to my left, and Blair was to my right. There was nothing out there, no danger. The air was clean, the sun was beaming down, and everything was wide-open. Yet for some reason, I opened my eyes after about thirty seconds, overtaken by the enormous fear that I was going to hit something. There was nothing out there, nothing at all, and I knew it for a fact, but still, I was afraid.

Come nightfall, the weather turned freezing cold, but there were no storms. All five of us ventured out into the city for our first real nocturnal adventure. The place was electric. Music, fire, and light. We bundled up and rode into the chaos. The city felt even more self-contained at night, when you couldn't see the emptiness of the surrounding terrain. The stars came out, millions of them, and the place became its own universe.

Naturally, there was no shortage of unfamiliar stimuli. We played with an oversized Lite-Brite set. We stood at the foot of a giant figure sculpted entirely of old books, while a group of people dressed in Day-Glo skeleton costumes danced wildly around a fire, accompanied by drums. Down the road, a sword swallower was swallowing swords. We said hello to a group of Oregon hippies massaging each other in a heated tent, whacked out on ketamine. There was an enormous boulder sitting in the middle of the open playa. It was ringed by fire and tended to by an enthusiastic team of belly-dancing girls. At the city's outer reaches, there was a giant tepee packed with bodies and pulsing with trance music—synthetic bird sounds and thundering drums.

Eventually, we found our way into a bar called the Green Monster, where we ordered up a round of absinthe. It was the first time any of us had ever tried the stuff. The absinthe was served with a splash of water and a spoonful of sugar. It was a milky green color, and it tasted like pastis. We sipped it and smoked cigarettes, waiting for something to happen. Ultimately, it made our faces feel somewhat numb, but otherwise, it was pretty mild.

absinthe *n.*

1.) A perennial aromatic European herb (*Artemisia absinthium*), naturalized in eastern North America and having pinnatifid, silvery silky leaves, and numerous nodding flower heads. Also called *common wormwood.*

2.) A green liqueur having a bitter anise or licorice flavor and
a high alcohol content, prepared from absinthe and other
herbs, and now prohibited in many countries because of its
toxicity.

According to published reports, Vincent van Gogh was high
on absinthe when he cut off a piece of his ear in December 1888.

van Gogh, Vincent (1853–1890)
Dutch postimpressionist painter whose early works, such
as *The Potato Eaters* (1885), portray peasant life in somber
colors. His later works, including many self-portraits, a
series of sunflower paintings (1888), and *Starry Night*
(1889), are characterized by bold, rhythmic brushstrokes
and vivid colors. His long struggle with depression ended
in suicide; van Gogh died of a self-inflicted gunshot wound
to the chest on July 27, 1890.

Sometime after midnight, we left the bar and ventured over
to a giant tent called "The Arena." A band was on stage playing
ambient music, accompanied by fire dancers. The music was terrific. Sonic liquid. The dancers were average. We stood in the
back watching the show for more than two hours. Blair danced
easily, spinning around and moving her arms in what appeared
to be a swimming motion. The rest of us just stood there, bobbing our heads and sipping whiskey from flasks. Horvak lit a
joint the size of his pinkie finger, and we each took a puff before
sending it out into the crowd.

At about 4:00 a.m., we made our way home, exhausted and

happy, wasted and cold. Henry was making us all laugh, bitch-ing endlessly about the weather. His Manhattan accent came out when he had too much to drink. And when he got pissed off, everything he said was somehow funny.

"I'm lost in a goddamn sand trap," he kept saying. "But I feel like a goddamn Eskimo. Is anyone else having trouble process-ing this?"

We cut across the playa on our bikes. To our left across the desert stood the Man, hovering in the distance, solitary and majestic, lit up brightly with blue and purple neon tubing. His presence was bittersweet. There was something wrenching about it, something lonesome and deeply sad. His death sentence was imminent, and there was no getting out of it. Everything was locked in. His ultimate fate was nonnegotiable. In less than forty-eight hours he would burn. I was stoned and feeling sentimental. Everybody's fate was nonnegotiable. I turned my head to the sky and took in a deep breath. Then I raised my hand above my head and waved at him.

15.

Theme camps formed the core of Burning Man's culture of participation. Hundreds of them could be found all over town, on every street, in every neighborhood. They were designed to blur the line between art and spectator. They were the lifeblood of the Black Rock City experience, facilitating interpersonal exchanges among festival-goers while creating an atmosphere rife with delirious overstimulation.

> **theme camp** *n.*
> A Burning Man campsite that presents an idea or concept in an artistic fashion and is designed to facilitate interactive participation.

Thunderdome was one example of a theme camp. It consisted of a huge, steel geodesic dome. It looked like something you might see on an elementary school playground, only it was ten times bigger, ten times weirder, and bungee cords dangled from its summit. Willing participants took turns strapping themselves into harnesses, hanging from the bungee cords, and engaging in man-on-man battles, armed only with four-foot foam lances. They swung across the expanse of the dome, trying to bludgeon one another. Spectators swarmed the dome's exterior, perched on its bars, looking in on the action, howling playfully for blood.

The crowd around Thunderdome tended to be a bit unruly— lots of people in leather, lots of biker types, sadomashochists, pyromaniacs, festishists, people with genital piercings. Two girls dressed in dominatrix attire could usually be found inside the dome, strutting around the desert floor, heckling onlookers. One would juggle fire while the other would offer to spank people with a riding crop. The place looked like a casting call for *Mad Max*.

The Picasso Camp encouraged participants to paint. It supplied two huge canvases and a wide variety of paints and brushes to anyone who felt like contributing to a mural.

Lynch and Henry and I walked over there at one point and picked up some brushes on a whim. Lynch painted the head of Elvis Presley. I painted a man in a cannon, about to be launched into the stratosphere. Henry painted what appeared to be a purple mountain goat.

The creators of the Astral Headwash theme camp offered dusty, dirty participants a full shampooing, just to be nice. I got my hair washed on two separate occasions by a topless woman who referred to herself only as Mother Inferior. She was a hairdresser from Seattle, a five-time Burning Man resident, and the tambourine player in a garage band called The Miracles on Ice. She also bore a striking resemblance to Charlotte Rae, the actress who had played Mrs. Garrett on the hit TV show *The Facts of Life*.

The Nipple Clamp Camp was devoted to nipple arousal through the use of clamps, ice, feathers, and other things. People went there to get their nipples aroused. Blair and Horvak made a trip over there together on a lark, as did Henry. They got the feather and ice treatment. Lynch and I opted against it, convinced that such activities were only semijustifiable in the company of a topless girlfriend.

The O.B.E. Camp reportedly helped facilitate out-of-body experiences through the use of light, sound, and artwork. People who wanted to try to have an out-of-body experience tended to hang out there.

Once again, my involvement was limited to observation only. My mere presence in Black Rock City seemed to be tantamount to an out-of-body experience all by itself. I felt no need to push the envelope, concerned that if I left my body any further, I might not ever return.

The Anonymous Camp offered twelve-step meetings of all kinds, both scheduled and impromptu. Anyone involved in a twelve-step recovery of any kind was encouraged to drop by for assistance and support. The place was somewhat anomalous, a beacon of sobriety and restraint amid a sea of remarkable decadence. And the tent was always packed.

The Black Light District was a Burning Man village, home to a collection of theme camps. My friends and I had wandered through it, wide-eyed and stupefied, on Thursday night, our first full night in town. The village was otherworldly, illuminated by more than 16,000 watts of black light, lending the entire area an eye-popping psychedelic glow.

One of the more notable theme camps in the Black Light District was the Body Hair Barbershop, where Burning Man citizens could stop by to get their body hair colored, styled, shaved, or trimmed. Henry kept threatening to get his back hair shaved there. That or he was going to dye it green. Ultimately, however, he never wound up going through with it, blaming his reluctance to participate on reservations he had about the overall professionalism of the staff.

The Oracle Booth was a simpler, more streamlined version of a theme camp. It consisted of a small wooden booth planted in the middle of the desert with the words THE ORACLE painted across the top. Random people took turns sitting there, playing the part of the oracle. Passing strangers would stop by, asking for insight and advice. Whoever happened to be manning the helm did his or her best to accommodate them.

I had gone by the booth on Thursday afternoon when I was out biking with Horvak and Blair. While they were off exploring some other spectacle, I saw a woman sitting there, wearing a Santa hat, a red bikini top, and thigh-high red leather boots. For some reason, I found her instantly annoying. She seemed to be a little bit too pleased with herself, a little too impressed with her own essential weirdness. She introduced herself as Sascha and demanded that I step right up.

"Ask me anything," she said. "Anything whatsoever. By the powers vested in me, I shall deliver to you the wisdom of the oracle."

Immediately, my mind went blank. I stood there thinking about it with my eyes closed for the better part of thirty seconds, but ultimately, I was unable to come up with anything decent.

"All right," I finally said. "What is the meaning of life?" I raised a hand in the air and motioned in the general direction of the cosmos.

Sascha laughed at me. She threw her head back and roared. "That is *such* a shitty question," she said.

"Hey," I said, "you said I could ask you anything."

"I lied," she said. "The Oracle Booth is now temporarily closed."

She rose from her seat and strutted off in the opposite direction.

I got back on my bike and pedaled off into the desert.

16.

Lynch and I were sitting in plastic chairs in the shade of a big white canopy, waiting to interview Larry Harvey. We'd been led to our station by an elfin woman named Julieta, whom we'd met over at Media Mecca, the hub of all press activity in Black Rock City. She was dressed like Tinkerbell and introduced herself as a high priestess of media relations. I found her attractive and was therefore inordinately shy around her. Lynch handled the conversation from that point forward, explaining his affiliation with *The Bomb* and passing me off as his esteemed colleague. Julieta had never heard of the magazine before.

"It's a men's magazine," Lynch informed her.

"Porn?" said Julieta.

"No, no. Not at all. Pop culture. Social trends. *Cosmo* for men, essentially."

"I like the name," said Julieta. *"The Bomb."*

"Thank you," we said.

At that point, she issued us press credentials. We hung them around our necks.

The credentials amounted to a small piece of paper in a plastic casing. The piece of paper read:

> *This entitles you*
> *to nothing in particular.*

This is paper and ink
stuck between plastic.

Immerse yourself.
Participate.
Lose track of time.
Tempt fate.

Ask before you shoot.
Leave no trace.
Whatever.

Ten minutes later, Larry Harvey stepped out of his trailer to greet us. We stood to shake his hand, and Larry gave us a warm hello. His voice was low and gravelly, and he was of average height and size. He was wearing black jeans, a tan safari shirt with big pockets, and tennis shoes. A walkie-talkie was clipped to his hip. He had sunglasses on, aviator shades with big dark lenses. The pearl gray Stetson on his head was the only physical demonstration of eccentricity. He wore it, he told us, as a loving tribute to his late father, who had worn it before him.

We handed Larry a bottle of tequila, a gift from our camp. He received it with a smile and passed it off to Julieta, and then he asked us a few questions about where we were from, why we were there, what magazine we worked for. Once again, Lynch handled all the talking, explaining our purposes briefly. Larry listened. He was friendly but appeared to be somewhat weary. He had a three-day beard, and his hands shook slightly as he lit a cigarette. He informed us that this was the sixth interview he had given today, with three more on the slate, and that he had only a few minutes to spend. Naturally, Lynch took this as his cue to get started. He opened up his notebook, uncapped his pen, and turned the recorder on.

Okay then. First things first. What the hell's going on out here?

(Laughs.) What do you mean?

I'm hoping you can explain this phenomenon to those who have never had a chance to come out here and experience it firsthand.

Well, first of all, it's not really a festival, although it's festive. It's a community. In fact, it's a very sophisticated and cosmopolitan city that is created in a remote desert upon one of the most barren plains on earth, in the midst of a sprawling grandeur of land and sky. Nothing else—not a bird, not a bump, not a bush—is here before we come. And it's a perfect and pristine nothingness when we leave.

It's also an experiment in social engineering, because we're trying to find out what kind of society will foster culture, since we don't seem to see enough of it outside our city.

It's a rite of passage. It's an opportunity for people to audition new ways of being, as irrational as that urge might be in a given instance. It's kind of like stalking the gene pool for culture.

And it's a ritual. Not only is it done every year, but ultimately, everyone in this city gathers, one great gathering in which everyone is present, and together we witness the sacrifice of the Burning Man.

And on top of that, it is, of course, an inspired party.

How do you spend your days here at the festival? How are you participating?

I give interviews. *(Laughs.)*

Is that the extent of what you do?

What we do here is a form of instant socialization. And really, the whole function of our city plan is to create a spontaneous phenomenon that no one can control, and that's culture. No one ever planned culture. It's a spontaneous, natural occurrence. It's just that it happens in some social circumstances and not in others. In mass consumer society, it doesn't happen much . . . increasingly less. You're not going to see an outbreak of culture while you wait in line at a concession stand. So we're trying to control only those forms of social structure that will foment this, at which point we quit trying to control it.

Why this location?

Well, we were looking for a place where we could burn things. And this environment being wholly denuded and virtually innocent of life, we were drawn to that. (To be technically accurate, there is a beetle that lives in some of the larger cracks, but we use a very small portion of this four-hundred-mile landscape.) Also, the Man was always meant to exist within a cosmic environment amid scales that magnify our sense of reality, scales that are larger than life. We came here to the Black Rock Desert and discovered a space so broad and empty and vast, it felt oceanic. Charmingly enough, it didn't move and you could walk on it! *(Laughs.)* So this is a site-specific event.

The population of Black Rock City is almost entirely white. Do you have any thoughts as to why?

It's because white people don't have any culture left. They're willing to travel six hundred miles, spend two thousand dollars on their theme camp, and camp in survival conditions in the middle of nowhere so they can connect with somebody else. If you're living in a ghetto, true, you may be afraid to leave it for fear of prejudice, but you're also connected to your aunts and your uncles and your cousins. What's the big rage in pop culture right now? White kids consuming rap music. Why did the rap people invent that culture? Because they couldn't afford mass entertainments and spectacles. They didn't even have a sound system, so they had to make sounds with their mouths. They created culture. They started imitating one another, emulating one another, and they invented a whole new art form. Now it's been ripped off, and it's sold as a product and a commodity out of its cultural context to white kids who are glad to embrace something that smells of style and culture and belonging, that has some kind of authenticity to it. And let's not kid ourselves. White people may be rich and we may be privileged, but we're isolated. . . . The white folks are coming here because they *need* it the most.

Do you feel that Burning Man is a religious experience? Is it a spiritual experience? Is there a difference between those two things?

Yeah, there is. I think it's the difference between faith and belief. I like to say that belief is faith commodified. Faith is an immediate experience. Belief is something that gets turned into dogma. Belief is something that gets controlled by all these intermediaries who say, "You can't talk to God right now, but I'm in communication with Him, and I'll get back to Him, and I'd like you to sign this contract." And we've got nothing to do with that.

The people who found religions are mystics. The people who run religions are administrators. And they end up being run for political purposes. That's merely my opinion.

Having said that, the fact of the matter is that many people do come here and respond with what you're forced to clinically describe as "conversion experiences." They change their entire lives. They'll quit their jobs. They'll get married. They'll get divorced. They'll come to terms with deep grief. They'll reorganize their entire existence. They'll reformulate their goals. They'll change their values. They'll change their *lives*. And it's really rather extraordinary, and certainly it's not anything you'd see if you went to a consumer event.

And, of course, if you look at the way the Man is presented, he is presented according to the conventions of religious iconography. I love temples and holy places. I always have. And I've tried to present this city in a way that creates certain kinds of perceptions, that allows people, if they so desire, to have a profound and transformative time.

Any final comments you'd like to make to the inquisitive general public?

Oh, no, not really, except that this is one hell of an outdoor experience! *(Laughs.)* It combines two things: survival camping with cosmopolitan living. You know? Seems to me that's the best of both worlds. The only thing I never understood was the suburbs. *(Laughs.)*

17.

Lynch and I finished the interview at around noon and met up with the rest of the group back at The Searcher for lunch. Henry had cooked up a big pot of pasta. We ate and told them all about Larry Harvey. Meeting the guy had been a curious thrill. He was a presence, no two ways about it, a captivating talker, a born salesman. Lynch played back some of the tape. Everyone sat there, rapt.

After lunch, Horvak and Blair suddenly announced that they were going on a naked bike ride. They stripped down, painted each other a variety of different colors, hopped on their bicycles, and left. Neither of them seemed to have any reservations whatsoever about being publicly nude. Henry, Lynch, and I just sat there, drinking beer and trying to act natural. It was odd seeing Horvak naked and odder still seeing Blair strip down. She had a terrific body. None of us knew where to look.

After they left, the three of us continued to sit there. We commented on Blair's body, and then we cracked a few jokes about how maybe we should get naked too. The conversation went on like this, but nothing ever happened. Nobody got naked. None of us had the guts. Whatever it took to get naked in public and ride around on a bike, we didn't have it. The confidence wasn't there.

With this in mind, it wasn't long before we decided to split up and head off into town on solo adventures. I think the realization of our nudity fears was what set us on our respective courses. We needed some time alone to contemplate our deficiencies. Aversion to being naked was a strangely depressing thing to realize. It made you realize how uncomfortable you were with yourself.

nudophobia *n.,* also **gymnophobia**
Fear of nudity.

yourself *pron.*
1.) That one identical with you.
    a. Used reflexively as the direct or indirect object of a verb or as the object of a preposition: *Did you buy yourself a gift?*
    b. Used for emphasis: *You yourself were certain of the facts.*
    c. Used in an absolute construction: *In office yourself, you helped push the bill along.*
2.) Your normal or healthy condition: *Are you feeling yourself again?* See usage note at *myself.*

It was Friday afternoon. The Man would burn the following evening. I made my way out to the playa and steered my bike down the long boulevard that led to his pyre. The boulevard was lined with wooden lampposts, and the Man was standing straight ahead beneath a darkening sky. The clouds were rolling in, slate gray and menacing. The sun was fading, and the wind was starting to kick up. The good weather had hung on through the early afternoon, but now the clouds were winning. In truth, the clouds had been winning for much of the week. The day before had been all right, but otherwise, we'd been under threat.

People were cruising around in art cars and on bicycles,

going this way and that, weaving in and out of installations and sculptures, talking about the weather, looking up at the sky. A lot of them seemed to be heading in the opposite direction, back toward the city, back toward their camps.

I didn't really care. I kept on riding toward the Man. I told myself that Horvak and Blair were somewhere on the playa, nude and probably freezing. That or they were back at The Searcher, washing the paint off of their naked bodies, putting their clothing back on. I figured they probably felt silly about having made the attempt and were huddled under blankets by now, cursing the weather and drinking hot tea. Meanwhile, I was out there on the playa, fully dressed and persevering, riding into the chaos, trying to make myself feel better about the fact that I was afraid to get naked.

A few minutes later, I was standing at the Man's feet. I had ascended the hay bales, climbed up onto his altar, and was standing beneath him, looking out on Black Rock City. It was something I'd been meaning to do ever since my arrival. The wind was whipping, dust was rising up all around, and visibility was poor. Rain appeared imminent. In the distance, through the growing fog, I could make out the arc of the metropolis.

The metropolis was large.

I needed a glass of water.

The climate was changing.

The climate was *always* changing.

Time passed. The weather worsened. Dust was burning my eyes. I shielded my face, stepped down from atop the hay bales, and remounted my bicycle. I zipped up my coat and rode away, across the playa and into the wind. On my way back to town, I turned around and looked to the Man again. By now, I could barely make out his figure in the distance. He was standing in the middle of the desert, in a milky gray haze, completely and utterly solitary. In the strangest of ways, it almost looked as if he weren't made of wood.

18.

Halfway home, the rain started falling. The weather kicked in full force. Suddenly, I was lost in a cloud. The wind stung my face, and my eyes were fried. I was in the thick of the city, and the ground was turning muddy. Pedaling was difficult, and I was having trouble seeing. Eventually, I dismounted my bicycle and ducked inside a large white tent. The tent was home to a theme camp called the Costco Soulmate Trading Outlet. The sign out front was prominent, inviting visitors to come inside and shop around. I'd ridden past it several times but had never had the courage or the inclination to enter. Now the weather had driven me in.

soulmate *n.*
One of two persons compatible with each other in
disposition, point of view, or sensitivity.

There were three people inside the Costco Soulmate Trading Outlet, a guy and two girls. The guy was battening the hatches, trying to keep the tent stable. The girls were tending to the tables, securing paperwork and computer wires. I could hear a generator running.

The guy saw me first. He walked over, shook my hand, and introduced himself. His name was Jerry. He had strawberry blond hair, a space between his two front teeth, and freckles on his arms.

The women were named Naomi and Courtney. Naomi was

tiny. She had short-cropped, curly blond hair and looked like a marathon runner. Courtney was heavyset and cheerful. Her face was painted blue.

The sales pitch began almost immediately. Courtney asked me if I'd like to find my soulmate. Naomi informed me that it was my lucky day. I wasn't exactly sure how to respond.

"Here at Costco," said Jerry, "we have one mission and one mission only: to offer quality name-brand and private-label soulmates at substantially lower prices than can be found through conventional wholesale sources."

He pointed to a banner hanging behind him. The Costco Soulmate mission statement was printed out across it in big red letters. He had just recited it verbatim.

I asked them what it would cost me.

"It all depends," said Naomi.

"We accept a wide variety of goods and services," said Jerry.

"Do you have anything specific to offer?" said Courtney.

I shook my head. Everything I owned was back at The Searcher.

"Not to worry," said Jerry. "It just so happens that we're accepting knock-knock jokes and songs this afternoon."

"I'd love to hear a song," said Courtney.

"As would I," said Naomi.

"I'm tone deaf," I said.

"Most people are," said Jerry.

"Sing your favorite," Courtney said with a smile. "Belt it out at the top of your lungs, and we'll be off and running. Pitch doesn't matter at all. All that matters is whether or not you sing it with heart."

"Enthusiasm," said Naomi. "That's all we're really looking for."

"I don't think you want to hear me sing," I said.

"Of course we do," said Courtney. "We would be *thrilled* to hear you sing."

"Just so long as it's done at the top of your lungs," said Jerry.

"Volume is really our only requirement," said Naomi.

"Go all out," said Courtney, "and we'll deliver your soul-mate."

"Think about it for a second," said Jerry. "One song. One soulmate."

"That kind of value is incomparable," said Naomi. "Where else can you find that kind of deal in America?"

"How about a knock-knock joke?" I said. "I know a few knock-knock jokes."

"I think we need to hear a song," said Courtney.

"Yes," said Jerry. "The weather being what it is, we're desperately in need of a song."

"A song?" I said.

"A song," they said.

"What song?" I said.

"Any song," they said.

I stood there thinking, trying to figure a way out of it. I had a difficult time saying no to anyone. It was one of my greatest weaknesses and one of my greatest strengths.

The three of them smiled at me.

"You can do it, Wayne," said Naomi.

"Yes," said Courtney. "We have the utmost faith in you."

I sang them the first verse of "Dust in the Wind," by Kansas (*Point of Know Return*, 1977). It was the most apropos song I could think of on short notice. I belted it out at the top of my lungs. My voice cracked. It sounded awful. I shut my eyes. Singing publicly felt deeply unnatural. I couldn't hit the high notes. I couldn't hit any notes.

"All my dreams, pass before my eyes, a curiosity. . . ."

Surprisingly, my dismal effort was greeted with generous appreciation. Jerry whistled and whooped. Naomi and Courtney applauded with gusto.

"Bravo!" said Jerry.

"Hear, hear!" said Naomi.

Courtney stepped over from the other side of the table, took me by the hand, and sat me down in a chair. Naomi walked over with a digital camera and snapped a head shot. Then she took the camera over to a laptop computer and downloaded the photo. Moments later, I was handed a clipboard containing the official Costco Soulmate questionnaire. My picture was printed at the top of the page in the upper left-hand corner. A battery of probing questions was printed down the length of the page. Jerry told me to fill it out carefully. Courtney informed me that they would process my information and issue me a soulmate within twenty-four hours.

"Go with your gut," said Naomi. "First thought, best thought. No holds barred."

I looked at the first question. It read:

Are you now, or have you ever been, a slut?

I picked up the pen and started scribbling.

19.

Sundown, Saturday September 2, 2000.
The oranges and pinks on the horizon were fading. The sun was
sinking out of sight, and the darkness was moving in. The clouds
overhead were starting to congeal, blanketing the moon and
stars. A cold wind blew in from the hills. A single red flare soared
into the sky over the playa. Slowly, citizens of Black Rock City
left their camps and ventured toward the Man in a massive herd.
It was a pilgrimage.

My friends and I were standing in the middle of a crowd,
directly in front of the Man, about seventy-five yards away. We
had arrived early in order to secure a good view. The preburn
ceremonies were already under way. Fire dancers and music. A
parade of crazy characters marching down the boulevard in costume. The big event was set to happen momentarily. The energy
in the crowd was electric. Henry had his video camera running.
Lynch was talking into his Dictaphone. Horvak and Blair were
cuddling like teenagers.

Romance was in the air.

I was wearing several layers of clothing. In the right front
pocket of my jacket was Mitch Baxter's coverage for *The
Grandeur of Delusions.* In my left hand was the teddy bear I'd
bought in the subway station at Union Square. Wilhelmina.
She'd been sitting in the bottom of my backpack for the past
month. I'd never bothered taking her out.

Sometime in the middle of it all, Lynch tapped me on the shoulder. I turned to face him. He extended the Dictaphone in my direction.

"Okay," he said. "Wayne Fencer. In ten words or less, I want you to describe exactly what you think you're doing out here."

"What I think I'm doing out here?"

"Yeah. I want you to make an official statement and sum up your experience of this moment as succinctly as you can."

I thought it over.

Lynch moved the recorder closer to my face.

"Okay," I said.

"Go ahead," said Lynch.

"Standing here in the desert," I said, "waiting for an epiphany."

"Standing here in the desert," Lynch said, "waiting for an epiphany."

"Yeah," I said. "I think that's ten words."

I counted the words on my fingers. It came out to nine.

Next, Lynch went around, one by one, asking each of us to describe how we were feeling in one word.

Everybody thought it over for a while.

Henry started out, saying he felt titillated.

Blair closed her eyes and said she felt awed.

Horvak said he felt discombobulated.

I looked at Lynch and told him I felt pregnant.

20.

It happened suddenly, without fanfare, well before any kind of official crescendo. A pyrotechnical glitch. Spontaneous combustion. One minute we were standing there, waiting. The next thing we knew, one of his arms was on fire. There was no announcement, no musical accompaniment, no drumroll, no crash of cymbals, no dramatic ignition. Just a sudden fire.

The Man was burning.

At first nobody believed it. Nobody reacted. But then the fire spread. Sparks shot forth, and the reality of the situation took hold. A gasp moved through the crowd like a secret. Then there was a period of confused conversation. And then the cheering began.

Next thing we knew, he was a torch in the night. His body was packed with fireworks, and he was crackling with successive explosions. Sparks were pouring from his frame like electrified confetti.

The Man was burning!

The crowd roared and surged forward, all of Black Rock City shifting in the direction of the fire, as if drawn by a magnet. I moved involuntarily, pulled by the Man and pushed by the force of the people behind me.

"Holy shit!" said Henry.

"This is it!" said Blair.

The cheering grew louder. Whistles and battle cries. Drums in the distance. Everything was happening fast. All around me, people were jumping up and down, screaming and hollering, letting off steam. It was a frenzy. The response felt a little disjointed to me. I couldn't match the crowd. Didn't have it in me. I was feeling a bit drier, a bit more subdued. The excitement seemed to have a manufactured edge to it. The moment had happened before anyone knew what was what, and then it took off into the night and left everybody behind, and now everyone was racing to catch up to it. I couldn't bring myself to jump up and down, couldn't bring myself to scream. All I could do was stand there.

Another crackling explosion. A shower of red embers burst from his chest like rose petals. Henry elbowed me in the ribs and raised his video camera above his head.

"Would you look at that!" he said.

I looked at that.

I looked around.

I was standing with approximately 26,000 people, in the middle of nowhere. A forty-foot-tall wooden man was on fire. Pyrotechnics and flammables were igniting throughout his frame. Raging flames and showers of sparks. A bright orange blaze against the black of night. People were going bonkers. People were feeling holy.

The Man was inside of the fire now. The flames had overtaken him. They were more than him, they were consuming him. He was engulfed, swallowed whole. He looked like a shadow of himself inside the blaze. The longer he burned, the more he got lost within the smoke and flames. He was disappearing.

As his legs burned away, he began to wobble back and forth, like a prizefighter with his bell rung. His knees swayed side to side, weakening. As the wobbling worsened, the roar of the crowd rose in anticipation. I felt anxious. My heart ran up into my throat, and my lungs went empty. An enormous wave of emotion welled up within me, suddenly, catching me off guard, and a kaleidoscope of memories swirled through my mind. Amanda. Pamela. My parents. My sisters. Benton MacKaye. Tony Robbins. Henry's mother. Uncle Brian. I stood there staring into the glow of raging flames, trying to maintain my composure. There was something tragic about this. There was something hypnotic and beautiful about this.

"He's gonna go!" Horvak screamed.

"Get ready!" said Henry.

The Man lurched to one side, fighting. He tried to stay up, but the fire was too much. He went. His legs gave out at the knees, and then the rest of him toppled over, his upper half falling over to the earth like a redwood tree, collapsing into a heap. It looked like it was happening in slow motion.

The hay bales ignited in a massive fury.

The crowd cheered and rushed forward. A hard charge.

My friends and I had no choice but to move with the flow. We all rushed in. The heat was fierce. I could feel it against my face as we got closer to the burn. Up ahead I saw the silhouettes of jumping, dancing people against the bright yellow light of the fire. Objects were sailing into the flames. Smoke and embers were rising up into the night. Women were on men's shoulders. People were hugging and kissing. The smell of marijuana laced the desert wind. A champagne cork went flying. People had tears in their eyes.

Lynch grabbed me by the arm. "Holy fucking shit!" he said.

"I know," I said. "I know."

That was all I could think of to say.

We never reached the fire. We got within about ninety feet of it, and then the forward momentum stopped. It was too hot on the front lines, and people stopped moving. There was no place else to go. The crowd was too much. Everyone was body to body. Getting up closer to the blaze would have taken work. None of us felt like battling our way in. We stood where we were and watched the burn unfold for about thirty minutes, and then we turned around and wove our way out of the crowd in the direction of the open playa. We needed space. Blair was feeling claustrophobic. So was Henry. So was everyone.

I lit a cigarette and looked heavenward. A wave of fatigue washed over me. It was nice to be out on the playa, nice to be out in space. It was colder out there, but that didn't really matter. At least there was room to move, room to breathe. Several smaller fires were flaring up all over the desert. People were burning whatever they could get their hands on. Impromptu gatherings were forming anywhere there was light and heat. Pyromania all around.

We headed toward one of the smaller fires. Some guy had set off a bunch of two-by-fours and plywood, remnants of a decimated installation. People were standing around it, warming themselves, watching it disappear. Music was blaring from two giant speakers hooked up to a generator—woodwinds and a harp. I felt it was a fitting selection.

It wasn't long before people started tossing things into the fire. My friends and I were soon to follow, stepping up to the blaze with our offerings. We each had something to burn. Horvak had decided to burn his American Express card. Blair had brought along an old diary. Lynch had a box of playing cards and one of his grandfather's old stogies. Henry brought his favorite T-shirt, the one that read THE FUTURE IS IN YOUR HEAD. I had the coverage and the bear.

Blair went first, tossing the diary like a Frisbee. It sailed into the flames and went up like a marshmallow. We all watched it go.

Afterward she turned to Horvak, kissing him on the cheek, and Horvak hugged her. He then walked up to the fire, laughing, and tossed his credit card atop the blaze. It disappeared almost instantly.

After that it was Lynch's turn. The stogie and the playing cards were offered to the blaze at the same time. Lynch did the sign of the cross half jokingly while it burned, and spat into the fire. Then he stepped away.

Henry's T-shirt went in next. It went up in a burst of fire and fell between a pair of two-by-fours. Henry watched it for a while, stone-faced. Then he turned his head to the sky and howled and sprinted out across the desert floor into the darkness, skipping like a little kid.

I was the last one to go. I walked up to the blaze, took the coverage out of my coat pocket, and dropped it in. All in all, it was pretty anticlimactic. I didn't feel much. The moment was too orchestrated, too forced. The heat was intense up close to the fire. I grimaced and watched the paper burn. It curled up at the edges and turned to black. Then it smoldered into ashes and vanished. I thought about Malcolm Faltermeyer and the tenets of accidental comedy. My belief in the concept was wholly undiminished.

After a while, I walked back over to my friends.

Blair asked me what I'd burned.

"Hate mail," I told her.

She asked no further questions.

I was still holding the bear. The bear was supposed to have gone in after the coverage. All along, I'd figured I would burn it, convinced it would be a nice, destructive, melodramatic thing to do. But now that the moment was at hand, I seemed to have lost all interest. I didn't really want to do it. The bear seemed too innocent, and the fire was too final.

Henry came back from his run.

"Go on, Fencer," he said to me, panting. "Chuck that fucker in."

"No way," I said. "The bear lives. I've granted her a pardon."

To our right, a few feet away, a girl was dancing by the fire, spinning around in a long flowered skirt. Her hair was tied up in a bandana, and she was wearing a big rainbow-colored scarf, and she was all alone. Her eyes were like saucers. I walked over to her and handed her the bear. She smiled and took it in her arms.

"For me?" she said.

"For you," I said.

"Thank you!" she said.

"You're welcome," I said.

She held the bear above her head, giggled, and did a pirouette. She wasn't alone anymore.

"Thank you!" she said again. "Thank you so much!"

A guy walked over. He had a big beard and mustache. Her boyfriend, I presumed.

"Look," the girl said to him. "A teddy bear!"

She handed it to him. He looked at it. His eyes were like saucers too.

The guy looked at me and smiled. So did the girl.

"Thanks," they said.

"Merry Christmas," I told them.

Then I walked back over to my friends.

21.

My soulmate's name was Caroline LeBlanc.
She was a member of the Stanford University swim team, and she wanted to be a pediatrician one day.

pediatrics *n.*
The branch of medicine that deals with the care of infants and children and the treatment of their diseases.

I had stopped by the Costco Soulmate Trading Outlet earlier that afternoon, shortly before the burn. Caroline had left a note for me. The note was written in pink ink:

To my soulmate Wayne:

Please be advised that my friends and I are going out on the town tonight, right after the burn, and we would be delighted if you would join us for cocktails, etc. If you're interested, be at the Center Camp Café at 10:30 p.m. sharp. If not . . . FUCK YOU!

I'll be wearing a big purple hat.

XXOO,
Caroline

Caroline was six foot three, 165 pounds.

My first thought when I saw her in person was: *I'm not attracted to her.*

I walked into the Center Camp Café a few minutes early, nervous and alone. My friends had offered to come along for the ride, but I had declined their offer. I didn't want an audience. It would've made me more nervous than I already was. Meeting my soulmate seemed like something I should do on my own. I figured if I was going to make an ass of myself, I should do it in private.

The café was crowded. Caroline was standing there in her big purple cowboy hat and platform shoes. She was huge. The platform shoes gave her another three inches. It was nothing short of startling. She towered over every girl in the café, and she towered over most of the guys, too. She was like a sunflower in a wheat field, and you could hear her all the way across the café. She had a big, booming voice and a big, booming laugh. I told myself that it wasn't her, that it couldn't be her, searching the café for another girl in a purple hat. No such luck.

Her face was somewhat attractive. Her eyes were big and brown, and she had nice skin, healthy-looking skin, skin that tanned easily. Her hair was dark—shoulder-length and straight. Her nose was long and thin. Her smile was enormous, and she he had a tiny space between her two front teeth. She was wearing bright orange bell-bottoms and a big blue puffy jacket. I couldn't see her chest. Her legs went on for miles. In a way, she kind of reminded me of Wonder Woman.

It crossed my mind to turn around and walk out, but I never really had the chance. Caroline caught me looking at her, and once we made eye contact, that was it. She said my name. My face gave me away. She screamed and waved me over. Two of her girlfriends turned and waved at me too. There were others around, some guys, some girls. It was a big group of people, and there was nothing bashful about any of them. They were all in costume—rhinestones, face paint, feather boas, glitter. Most of them were Stanford students. They had strength in numbers. I was all by myself.

Nervous, I walked up and said hello. Caroline smiled and greeted me with a mammoth hug. She had to crouch down to get her arms around me. I had to get up on my tiptoes to avoid sticking my face in her chest. It was pretty uncomfortable.

"Sorry," she said. "I'm a giant."

"It's no problem," I replied.

I had to look up at her to make eye contact, which was awkward. I didn't know what to say to the girl. My stomach was in knots. I felt like my uneasiness was visible on my face.

One of Caroline's girlfriends was standing off to the side, eavesdropping. It wasn't long before she stepped in, handed me a glass of champagne, and introduced herself as Tori, Queen of the Magpies. She was wearing a red Lycra bodysuit, an Indian headdress, moon boots, and a blue-jean miniskirt. She asked me where my costume was. I told her I didn't have one. I told her I wasn't aware that a costume was necessary. She told me that a costume was *always* necessary. I apologized and told her I wasn't aware of the rule. Tori turned her nose in the air and walked away. A few minutes later, she returned with a blue PUMA headband and a pair of big pink earmuffs. She told me it was the best she could do on short notice. She handed them to me and ordered me to put them on. Naturally, I obeyed.

The three of us talked for the next hour. The conversation went all right. I smoked an endless series of cigarettes and tried to be polite. All throughout, the girls kept introducing me to a steady stream of friends, upwards of fifteen people. Some of the girls were on the swim team. One of the guys was on the baseball team. A couple of other guys were strangers, new to the group, soulmates just like me, recruited off the streets. And one of the girls was a soulmate too.

A little while later, the group made motions to leave the café and head out into town. By then, it was about 11:30. I had arranged to meet up with Lynch and the rest of my friends at the absinthe bar at midnight, just in case the soulmate thing didn't work out. This was officially the point of no return. Making a break for it sounded like an enticing option, but leaving would require a kind of social delicacy that had always eluded me.

"So," said Caroline, "are you coming along for the ride?"

"Of course he's coming along for the ride," Tori said. "Look at him, for God's sake. He's wearing your earmuffs. There's no turning back now."

"You want me to come?" I said. I'd been hoping for a total rejection.

"*Of course* we want you to come," said Tori. "You passed the test, Wayne. Didn't you hear? We've decided you're not a sociopath. That's our only real criterion."

"You're more than welcome to join us," said Caroline.

They looked at me and smiled. I told them I'd love to go along. The girls squealed and hugged me at the same time. There was something highly obnoxious about them, something manic and uncontained. I couldn't decide if it was endearing or annoying. They seemed to lack all manner of self-consciousness.

I lit a cigarette and asked for another glass of champagne. Tori handed me the bottle she was holding. There was hardly anything left. I drained it.

A few minutes later, the group started moving. We fell into

the pack and moved out of the café, out into the darkness of the open playa. The weather was terrible, windy and cold, but nobody seemed to care. Some people in the group were singing "Riders on the Storm." A couple of the girls hooked arms and started skipping. There were more bottles of champagne going around and a bottle of whiskey. Everyone seemed to be in a good mood. We were headed for the dance camps at the outer reaches of town.

Somewhere along the way, one of the guys in the group started scurrying around, distributing little white pills to everyone. He was a tiny guy, about five feet four inches tall, a Stanford biochemistry student. His name was Gregg. He was wearing a bright white fake fur coat, and he moved and talked at an insanely rapid clip. Next to Caroline, he looked like an elf. I'm pretty sure he was gay. "Treats for everyone," he said. "Happy travels, happy travels." He kept repeating that over and over again. Tori took one, as did Caroline. I took one too. I watched as Caroline and Tori washed their pills down with champagne. Then they passed me the bottle. I popped the pill and washed it down in one motion.

"This is going to be fun," said Tori.

"I can't fucking *wait,*" said Caroline.

"What did we just take?" I said.

The girls looked at me and died laughing.

22.

The "Godfather of Ecstasy" was a man named Alexander Shulgin. Years earlier, I'd read a magazine profile of him while sitting around the Denver airport, waiting for a flight back home.

Shulgin was born on June 17, 1925, in Berkeley, California, the son of two public schoolteachers. His earliest passions included marbles, stamps, and books. At around the age of seven, he became interested in chemistry. He set up a small laboratory in his parents' basement and started paying frequent visits to a local chemical supply store. He rode there on his bicycle. He was a very bright boy.

In 1942, at the age of sixteen, Shulgin went to Harvard University on a full scholarship. He really hated it there.

"It was a total disaster," he later said. "The people around me were sons and daughters of important people, with money and property, position and stature. I was not, and there was no social blending at all."

Lonely and miserable, Shulgin dropped out of Harvard in the middle of his sophomore year and joined the navy, hoping for happier times.

World War II was in full swing.

Shulgin served on a destroyer escort in the North Atlantic.

During this time, he suffered a painful infection. The treatment he received involved the drug morphine. The morphine was administered, and the pain went away instantly. It was like *magic.* The experience had a profound effect on him. It marked the beginning of his dual fascination with pharmacology and the nature of human consciousness.

pain *n.*
1.) An unpleasant sensation occurring in varying degrees of severity as a consequence of injury, disease, or emotional disorder.
2.) Suffering or distress.
3.) *Plural:*
    a. The pangs of childbirth.
    b. Great care or effort: *take pains with one's work.*
4.) *Informal:* A source of annoyance; a nuisance.

I was familiar with ecstasy. It was popular back in Boulder. People took it on the weekends, went dancing, and rubbed each other. I never really did.

Generally speaking, I didn't handle drugs well. I was a happy drunk, but I tended to get a little sloppy. Marijuana delivered a low-grade, somewhat amusing level of paranoia. Anything stronger than that and I wound up blowing fuses.

Case in point: One night toward the end of my freshman year, A.B. and I got our hands on some psychedelic mushrooms. We each ate a handful and went to a George Clinton concert over at the Fox Theatre, thinking it would be an interesting experience. It was the first time either of us had ever taken them.

Everything went fine until the mushrooms kicked in. Once that happened, I started having problems. I couldn't stop thinking of dark and terrible things. I kept looking over at A.B., who appeared to be having the time of his life. He was clapping his hands, jumping up and down, and laughing his ass off. I tried to talk to him, but I couldn't really make any sense. Every communication was a miscommunication. Every miscommunication spawned another layer of miscommunication. My powers of articulation were gone.

From there, things spiraled downward. I quit trying to talk to others and started trying to talk to myself. I had nothing good to say. I talked myself into corners. My thoughts were looping. The more they looped, the more they degenerated. I started telling myself that everyone was mad at me. I imagined that I was letting everybody down, because I didn't like the music and I wasn't having a good time. I told myself that I was a cancer. I thought about cancer. George Clinton looked like an alien. He was genuinely hostile and clearly dangerous. A cocktail waitress came by and asked me if I wanted a drink. I thought she was an undercover cop. I told her to leave me the fuck alone. In the ensuing thirty minutes, I gave some serious consideration to things like death and blood and diarrhea and war. Eventually, I ran out of the theater and went on a ferociously contemplative five-hour walk. It was twenty degrees outside. I wasn't wearing a coat.

After his military service ended, Alexander Shulgin went back home and studied biochemistry at the University of California at Berkeley, where he received his Ph.D. in the mid-1950s. Not long after graduating, he landed a job at Dow Chemical as a research chemist. There he created Zectran, the world's first biodegradable insecticide. Zectran generated windfall profits, and Shulgin's bosses were ecstatic. In consequence, he was given the freedom to study whatever he wanted. His superiors considered him a shining star and left him alone to do his work. They wanted him to tinker around in their laboratories and invent things that would make them large amounts of money.

"Dow said, 'Do as you wish,'" Shulgin later remarked. "I did as I wished. I did psychedelics."

Twenty-five minutes after I downed the pill, my stomach started hurting. That was the first official sign that the drug was working. It was a subtle ache, a funny feeling, nothing too serious. Something was happening to me, no two ways about it. But I wasn't quite sure what.

From there, I started to notice that I could hear a little bit better than usual. I could pick voices out of crowds with ease. I could hear the wind. I could hear the sounds of music. My vision was improving too. Objects looked solid and defined, colors were more vibrant. I felt warmer. The city seemed friendlier than before, more open, more receptive, and a great deal more mysterious.

From what I could tell, my new friends seemed to be undergoing similar transformations. The dynamics of the group had shifted. People weren't talking so much anymore, and if they were, they were talking quietly. Even Tori had gone silent. Everyone was starting to feel something.

onset *n.*

1.) An onslaught; an assault.

2.) A beginning; a start: *the onset of a cold.*

3.) *Linguistics:* The part of a syllable that precedes the nucleus. In the word *nucleus,* the onset of the first syllable is (n), the onset of the second syllable is (kl), and the last syllable has no onset.

The technical name for ecstasy is 3,4-methylenedioxymetham-phetamine, or MDMA for short. It was first patented in 1912 by the German pharmaceutical company Merck and was initially used as nothing more than an intermediary. At the time, nobody thought much of it, and for many decades, it lay dormant in the pages of chemical literature.

On September 12, 1976, Alexander Shulgin created a new synthesis for MDMA in his home laboratory and soon became the first human being on record to consume it. The initial dose was conservative, measuring approximately 15 milligrams. Shulgin ingested it and waited. There was no noticeable effect. In the coming days, he upped the dosage in carefully controlled increments, documenting everything. At a dose of 81 milligrams, he started to feel something.

He described the initial experience in his lab journal:

> First awareness at 35 minutes smooth, and it was very nice. Forty-five minutes still developing, but I can easily assimilate it as it comes under excellent control. Fifty minutes getting quite deep, but I am keeping a pace.

Then the MDMA took hold. Alexander Shulgin experienced what the scientific community often refers to as a "eureka moment." He went on to write:

> I feel absolutely clean inside, and there is nothing but pure euphoria. I have never felt so great or believed this to be possible. The cleanliness, clarity, and marvelous feeling of solid inner strength continued throughout the rest of the day and evening. I am overcome by the profundity of the experience.

24.

We arrived at a big tent on the edge of town
and went inside. Drums and bass were booming from giant
speakers. Colored lights were flashing. The place was filled with
people in all manner of costume. A DJ was on stage. I could
smell incense. My friends started dancing immediately. They
dove right in with zero hesitation. Tori and Caroline walked right
into the thick of the mob, held hands, and took turns twirling
each other around. Gregg was running around like a maniac,
passing out lollipops to total strangers.

I stayed toward the back of the tent and watched everything.
My shoulders moved a little bit. My foot tapped. I was feeling
pretty good about things. Under normal circumstances, this
wasn't my kind of scene. I didn't like electronic music, the rave
culture gave me the creeps, and I couldn't dance for shit. Now,
for some reason, the music was agreeing with me. Everything
was starting to agree with me. Nothing was uncomfortable. I felt
warm, simple, effortless, at ease. The feeling was like a beam of
light. It started in my stomach and rose up within me. Without
even realizing it, the drug had taken over. It kicked in, full force,
and that was it. The transition happened quickly and seamlessly.
It was meteoric, and it fooled me entirely. The exaggerated nature
of my mental state felt crystalline and true. I never doubted it for
a second. Everything was all right, everyone was my friend, life
was beautiful, and there was nothing to be afraid of. It was as
though my spirit had been unlocked. It was magical.

With this in mind, it wasn't long before I dropped my last remaining shreds of inhibition and ventured into the thick of the crowd. I was even dancing a little bit, hopping around from one foot to the other, moving my shoulders from side to side. Up ahead I could see Caroline's purple cowboy hat, bobbing above the crowd. I made my way over to it and found her and Tori, dancing like maniacs. When they saw me, they went wild. They reached out for me and hugged me again. It was as though we were old friends, reunited after years apart.

"HOW DO YOU FEEL?" said Caroline. She had to scream to be heard.

"GREAT," I said. "I FEEL PERFECT!"

Tori squeezed my hand and squealed. Her palm was warm and sweaty. So was mine. It felt great to touch someone. I twirled her around. Caroline massaged my neck and shoulders. That felt great too.

"THANK YOU SO MUCH FOR INVITING ME OUT!" I said. "I'M SO GLAD I CAME!"

The girls hugged me again and told me I was welcome.

"YOU'RE TWO OF THE NICEST GIRLS I'VE EVER MET!" I said.

The girls smiled and told me that I was one of the nicest people *they* had ever met. We hugged again. We were flying.

"THIS IS THE BEST I HAVE EVER FELT AS A HUMAN BEING ON PLANET EARTH!" I announced.

The girls laughed and said "ME TOO!"

We danced.

25.

In the late 1970s, Alexander Shulgin's first wife died of a stroke. He had been married to her for thirty years. The following year, he met a woman named Ann. Ann was divorced and had four children. She was a big fan of peyote.

Alexander and Ann were married on July 4, 1981, in a small service in Shulgin's backyard.

The gentleman who conducted the ceremony was an employee of the United States Drug Enforcement Agency (DEA).

By the time the mid-1980s rolled around, MDMA was being used in experimental therapy sessions across the country.

Talk show host Phil Donahue devoted an entire hour to the drug's medical possibilities in February 1985.

There were other possibilities for the drug as well. New uses for it had been manifesting across the country, most notably in Dallas, Texas, where word of MDMA had spread like wildfire and an underground market was rapidly developing. Nightclubs in the area were selling the new drug like hotcakes. People were taking MDMA and dancing the night away. They were high as lab rats, bug-eyed and euphoric, and it was all perfectly legal.

Officials at the DEA later estimated that Dallas residents were consuming an average of 30,000 hits of MDMA per month during the mid-1980s.

• • •

A few enterprising Texans were quick to pounce on MDMA's inherent profit potential. They realized that it filled a void in the marketplace. And they capitalized.

One dealer even decided to give MDMA a new nickname, in an effort to make it sell better.

ecstasy *n.*

1.) Intense joy or delight.

2.) A state of emotion so intense that one is carried beyond rational thought and self-control: *an ecstasy of rage.*

3.) The trance, frenzy, or rapture associated with mystic or prophetic exaltation.

4.) *Slang:* MDMA.

Shulgin, it should be pointed out, was never a big fan of the nickname "ecstasy."

He always felt the drug should have been called "empathy."

26.

I was high. I was screamingly high. I was miraculously, screamingly high. I was so high that I didn't even know that I was high. I was dancing like a fool and didn't even care. I was smiling at strangers, doing karate moves. I rarely smiled at strangers, and I knew nothing about karate. I was jumping around like a moron. People were smiling back at me. Everyone seemed to be in the same condition I was in. A lot of people seemed to have swallowed little white pills. The music was a miracle to me. Sound had never sounded so good. I felt at home in the universe. I felt my affection for humanity growing by leaps and bounds. I felt I understood people. I felt they understood me. I ran into Gregg on the dance floor. He was jumping up and down. His eyes were dilated and his jaw was grinding. I gave him a high five and told him he was my hero. He hugged me and said, "WELCOME TO THE STRATOSPHERE!"

Time went by. At some point, I felt like having a cigarette. I wanted to go outside and have a cigarette and get some fresh air, and I didn't want to go alone. I decided I wanted Caroline to come with me. She was my soulmate. She was prettier than I had given her credit for. She looked like Wonder Woman, and she had a heart of gold. There was far more beauty to her than I had initially realized. I went up to her and extended my hand and asked her if she wanted to take a walk with me. She said yes. She turned to Tori and told Tori that we were going to go for a walk.

Tori smiled and hugged her, and then she blew me a kiss.

We went outside. I lit a cigarette. It was the greatest cigarette I'd ever smoked. Caroline produced a bottle of water and a bottle of champagne from her backpack. We each took a sip of water and talked about how great water was. Then Caroline handed me the bottle of champagne. After I finished my cigarette, I popped it open. Champagne shot out onto the desert floor. Passersby cheered. I laughed and took a bow.

I took Caroline by the hand, and we started walking. I didn't know where we were going, I just felt like moving. She was right there with me, squeezing my hand the entire way. I took a sip of champagne and handed her the bottle. She took a sip and handed it back to me. It was nice to be out of the dance tent. The weather was acting up, but the air felt good anyway. I had pink earmuffs on. A blue PUMA headband. Caroline's hand was warm. My jacket was warm too.

We wound our way around for a while, and then we cut across town and walked out onto the open playa. It felt good to be outside, good to be in open space. Up ahead there was a big fire burning and a few people milling around it. The fire was the size of a large car. We moved to it instinctively. I could hear classical music in the distance. The whole scene seemed like a dream to me. A strange and spectacular dream.

Caroline and I sat down on the ground in front of the flames and held hands. We talked about the heat of the fire as if it were a great miracle. I took a big drink of champagne, and it went down easy. Caroline put her head on my shoulder. We watched the fire for a while. I thought about things. Everything seemed clear to me. My heart was in my throat.

And then I started talking.

"I have to tell you something," I said.

Caroline lifted her head and looked directly at me. Her eyes were like a doll's eyes in the firelight.

"I want you to know how glad I am that you're my soulmate," I said. "This is one of the all-time best nights of my life. I honestly feel like we've known each other for such a long time, and I feel incredibly lucky to know you."

"Oh, thank you, Wayne!" she said.

She reached over and gave me a hug. I kissed her on the cheek, and then she took me by the hands and looked into my eyes.

"I feel exactly the same way," she said. "You're such a sweetheart. I knew it the minute you walked into the café. You have such a good spirit."

"You've just been so welcoming to me," I said. "I haven't felt this way around anyone in so long. I've been so guarded for so long, and I didn't even realize it. It's not that I don't like people, it's not that I'm not nice to them, but I'm always keeping them at arm's length in one way or another. I never really open up to people completely or feel like I'm able to."

"Why?" said Caroline. "You should always open up to people. You're a great guy. You can always open up to me."

"I don't know," I said. "I think it's at least partially because I've been through a lot this past year. I lost an ex-girlfriend to suicide, and it's been pretty tough to deal with at times."

"Oh no," said Caroline. She squeezed my hands.

"It's been hard," I said. "It's one of the hardest things I've ever had to deal with. I wasn't prepared for it at all."

"How could you be?" said Caroline.

"And then, to make matters worse," I said, "when I was at her funeral, I found out that she'd had an abortion while we were dating. It happened a little over three years ago. She never even told me about it."

"Oh my God," said Caroline. She squeezed my hands tightly. Somehow the news didn't make her uncomfortable. Somehow it drew her closer to me. Somehow I felt all right talking about it. I wasn't uneasy or afraid. Everything seemed simple and completely natural.

"I've just been struggling to find a way to come to terms with it," I continued. "I've been blaming myself a lot. I've spent too much time overanalyzing. I've been telling myself that I could have done things differently, that it was my fault in a lot of ways that things turned out how they did. I've been telling myself that my actions were harmful, and I've been worried that my life is now stained in some kind of irrevocable way. It might not make much sense, but at times I've kind of lost my faith in my ability to live. Because she's gone, and because my kid is gone, I didn't feel like I had any right to be here."

"You can't blame yourself," said Caroline. "You can't give up. It's not your fault."

"I know," I said. "That's what I'm realizing. I realize I can't blame myself. I realize that it's not my fault. I realize that all of the overanalyzing is pointless. The answers are actually a lot simpler than that. I think that's a lot of the reason why I feel so good right now. It feels like such a *relief*. I mean, I see that I didn't handle things perfectly. It's not as if I'm absolving myself of everything. I realize that my actions caused her pain. I realize that I could've been more responsible. I broke up with her, and I didn't do the greatest job of it, and it really hurt her."

I paused for a moment to light another cigarette. My eyes went up to the sky. There was a break in the clouds and a sea of stars inside it. Everything seemed to be trembling.

I turned back to Caroline and continued.

"I was scared," I said. "I didn't want to hurt her. I realize that now. That was never my intention. And I had no idea that she had been pregnant. I had no idea that she was as fragile as she was. I couldn't have known. She never told me. She never really told anyone. The people she did tell, she swore to secrecy. I never had a clue. I was nineteen years old then. I was just a kid. I was a baby myself. And so was she. I mean, Christ. I'm only twenty-three now."

"Exactly," said Caroline. "There's no way you could have known."

"I've been in a lot of pain," I said. "I knew it, but I didn't *realize* it until right now. So much of what I've thought and said and done these past few months is a response to pain. And I haven't really acknowledged it properly. And I haven't been able to move past it because up until this moment I haven't confronted it directly and admitted that it's there."

"Exactly," said Caroline. "That's exactly right. You have to see what it actually is. You have to diagnose it. You have to have that moment."

"And what's weird about that realization is the fact that it also makes me realize something about Amanda that I never realized before. I realize now that when she killed herself, she didn't really want to die, she just wanted her pain to end. She was in pain too. It was about pain, not death. She had pain, and she convinced herself that she couldn't handle it any other way. The pain became unbearable in her mind. And it might have only been that one night. It overwhelmed her, and she made a terrible, rash decision. She made such a big mistake. And there's nothing anyone can do about it now. That's the hard part. It's such a difficult thing. But it's something that I have to live with. And the only sane thing I can do is learn from it and move on."

Caroline put her arm around me. "I'm so sorry," she said.

"Me too," I said.

"So, so sorry," she repeated.

"I'm so sorry for Amanda," I said. "And I'm sorry for her friends and family. I'm sorry for everyone."

Caroline took me in her arms and pressed my head against her chest. "You poor thing," she said, and kissed me on the forehead.

Tears formed in my eyes. I thought I felt one fall.

"I don't mean to dump all of this on you," I said. "I know it's pretty heavy."

"Not at all. I'm glad you told me. I feel honored that you would trust me enough to tell me."

"Thank you."

"You're welcome."

"I appreciate it."

"You have a good heart."

"Thank you."

"You have to understand that."

"Thank you."

"You're a sweet human being, and you deserve to have a happy life. You have to promise me that you'll allow yourself to have a happy life."

"I will," I said. "I will. I will."

I turned my head and kissed her. She tasted like lollipops and champagne. We reclined on the desert floor and made out for a while. It felt good. It felt better than anything had felt in a long time.

"You're so easy to be around," I said. "You're such a beautiful person. You're so easy to talk to."

"Same with you," she said.

My heart was pounding and my palms were sweating. The

fire was bright. I was lying on top of Caroline. Our faces were inches apart.

"I know that this is going to sound really crazy," I said, "but I honestly feel like I love you right now. I really feel like I love you. Is that incredibly weird?"

"No," she said, squeezing me. "It's not weird at all. I feel like I love you, too. I feel close to you."

We kissed again.

"I feel like I love so many people," I said. "And I never tell them. And if I do, I don't tell them enough. And sometimes I just feel like I love everyone."

"Me too," said Caroline.

"That doesn't trivialize it, does it?" I said.

"No way," she said.

I reached over and picked up the bottle of champagne and proposed a toast to the two of us. We each took a sip, then we kissed again. I took the cork out of my pocket and tossed it in the fire. We watched it burn. A few minutes later, Caroline stood up. She took me by the hands and helped me to my feet. We hugged for a long time, then we kissed for a long time. I told her that I loved her. She told me that she loved me, too. Then we started walking.

"Where are we going now?" I said.

"My place," she said.

We walked back into the city and found our way to her tent. The tent was big and red, and it was pitched between two campers.

She unzipped the door, and we climbed inside.

27.

We tried to have sex. It was useless. I was too wasted and couldn't get it up. Too many chemicals. I apologized profusely. Caroline gave me a hug and told me not to worry. We talked and kissed for the next two hours. And at some point, we drifted off into a drug-addled half sleep.

A couple of hours later, the sun broke the horizon and the light inside the tent turned pink. I sensed it and sat up. I had no idea how long we'd been lying there. The air around me was stale and cold, and my face felt numb, and my nose was stuffy. I blinked, looking around, trying to get my bearings. I was light-headed and surprised to be naked. I felt nauseous. Things were different now. The high was gone. So was my sense of comfort. So was my confidence. I was dizzy and felt strange.

I looked down at Caroline. She was sprawled out on the air mattress, six feet three, asleep. Her hair was mashed against her face, and her mouth was slightly open. She looked like a hangover. The attraction was gone. So was the sense of familiarity. So was everything. I sat there, remembering. The night came back to me in a flood. I remembered the dancing and the walk and the conversation by the fire. A strange uneasiness washed over me. I put my clothes on in a hurry. Then I started to feel sick. The feeling took hold of me in a terrible wave. I unzipped the door of the tent, stuck my head outside, and vomited.

I heard Caroline stir. I finished vomiting, pulled my head back inside the tent, and turned to her. She was lying there, looking at me.

"Are you okay?" she said. Her voice was scratchy.

"Yeah," I said. "Just a little under the weather."

She grimaced.

"I have to go," I said. "My ride is leaving for Vegas any minute now."

"Vegas?" she said.

"That's where we picked up our camper."

She rubbed her eyes and propped herself up on one elbow. She yawned and brushed her hair out of her face. She removed a piece of paper and a pen from her backpack and wrote down her address and phone. I took it from her and put it in my pocket.

"That's my number in Palo Alto," she said.

"Okay."

"I'll be swimming down at UCLA later this year. Maybe you could come. Maybe we could have dinner or something."

"Sure. That sounds good."

There was a brief silence. The two of us looked at each other.

"I feel like shit," she said.

"Me too."

"Last night was crazy."

"I think it was one of the craziest nights of my life."

"You were so sweet."

"I was out of my tree," I said. "I don't think I've ever been that happy in my entire life."

"Yeah." She laughed. "I know. It was great. I had so much fun."

"I did too."

We hugged. I told her I'd write. She picked up the earmuffs off the floor of the tent and handed them to me. She insisted I take them. I put them on. She laughed. Then she leaned over and hugged me again.

"I'm glad I finally got to meet my soulmate," she said.

"It's about goddamn time."

"You take care of yourself, Wayne."

"You too."

She kissed me on the cheek.

I waved good-bye and crawled outside into daylight.

28.

There was a stiff wind blowing across the desert as I made my way back to The Searcher. The sky was coming alive. The wind was roaring in my ears, and the magic of the darkness was gone. The night was officially over, one of the strangest nights of my life. My neck and back ached. My brain felt like it was made of mashed potatoes, and I hadn't eaten anything in twenty-four hours. I figured I should probably take some vitamin C.

The remnants of the Man were lying in the distance behind me, a forgotten heap of ashes. The desert was spotted with forgotten heaps of ashes. Fires were smoldering, and streams of smoke were billowing into the sky. It looked like a battleground, like the aftermath of a meteor shower. My eyes hurt. The sun was rising. The sun was always rising. The night before had been like some kind of dream. I was having a hard time figuring out exactly what had happened. I was all out of cigarettes. I figured that was probably natural.

My friends were no doubt back at The Searcher now, waiting for me, in all likelihood. Maybe they were pissed off. They had probably cleaned up camp without me. They were probably looking at their watches, cursing my name, wondering where the hell I was, what the hell I was up to. They were probably contemplating whether or not they should break up into search parties and go looking for me. Perhaps they were contemplating leaving me. We were scheduled to roll out of there any minute now. Lynch and I had an eight-hour drive ahead of us. Traffic would potentially be a factor. We had to be back in Las Vegas that night no later than 9:00 p.m. My flight departed at 9:30. Lynch was catching the red-eye back to New York at 10:00. He had to be at work first thing the following morning. He had to show up at the office and be professional, ready to tell his boss what the hell had happened all week.

I felt like I had just come back from the moon.

Lynch was standing out in front of our camper when I rolled in. He was alone in the dawn, standing with his hands in his pockets, yawning, wearing his cowboy hat and shades. He told me I looked like hell. I thanked him. He asked me about my earmuffs and the details of my evening. I gave him a brief rundown. We loaded my bike onto the rack on the back of the camper, and then we climbed inside the cab. Lynch took the wheel. I rode shotgun. The others were in back, out cold, dead asleep. At that point, I was too scrambled to sleep. My hangover was monstrous. My insides felt hollowed out, and my brain felt like it had been erased. My throat hurt, and my lips were chapped. I was dehydrated to the core, my body ached, and yet somehow the notion of drinking water seemed revolting. Lynch turned the key and started the engine. I stuck my head out the window and vomited again.

We rolled away across the desert. The sun was up, and traffic wasn't bad. We'd made it out ahead of the rush. A staggered line of vehicles was moving along the old dusty road in the sunshine. An assortment of costumed volunteers was lined up at the exit gate, bidding people farewell in the morning light. There was a guy on a megaphone standing off to the side of our lane. He was dressed up like the Tin Man from *The Wizard of Oz.*

"YOU ARE NOW ENTERING THE REAL WORLD," he said. "WE APOLOGIZE FOR THE INCONVENIENCE. . . ."

Lynch gave him the finger.

29.

Later that morning, we pulled into a Denny's restaurant somewhere south of Reno. At that point, it was just Lynch and me. We had dropped off the rest of the crew back at the Super Kmart an hour or so earlier. Everyone was terribly hung over. Blair was feeling sick. Horvak and Henry looked haggard. Good-byes were said quickly, in a fog, without ceremony. Lynch and I helped them unload and wished them well before setting off on our long day's drive to Vegas. We headed down the road in a stupor before stopping off at Denny's in search of caffeine and nourishment. At the time, it seemed like the logical thing to do.

"You don't look good," said Lynch.

"I don't feel good," I said.

We were sitting in a greasy booth in the corner. I was leaning against the window, trying to keep myself upright. Lynch was leafing through a *USA Today* in slow motion. It amazed me that he was even able to read. I closed my eyes and tried my best to focus on my breathing in an effort to stave off nausea.

A few minutes later, our food arrived. Lynch had ordered a plate full of bacon and eggs. For some reason, I'd ordered the Denny's fruit salad in a worthless attempt to make amends for the previous evening's ingestions. It was a lost cause. My stomach was ravaged, and my appetite was shot. I looked down at my plate and grimaced and sank back into my seat.

"You gonna be okay?" said Lynch.

"Potentially," I said.

Our waitress reached over and poured us some more coffee. She was twice my age and twice my size. Her name tag identified her as BETTY. She asked us how we were feeling this morning. Lynch said the word "fine." I nodded and said, "Thank you." Betty shook her head and grinned at us, and then she walked away.

I picked up my fork and played around with my fruit a little bit, trying to come to terms with it. I stabbed at a grape and ate it, but it didn't really agree with me. None of my food was agreeing with me. There were some cantaloupe slices and watermelon slices and banana slices. None of it looked any good to me. All of it looked like alien food.

I set my fork down on the table and asked Lynch to hand me our travel bible, a Rand McNally road atlas we'd picked up last Wednesday on our way out of Vegas. He reached inside his backpack and slid it in my direction. The atlas was red with a picture of a desert highway on the cover. I sat there staring at it for a while, contemplating the act of actually opening it. Lynch was staring down at the sports page.

"It's gonna take me a week to get over this," I said.

"It's gonna take me a month," said Lynch.

"I think I made an ass out of myself last night," I said.

"You and twenty-five thousand of your closest friends," said Lynch.

"I think this might be the worst I've ever felt."

"Consider it an achievement."

"I think I'm gonna start getting healthy when I get back to L.A."

"Right."

"I'm gonna get myself into shape," I said. "I'm gonna get my shit together. I'm finally gonna quit smoking—end of story, once and for all."

"Eat your fruit."

"I'm gonna get a gym membership," I said. "I think I might even start taking karate."

Lynch looked up at me and roared. "Oh, Christ," he said. "You have officially fucking lost it."

"I'm serious," I said. And then I started laughing too.

We went on this way for a while, and then the laughter petered out and both of us were quiet again. There was Muzak playing overhead, a vaguely familiar pop melody, light rock, adult contemporary. Maybe it was Foreigner, maybe it was Phil Collins. Maybe it was neither. I was having trouble placing it. Lynch turned his eyes back to the newspaper, scanning the statistics and the box scores. I picked up the atlas and made a half-hearted attempt to trace our route back to Vegas, flipping from page to page before stopping at a profile of a town called Goldfield. According to Rand McNally, it was located right off of Highway 95, in between Reno and Vegas, an abandoned gold rush settlement in the heart of the desert wastelands.

"Hey, Lynch," I said. "There's a ghost town on our way back to Vegas."

"I know," he said. "We passed right by it on the way up. I remember the signs."

"I didn't see any signs," I said.

"You were probably asleep," he said.

"I was never asleep," I said.

"Bullshit," said Lynch. "You slept all the way through midday."

"It doesn't matter," I said, "I wanna make a stop there. I wanna take a little side trip."

"No, you don't," he said. "Trust me. The place is a boneyard. There's nothing left to see."

"I don't care," I said. "I just want to stop and check it out for a second. Get out and stretch my legs. It won't take long at all."

Lynch turned his eyes up from the paper and stared at me, waiting for some kind of punch line. But I never gave him one.

"You're kidding me," he said.

"I'm not," I replied.

"You really wanna go and see a ghost town?"

"Yeah. I really do."

"What in the hell for?"

"I don't know," I said. "I guess I just want to see if it's there."

Lynch kept staring at me, waiting for a better explanation. I kept my mouth shut and held my ground.

"You're serious about this," he said.

"Pretty much," I said.

"This is mandatory," he said.

"Essentially," I replied.

"Well, if that's the case," he said, "we'd better get on the road, then. We're making it to Vegas by sunset, no matter what. That's my only stipulation. If I don't catch my flight, I'm a dead man."

"Fine," I said. "Let's go. It's not like I'm gonna eat anything, anyway."

With that, I raised my hand and signaled to Betty for our check. She waved back and smiled and made her way over toward the register to ring us up. Lynch and I sat there in silence for a moment, both of us staring blankly at our food, and then Lynch started up the conversation again, inquiring about my plans for the immediate future, curious to know what I was going to do with myself when I got back to L.A. He wanted to know what my overall strategy was.

"So what's the deal?" he said. "You fly back to L.A., and then what?"

"And then I'm not really sure," I said. "Probably just deliver pizzas for a while and try to figure it out as I go. Maybe get back into the market. Maybe try to get a job in the movies. Maybe write a script. Blah, blah, blah. It's kind of a gray area. I just know it's not gonna involve anything corporate or conventional. Nothing soul-crushing. Nothing nine-to-five."

"Sounds like a plan," said Lynch.

"No, it doesn't," I said.

We laughed again, briefly. I tried not to wince. Lynch cleared his throat and slid out of the booth, excusing himself to the bathroom. I leaned back into my seat, resting my head against the window, and looked out to my left, through the tint, into daylight. Cars and trucks were rolling by. People were headed off in every direction. The sun was beating down, and the sky was blue. Another blazing sunny day in the high country. I whistled through my teeth—a long, soft-dying note—and stared out at the hills and the trees. Betty came by with the check, and I handed her a twenty and told her to keep the change. She filled up my mug and thanked me, told me to be good, to stay well, to take care of myself. She told me to stay awake. I smiled at her and told her that I would.

"You do that, sweetheart," she said to me. "You be careful on the road."

And then she winked and walked away.

I ripped open a sugar packet and dumped it into my coffee. And then I lifted my spoon and stirred.

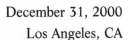

Dear Mr. and Mrs. Anaciello,

I've been meaning to send this letter for a while now. On any number of occasions I've made the attempt to write it, but every time I've done so I've found myself frozen, unable to get the words out. I suppose, in retrospect, that I just wanted to make good on the moment, to come up with some sort of definitive statement, to somehow say all the right things. Thinking about it now, though, I'm not so sure if that is even possible. I'm not so sure if fully defining a situation like this is something that can be done. And so with this in mind, I'm just going to do my best to speak as plainly as I can here. I'd like to say a few words about my relationship with your daughter and what she continues to mean to me.

I dated Amanda during college for a year, as you'll probably recall. I met her at a party in Boulder early in the fall semester, and we went on our first date the following weekend, down at this restaurant off of Pearl Street called Potter's. I remember being a little nervous going into it, but Amanda didn't really seem fazed. She was talkative right out of the gates, funny and completely composed. She handled the conversation throughout much of the early going, and by the time we got to the restaurant, I found myself feeling much more at ease. Looking back on it, that was always one of my favorite things about your daughter—she really had a way of making people feel instantly comfortable around her. Didn't matter who it was or where they were. She could always find a way to talk to people in a manner that made sense to them. I remember, for example, how she absolutely owned our waiter at the restaurant that night, even going so far as to con him into bringing us each a free glass of wine with our meal. I just sat there laughing to myself, stunned by the entire transaction. We were both underage at the time, and the guy didn't even appear to be in a good mood. But Amanda charmed him senseless in a matter of minutes, and what's more, she made it look easy.

It's also worth mentioning that later in the evening, when it came time to pay the check, I reached down into my back pocket and realized that I'd forgotten to bring my wallet with me. Somehow in my rush to get out the door, I'd forgotten to grab it off my desk. It was awful. I remember sitting there, terribly embarrassed, trying my best to act normal, debating back and forth about what to do. Amanda, of course, read right through me in a matter of seconds (another thing she was great at). She demanded to know what the matter was, why I was acting funny, and she wouldn't let up until I told her. So naturally I came clean, lowered my head and admitted that I'd forgotten my wallet, that I had no credit cards, no money, no cash. I stuttered and told her that I was sorry, that I didn't know what else to say. And of course Amanda thought that was hilarious. She threw her head back and laughed, slapped the table and told me I was an absolute moron, that I didn't know how to impress a lady. And then she pulled out her purse and paid for dinner without a second thought. As a matter of fact, I think she put it on your credit card.

Sorry about that.

Our relationship, just so you know, was filled with funny times like that. So many good times. So many laughs. Too many to keep track of, really. It's been amazing this past year, how often I've found myself hit with memories about her that I didn't even know I had. Nine times out of ten, the recollections are good ones—some laugh, some inside joke. Epic conversations. Comic misadventures. Trick-or-treating for beer. Getting a flat tire up in Telluride. Throwing spaghetti at the television set.

I want you to know that these are the kinds of things that I recall most often about your daughter. These are the memories that live on with me. I remember how contagious her laughter was and what an amazing way she had with people. I remember what a terrible driver she was and how she would never come close to admitting it. I remember how bawdy her sense of humor was and how much fun she could be at a party. And every time I do, it makes me smile. It's pretty much guaranteed.

At the same time, these kinds of memories are bittersweet for me. In remembering the best of Amanda, it's impossible not to be somewhat saddened by it as well. I sit back and think of the way she lived, what a force of nature she could be, and her manner of death becomes all the more tragic and perplexing. I imagine that this is a pretty common paradox for all of us who knew and loved her.

As you probably know, Amanda and I broke up back in 1997, after about a year or so of being together. This, for the most part, was my doing. Like any breakup, it was complicated and difficult, a matter of bad timing more than anything else. I was young and noncommittal, not quite sure of what I wanted, and I did a poor job of handling the situation. I communicated badly—or maybe I failed to communicate at all. I didn't listen well. I didn't do the right things. And Amanda was heartbroken. I never intended to hurt her feelings in any way, but it happened. And I am terribly sorry for that.

With this in mind, I've spent a lot of time this past year wondering if my actions back then might have in some way played into

Amanda's decision to end her life. I've spent a lot of time mired in guilt and hypothetical thinking, trying to come to grips with the situation and its possible implications. It seems likely that everyone who feels Amanda's loss has gone through a similar kind of thought process this past year, wondering if there was anything they had done (or not done) or said (or not said) that may have contributed to her death, or if there was anything they could have said or done that somehow would have helped prevent it.

Obviously I sit here today wishing that I had the answers for you. I wish so badly that I had the wisdom on hand to fix this situation, to somehow make it all make sense. But I don't. The questions that lie at the heart of this experience are beyond my understanding right now.

That being said, I'd like to offer up a few simple thoughts that will hopefully do some small bit of good. First and foremost, I want you to know how much I loved your daughter. I want you to know how deeply sorry I am for your loss and how much I've been thinking about you this past year. Amanda's death was great shock to us all, and the sense of personal loss that I feel in her absence is difficult to describe. She will always be greatly missed.

In response to this tragedy and its resulting grief, much of my time this past year has been spent in a dual state of contemplation and motion, as I've been trying to untangle the contents of my heart and come to terms with how I really feel about things. I've been interested, as silly as it might sound, in trying to figure out what everything means.

And as far as that goes . . . well . . . the best I can tell you at this point is that I've come to no conclusions. I've had no grand epiphany or definitive success of any kind. But then I guess that shouldn't come as any big surprise. I'm human.

Along these same lines, one of the things that has brought me the greatest amount of comfort recently has been the idea that nothing in this world has any inherent meaning, that nothing means anything until we ascribe meaning to it in our minds. If this holds true (and I tend to believe that it does), then maybe my quest to uncover some kind of underlying explanation for every-thing isn't as fruitless as it can sometimes seem. Maybe the answer is that there are no answers. Maybe instead of looking for certainty and exactitude in the universe, I'm better off trying to build meanings within myself that give me and those around me the greatest possible sense of peace and happiness, and letting that alone serve as my guide.

And so in writing this letter today, I suppose that this is what I'm attempting to do. I suppose that I'm making a humble effort to imbue your daughter's death with a little bit of light. I suppose I'm writing to let you know that I am committed to ascribing the tragedy of her passing with a deeper and more positive meaning. And I'm convinced that if enough of us do this we can transform the pain of our grief and the legacy of her loss into something that comes close to being as beautiful as she will always be.

Please know that you and your family are forever in my thoughts and prayers. I sincerely hope that this letter has brought you some small measure of comfort as we head into the New Year. And I wish you peace.

Wayne